MW01532079

Scars We Didn't See

AUBREY WHITTEN

HUE PRESS

Copyright © Aubrey Whitten, 2025.

This novel is entirely a work of fiction. The story, all names, characters, locales, and incidents portrayed in it are the work of the author's imagination or are used fictitiously. Any resemblance to actual persons, living or dead, or events is entirely coincidental.

All rights reserved.

No part of this publication may be reproduced, distributed, decompiled, reverse engineered, stored, or transmitted in any form or by any means, including pho-tocopying, recording, or other electronic or mechanical methods, now known or hereinafter invented, without the prior express written permission from the author.

Aubrey Whitten asserts the moral right to be identified as the author of this work.

Cover beautifully illustrated and designed by The BookShelf Studio.

HUE PRESS

eBook ISBN – 978-1-7636050-7-7
Paperback ISBN – 978-1-7636050-5-3

NATIONAL LIBRARY OF AUSTRALIA
A catalogue record for this book is available from the National Library of Australia

To the little man who discovered Richmond with me and chose Lola's forever home

1

She Didn't See What
Could Be

Lola

"I ain't seein' no *lady* doctor!"

The mechanic stood with his arms crossed, an oil-stained shirt stretched tight over his belly, and a scowl already carved into his weathered face.

Clutching the chart with his name on it to my chest, I nudged my gold-rimmed glasses up my nose. "Mr. Barnes—"

He snorted. He wasn't listening.

This wasn't exactly the start I'd hoped for.

I didn't move, hiding under a limp blonde fringe, my shaky knees betraying my nerves. The waiting room was too quiet, too quaint, for a medical clinic. And as odd as the crocheted *Welcome* sign looked above the shelf of glossy pamphlets about flu shots and erectile dysfunction, I was the one thing in the room that didn't quite belong.

And this man wasn't about to let me forget it.

"Mr. Barnes, I know it's my first day," I said, relieved my voice didn't shake as badly as my knees. "But I've been a GP for more than ten years—"

"You listen here, Lola from the City. March yourself back to your room and shut the door. I *ain't* seein' you."

My fingers tightened around the chart, but I stayed quiet. He might have been the first patient to flat-out refuse to see me, but even the ones who shuffled in without protest watched me with an uneasy curiosity. My new neighbours paused every time I pushed open the gate of my cottage, too.

The locals were suspicious.

Of me.

Lola from the City. The newcomer. The *outsider*.

"Evan Barnes!" Brooke shot up from behind the reception desk. "Are you causing trouble in my waiting room?"

"Sit that perky rear down, Goldilocks," he said. "You ain't part of this."

"Wanna bet?" She planted her hands on the hips of her stiff teal uniform. Her military precision running the clinic's appointments clearly didn't include any disruptions from him. "Look how busy we are this morning!"

My gaze skipped over the handful of people in the waiting room. One, two, three... Yep. Only four patients.

This was...*busy?*

At the clinic where I used to work in Sydney, just claiming a seat was a battle. Coughing, crying toddlers, and the hum of too many voices had overwhelmed me from the moment the doors opened.

Richmond was the opposite. Here, the quiet wasn't just a relief—it was the point. It was why I'd chosen it.

Safely tucked at the bottom of the world, tourists trickled through the small town, snapping photos of the sandstone cottages and convict relics cradled by the Coal River Valley. Only a thousand or so called this place home. Three days ago, I'd slipped into town unnoticed, a single suitcase bumping along the path behind me, hoping to become one of them—despite every odd stacked against me by a man who'd made staying with him impossible.

I took a steadying breath. Apparently, I hadn't run far enough to avoid men like him.

Evan still stood there, arms folded, unimpressed. Brooke tried again. This time, she dialled up the charm with her sweetest, red-lipped smile.

"You know we wouldn't let any old city girl work here," she said. "Dr. Hughes has a sensible head on her shoulders."

Evan flopped onto a chair. "She can have ten heads on her shoulders. I ain't seein' her." He grabbed a magazine and thumbed through the pages. "My rear's parkin' right here until the other doctor is free."

And that was that. There was nothing left to say.

Sighing, I slunk down the corridor, opened the door to my room, and let it click shut behind me. My back hit the wall. I didn't have the energy to lift my eyes, much less admire the space I'd so proudly decorated the day before.

My consultation room.

I'd never had much that was truly *mine*. Growing up, my older sister devoured the spotlight, testing my parents' limits and breaking all the rules while I drifted unnoticed in her shadow. Later came medical school, then shared houses, and a string of failed relationships...

Until Chris.

But our terrace on the harbour had never been mine. Right down to the eggshell-coloured walls I'd mistakenly called *white* only once, that prison had only ever been his. He'd taken so much pleasure in reminding me I had nowhere else to go. I belonged to him.

But not anymore.

Decorating my room at the clinic had been a labour of love. A symbol of my fresh start. Of me.

With my sleeves pushed up and masking tape stuck to nearly every finger, I'd painted one wall a soft powder blue. Cheerful prints hung in a neat line, and I'd set up a children's nook in the corner—a tiny table, matching chairs, and boxes spilling with toys and picture books I'd bargain-hunted from the local buy-and-sell group.

The seller had dropped everything off at the clinic for me, and I'd offered extra for the delivery with a tray of freshly iced cupcakes as a thank you. I couldn't afford more.

Pride bloomed in my chest each time I opened my purse and glimpsed the bank card tucked inside—the first I'd touched in years—but my account was empty.

Money disappeared fast on the run. A month hiding in cheap motels down the Australian coast, an airfare, rent, and one last basket of groceries had swallowed nearly every cent I'd stashed away. My escape fund was gone. The only thing left in the bottom of the faded pink pillowcase was the engagement ring from a proposal I wished I'd never accepted.

But I could survive. I *would*.

My freedom from Chris was worth eating peanut butter sandwiches for another week.

I didn't shuffle to my desk straight away. I stayed standing, letting the quiet of the room hold me for a moment. Even if I hadn't earned my patient's trust just yet, I'd earned the right to pause and take a breath, at least.

A knock rattled the door before it creaked open.

Brooke poked her head in. "Got a sec?" Without waiting for an answer, she stepped inside.

My fingers twisted the faded pleats of my black skirt. "I'm sorry I let you down—"

"What are you going on about, Doc? You haven't let anyone down!"

"But the patients..." I bit my lip.

"Are acting as difficult as they do for *any* new face in town. I've been here a year, and people still joke about me being a blow-in."

"Really?"

"Cross my heart. Look, I know this morning has been a hot bag of garbage juice, but your afternoon will be busy. *Believe* me."

I flicked a look at the computer. "There aren't many appointments scheduled in..."

"*Yet*. I've got about ten sticky notes I'm still juggling! The phone started ringing off the hook for women's health checkups since word got out you're here. Wait." Brooke's mouth dropped open as some realisation hit her. "Does this mean you'll end up seeing everyone's vag in town?" A faint line settled between her brows. "Is that weird?"

"It is now you said it." I laughed. "It may shock you to know I've seen one or two before."

She grinned. "How many crusty old dicks have you seen?"

"If you've seen one, you've seen them all."

"Isn't that the truth?" She rolled her eyes. "Well, thanks to the biggest dick on this side of Tasmania, you have a twenty-minute break before your next appointment. Make the most of it."

"I suppose I could get started on those blood results—"

"What? No!" She barricaded me from getting closer to the computer. "Forget those! Grab a tea or coffee." She shooed me to the door. "I'll have you know I splurged on the expensive coffee pods this week, and I even managed not to scoff all the fancy biscuits the ladies from the church dropped off for you."

"For...me?" Biting back a smile, my eyes danced around the scuffed toes of my ballet flats, but my heart floated somewhere in the clouds. "That's very kind of them."

Brooke snorted a laugh. "Don't let your guard down just yet. Those scheming old ducks *always* have an ulterior motive.

They're probably trying to win you over so you'll agree to a date with one of their grandsons. But if you need a protector against the grannies of the valley, I'm officially on duty!" She saluted me with a wink before darting a guilty look at the door. "Right after I check in the next patient."

Brooke disappeared to reception, and I took the quieter route, slipping down the maze of corridors towards the break room hidden at the very back. A cup of tea *would* hit the spot. What type of fancy biscuits did church ladies bake? Something sweet and crumbly with fluffy icing in the middle? I pushed open the door. Maybe I could sneak one—

"*Oh!*"

My eyes widened as I sucked in a panicked breath—or, at least, I tried to. My lungs locked up. I stumbled back a step, then another, until I collided with the wall, spine first.

A man crowded the other side of the room.

Not just any man.

A beast of a man.

He was tall, with broad shoulders wrapped in a red-checked flannel shirt, the sleeves folded up to reveal muscular forearms dusted with dark hair. Actually, he had lots of dark hair everywhere—thick and wavy on his head, tamed on his brows, but slightly bushy on his beard. He had grey eyes, though, and they tracked me as I crept along the wall, my hand fumbling along the tiles, desperately searching for the doorknob.

The man cleared his throat. The rough noise forced my eyes down.

Someone. Help me.

My pulse picked up. I had to get out of there. That man would snap me like a twig. He'd crush me even if I stood as proud and strong as the ancient eucalyptus dotted through the valley.

"We're just..." Sounding almost nervous, his voice trailed off.

I dared to lift my eyes again. The man had worked himself into the opposite corner of the room, his gaze fixed on his tan work boots. Uneasy, almost as if his heart thumped as fast as mine, he hopped a white tile from hand to hand.

I glanced at the wall behind him. Still almost bare like it was yesterday. But now, tiny red spacers dotted the gaps between rows of freshly laid subway tiles. On the wooden counter, a faded blue towel had been thrown down, with an assortment of tools lined up neatly on top—absolutely none of which I could name.

Balls.

Shame curled a slow, fiery path up my neck. The poor man wasn't a villain lurking behind the door, waiting to attack. He was finishing the break room renovation.

My glasses hadn't budged, but my finger trembled when I pushed them up anyway. "I—I'm s-sorry." A gulp of air didn't help get the words out any easier. "I wasn't expecting..." *An enormous brute to be lurking in the break room.* "You." *Or anyone else, for that matter.*

"Yeah, uh... We were supposed to finish—"

The back door swung open.

My heart jumped when a second man barrelled inside. He was much younger and impossible to miss, with a bright crop of ginger hair and a blinding neon safety shirt. His khaki shorts were the only dull thing about him.

"Lola from the City!" he cried.

My eyes bulged.

Did *everyone* call me that?

He dropped a toolbox on the floor. "Everyone in town is talking about you! I'm Harry." Grinning, all dimples, he jerked a thumb over his shoulder. "The old man is Aiden. Has he talked yet? He *does* talk."

I masked the tremble in my hand with a tight fistful of skirt but stayed pinned to the safety of the wall.

Harry hooked his thumbs in his toolbelt. Tilting his head, his ginger brows squished together. His eyes went from me to Aiden. We must have looked ridiculous—each of us squashed into opposite corners, refusing to say a word, barely looking anywhere but at our shoes.

Harry sighed. "Did you already scare the new girl?" His pointed look fell on the man wearing red-checked flannel. "What the hell, old man? Were you raised in the Hollyoaks' barn or something? Say *hello*."

"Oh, uh..." Aiden stood taller and squared his shoulders. He dipped his chin and ground out a simple "Hello."

"Frigging hell," Harry muttered. "The cows would do a better job than that."

Aiden glared at him.

A cautious smile spread across my face. I didn't mind Aiden's awkward greeting. His deep, gravelly voice was the kind that should've set me on edge, but instead, it calmed something in me. I raised a hand in a clumsy wave, even though we'd already been introduced. It just felt like the right way to say hello...*officially*.

"It's nice to meet you, Harry." I edged away from the wall. "And...Aiden."

Crinkles touched the corners of his grey eyes. Was that the start of a smile? Maybe.

Feeling braver, I asked, "Are you a carpenter, Aiden?"

Dead silence.

Harry slapped his hand against his forehead. "Why are you like this?" he hissed at his friend.

Aiden's dark brows furrowed as he glanced from Harry to me. "No, I'm a cabinetmaker." Each word came out rusty. Harry said Aiden talked, but I got the sense he didn't usually say much. "I build furniture and do renovations like the, uh..." He waved a hand at the unfinished kitchen.

My eyebrows shot up. Aiden could make things? His own furniture? Impressive!

Other than cooking and perfecting the feature wall in my consultation room after watching a hundred online tutorials, I was rubbish at anything creative. Watercolours? Forget it. I'd tried pottery once, too. What a disaster. The coffee mug I'd laboured over for hours had come out of the kiln resembling a perfectly wonky lump of poop.

"We were supposed to sign off on this reno before you started," Harry said. "We're running behind schedule because *someone* couldn't decide what finish he wanted on the cabinets." He shot an accusing glare in Aiden's direction. "But the old man finally settled on wangdang—"

"Wainscot." Aiden's correction was gruff.

Harry shrugged. "What do I know about wood? I'm an electrician." His chest puffed out with pride. "I share a workshop with Aiden. I also dabble in a bit of tiling and stuff. Whatever the old man needs—"

"Stop calling me old."

"Dude, you're—what—pushing forty?"

"Why don't you get back to work instead of wasting the doctor's time talking about how many steps I am away from the grave?"

Harry grinned. "See?" he said to me. "He doesn't deny it. *Old*. But don't worry—we'll be out of your hair soon enough. Damn, even sooner if I get one of these biscuits in me!" His hand shot out for the plate on the counter. A melting moment stuffed with lemon icing disappeared from the pile. "Where'd these bad boys come from?"

"Brooke said they're from the, um... ladies at the church," I said.

"Thought so." Most of the biscuit disappeared in Harry's mouth in one big bite. "Yolanda Briggs once convinced me to escort her granddaughter to the church dance with a plate half the size of this. It was totally worth being stepped on for three hours." He chewed, eyes on the ceiling, before popping the last of it in his mouth. "Whose grandson did you have to promise to meet for coffee? Geez, a haul this big, and they might bribe you into a date with the old man!"

Aiden sighed. "Kid, come on—"

"Nah, I'm just fooling around." Harry wiggled his eyebrows. "A whole basket of goodies couldn't convince a woman to be alone with you, smooth talker!"

Aiden grunted, but he leant over the counter, careful not to get too close, his gaze flicking up just once to meet mine as he slid the plate of biscuits across the wood.

"You better grab one before Harry eats them all," he said. "You'll need to keep your strength up to fight off all the invitations." Another twitch tugged at the corner of his mouth. Maybe that was his smile, after all.

Whatever the expression was, it was enough to coax a genuine smile from me. I reached for a biscuit but couldn't quite get my fingers on a melting moment.

Aiden nudged the plate closer. "The ones with pink icing are the best."

A soft laugh escaped me. Maybe I'd been wrong about him. He wasn't a brute or a man I needed to cower away from. He was just...

Aiden.

2

He Didn't See a Future

Aiden

NIGHTS WERE ALWAYS WORSE.

My eyes stayed locked on my boots as I headed along the stone path to the village store. I didn't need anything. I shouldn't have stopped in town at all. The prickly red dusk set me on high alert, and the faint scent of woodsmoke clung to the chill already creeping over the valley.

But the chance of seeing *her* was worth the risk of stumbling on old ghosts.

Lola.

Looking at her made my heart beat fast—like a panic attack, but good.

She was all shy smiles, with a cherub face half-hidden behind a veil of champagne hair and tiny blue eyes peeking out from behind glasses too big for her face. She kept her head down, her shoulders always curling in like she wanted to tuck herself out of sight.

Yeah, Lola tried to hide, but I noticed her everywhere.

She wandered around town after the clinic closed. We'd stammered through a few awkward hellos at the village store. A wave hello at the coffee shop. Sometimes, I spotted her on the bench by the riverbank reading a book.

Yesterday, she'd clutched a copy of *Flowers for Algernon* under her nose, only pausing between pages to nibble her sandwich. I'd gawked at her for so long that Rose had sidled up beside me on the street.

"And what's caught your attention over there?" she asked, craning her wrinkled neck to peer around me, desperate for gossip to share with the other old crows at church.

I stuffed my hands in my pockets and shrugged.

"And here I was thinking it might have been the pretty doctor catching your eye," she said. "What's her name again?"

"That's, um..." I coughed into my fist, but my voice didn't grind out the name any easier. "Lola."

"That's the one. She rents the place next to Yolanda Briggs, you know. The poor thing is living all on her own without a friend in the world! What do *you* say about that?"

Nothing. That's what I'd said.

A nod goodbye, and I'd gone about my business... but not without one last look at Lola over my shoulder. Maybe if I got my hands on that book, we'd have something to talk about beyond awkward hellos.

I cursed myself for still not ordering a copy as the door to the village store loomed in front of me. My palm landed on the flaking green paint. I gritted my teeth.

Harden up, you weak bastard.

I could hear the almost two hundred years of history when the door groaned open, but it was the jingle that always turned my gut.

I hated that damn bell.

Ashley was crouched on the wooden floor. She hummed as she slid a cereal box onto the shelf, swaying to the music, her dark ponytail swinging in time. I was too big to sneak past her. My boots were heavy, and her head whipped around before I'd made it two steps.

"Back again, Aiden?" She slid another box onto the shelf like nothing was out of the ordinary. "That's the fourth time this week."

"I...forgot..." What? I never forgot a damn thing. Routines ruled my life. They had to. One misstep, and my world could unravel. "Something."

Her mouth curved as if she were about to laugh, but instead, she only nodded. "You've been forgetting things a lot lately."

I grunted and picked up a basket.

Ashley went back to stacking cereal, and I wandered around the cramped aisles, wasting time, picking up junk I didn't need. Laundry detergent to add to my growing stockpile. A box of pasta that would sit untouched in the pantry.

Minutes ticked by.

The store was silent except for the thump of my pulse and the croon of some feel-good playlist Harry would like. I kept my mind occupied rehearsing what I'd say to Lola. She wouldn't get any jokes from me, but something casual could work. How was she settling in? How many invitations had she dodged from the matchmaking busybodies? I raked my fingers through my hair. Nah, I couldn't ask her that. What about the weather? Yeah, the cold front expected over the valley was a safer option than imagining Lola smiling at some other man.

The bell never jingled.

No Lola tonight.

Sighing, I headed for the checkout, my footsteps slowing as dread turned my muscles to lead.

Man up. You've gotten through this plenty of times before...

My chest swelled from the breath in. The tremor threatening to shake my hand steadied.

Ashley beat me to the register. She wiped her hands down the front of her apron and glanced at the random items I started unpacking on the counter.

Her eyebrows pinched together. "Angel hair spaghetti?" she asked, holding up the box.

I shrugged. "I like pasta."

"Do you? This one seems a bit—I dunno—dainty for you. I'd guess you're more of a pappardelle kinda man."

I was more of a make-pasta-from-scratch kind of man, but Ashley didn't need to know that. I'd seen her huddled with the church ladies at the village markets. *Gossiping.* I didn't want anyone to know my business. Any of it. Not even pasta business.

Ashley picked up the box of spaghetti and sent it soaring for the scanner.

My jaw clenched.

Just breathe—

The beep pierced my ears like a scream. The breath I forced into my lungs did nothing, and my hand only stopped shaking when I clenched gnawed fingernails into calloused skin.

I knew better, but there I was, risking my damn dignity over a woman who didn't know I existed. My triggers weren't a secret. The bell. The scanner. Sharp, high noises were a one-way ticket to a flashback I couldn't risk having in the village store.

But I battled to keep my face neutral. No one knew about the shit going on inside my head, and I planned to keep it that way.

Oblivious, Ashley kept scanning the rest of my groceries. "How's work?" she asked. "Busy at the moment?"

"Yeah."

"How's everything on the mountain?"

"Quiet."

My eyes tracked the canned tomatoes as they torpedoed across the counter. I squeezed my fist tighter as the scanner squealed. My breaths evened out.

Another one down.

"Harry stopped by this morning," Ashley said. "He was telling me you've built a deck out the back of your place."

"Yeah."

"I bet you've got a nice view of the valley."

"S'pose."

Ashley grimaced.

I couldn't blame her. Talking to me was like getting blood out of a stone. But what was the point of asking and answering pointless questions like "How are you?" anyway? What a waste of time. It wasn't like I could answer honestly and say, "I'm exhausted, lonely, and wish this whole merry-go-round was just...*over*."

People laughed nervously and looked for the nearest exit if I said shit like that. I'd learned that the hard way. My father passed away after seven years of silence between us. Once upon a time, I'd lived a life of service that made him—my family—proud. And I ruined it.

Ashley slid the full shopping bag across the counter. "I'd say see you next week like I used to," she said, "but I've got a feeling you might forget something tomorrow."

"No idea what you're talking about," I lied.

"None, huh?" She smirked. "So, you're not interested to know your girl just headed for the post office?"

"I don't have a girl."

"Uh-huh."

I grunted. The less I said about Lola, the better.

"She's nice, the doctor," Ashley said. "It's funny, though. Everyone sure was convinced you were sweet on Ruth Wilks for a while there."

My hand froze midair before I could grab the bag of groceries. People speculated too much about Ruth. About me. We were no one's business. If everyone had stopped sticking their noses into our lives, maybe Ruth would still come to town.

I jerked my chin down in a nod goodbye to Ashley. I needed to get out of there before I said something I'd regret. The bell jingled as I barged through the door, but for once, I didn't notice.

My boots nailed to the path outside.

Lola.

The sight of her gripped around my chest and dragged me closer. Fear didn't slow my steps. The only place I needed to be was beside her, holding open the post office door so she didn't have to shoulder her way out under a mountain of boxes and bags.

I could carry her packages. Maybe I'd sneak a touch on the sleeve of the pink cardigan she'd thrown over that loose black sack she always wore and ask about her day...

"What the bloody hell is wrong with me?" I muttered.

Relationships? Not on my to-do list. But my vow to spend my life alone didn't stop me from walking in the opposite direction from where I'd parked my truck.

If Lola heard me coming, she didn't show it, and there was no way she'd see a thing over the haphazard tower of packages in her arms. She also didn't notice the gap in the worn stone pavers. She wobbled from foot to foot along the path until the toe of her shoe caught. Parcels hurtled through the air. I dropped my groceries and lunged forward, catching her just before she hit the ground.

Her fingers clung to my side, and, shaky, a little uncertain, she lifted her chin and pushed her glasses up her nose.

"Oops," she whispered.

My heart pounded too fast in my chest—another one of those panic attacks, but good.

"Oops," I whispered back.

No idea why. My smile was unexpected, too.

Lola untangled herself with a guilty smile. The scent of coconut shampoo clung to her, reminding me of beach holidays

I never take anymore. I wanted to pull her back and trap all her sweetness. Instead, I stuffed my hands into my pockets. Nervous? Nah...

"Been doing some online shopping?" I asked.

"Um..." She nibbled on her lip. "No..."

I cocked my head. She was even worse at lying than I was.

"Okay... Yes!" A dizzy smile burst across her face. "I got my first pay! I needed a few things for my cottage." Hands flying to her cheeks, she blinked down at the explosion of packages scattered outside the post office. "I guess I got a bit carried away."

"A bit, huh?"

"A *teensy* bit." She laughed, and it was just about the sweet-est sound I'd ever heard. "I bought cooking utensils, candles, fluffy towels, and fancy pink sheets that aren't scratchy. Oh! New clothes and a pair of shoes." Her eyes sparkled. I'm not exaggerating. *Sparkled*. "And it was all brand-new! I didn't even have to wait for anything to be on sale!"

Lola darted around picking up her boxes, smiling like it was Christmas morning. And somehow, it didn't feel right. The emotion was too raw. Too *new*. I ignored the knot twisting in my gut. The sun was dying over the horizon, and when night closed in, I hovered at the edge. I was overthinking it...

I crouched down to help her, holding up a white box marked with the logo of one of the big bookstores. "And this?"

Lola took the package from me and hugged it against her chest. "I love reading," she said.

Me too.

I ached to tell her I loved books and cooking, just like she did. I wanted to sniff her smelly candles and wash her fluffy towels. I didn't give a damn if her sheets were pink or if they itched worse than the woollen jumpers my Nan had knitted for me. I wanted to cuddle Lola on her sheets all night.

But I didn't say a word.

My arms buried under a mountain of packages, I straightened up and swept my gaze along the street. No cars. Just my truck. All the spots outside the post office were empty, too.

"Where are you parked?" I asked her.

"I, um, well..." There she was, biting down on that pink lip again. "I don't have a car...yet."

How the hell was she getting around? On foot? Over my dead body. "How did you get here from Hobart?"

"The...bus..."

"What about all your stuff?"

"Oh, you know..." She waved her hand about like this conversation wasn't a big deal. "I didn't want to haul all my junk from the mainland when I moved." The nervous laugh that followed didn't convince me, either. "My cottage came furnished... Sort of..."

My eyebrow crept up. She was acting more than a little skittish. Was it me? Was I being awkward again? Goddammit. I wanted Lola to tip her chin up at me and bless me with another smile. Or let out another one of her airy laughs. I liked those the best. Pure heaven.

"I'll drop you home," I said, turning to head for my truck.

Lola's hand darted out to grab one of her packages. "No. It's okay. I can manage," she insisted. "I know you're busy."

I took the box back and carefully balanced it on top of the pile. Ignoring the bruising sky, I said, "I've got time." Not much, though.

Lola fidgeted with the hem of her cardigan. "Are you sure?" She whispered her address to her shoes. "I don't want you to go out of your way."

"That's on my way."

"Really?"

Not really. "Really."

Stumbling through another insistence that it was no trouble to drop her home seemed to settle it—or maybe Lola was just too nice to say no. Either way, she kept close behind me, her silence the same quiet relief it always was. I moved slow, careful not to jostle her precious cargo, and grabbed the discarded bag of groceries on the way. When I opened the passenger door, Lola's fingers curled over my forearm.

Surprised, my heart already hammering, I dropped my gaze to stare at that soft touch.

Oh, those little hands...

Blue eyes blinked up at me. "Thanks, Aiden."

Tongue-tied, I nodded. Truthfully, I almost died.

The pretty curve of her lips cracked my chest wide open and knocked out any wind left in my lungs. But instead of feeling like my life was a one-way trip to hell, for the first time in a long time, I didn't want to jump off the merry-go-round anymore.

I wanted her on it with me.

3

She Didn't See His Attempt at Flirting

Lola

EARLY MORNING SUN PEEKED under the front door. The tag on my dress had nearly made it out with me, but I'd yanked it off just in time, grabbed my bag, and reached for the knob.

My phone buzzed.

Please... Not yet...

I blinked at the message lighting up the screen.

Mum

> Thank God you're okay! It's been two months! We've all been worried sick!

> Where are you?

My forehead fell against the door, and I sighed into the wood. This was my own fault. I'd sent a message letting my parents know my new phone number, washed up the breakfast dishes, headed for the door, and—*ding!*—there was my mother.

Two calls from Mum had gone unanswered. The text—I couldn't decline. Despite her accusations, I *did* love her, but she'd asked me the one question I couldn't answer: Where was I?

A thousand miles from where I should be. Exactly where I wanted to be. Safe.

I'd never wanted my family to worry, but I couldn't risk telling them the truth. Not this time.

Chris was intelligent. Driven. *Relentless*. Those traits made him a formidable lawyer, but his perfect shell was fragile, cracked in ways I didn't understand. No amount of my love patched him up. A lesson learned the hard way. I also knew I couldn't risk him finding me. The day I'd fled Sydney, I'd deleted every trace of my existence from my old phone, dumped it in a bin under the flashing neon sign of a greasy takeout place, and disappeared.

I had to. Four failed attempts. Chris had always found me. My parents would have to wait.

Lola

> I'm okay, Mum. I'll try to call you tonight. Love you xxoo

I wouldn't call.

After slipping my phone into my bag, I sucked in a breath deep enough to conquer the world and turned the knob. The door cracked open. Sunlight poured in a gap just wide enough for me to peek outside. If I scrunched into the corner and angled myself just right, I could see a sliver of my front garden.

Yolanda often hovered near the gate...

My next-door neighbour loved to chat. The day I'd moved in, she'd announced that her roses were the best in town, and I quickly realised her prize-winning blooms needed an awful lot of extra love around the time I left for work each morning.

I squeezed the doorknob tighter to stop the tremor in my
fingers. This wasn't the morning for one of Yolanda's chats.
Anxiety left my nerves dog-eared and worn, the battered pages
of a story I'd read too many times. I thought I'd have longer
before the reality of my old life collided with the fantasy I was
creating in my new one.

I inched the door open a little wider. I glanced left. Right.

All clear.

Diving outside, I pulled the door shut, checked the lock
twice, and raced for the gate.

"Morning, pet."

Balls.

I plastered on a smile before I turned my head. The wafer-thin
skin around Yolanda's eyes crinkled when she smiled back. Her
hair was a puff of steel-wool curls, and after she popped the
cigarette in her mouth, her hands were free to cinch the belt of
her purple bathrobe tighter around her waist. The tips of bunny
ear slippers peeked from underneath.

"I couldn't help noticing you had a visitor yesterday," Yolanda said, a grey eyebrow arching as she took a drag of her cigarette.

No doubt she'd seen plenty when she'd hung out her front
window gawking as Aiden's black beast of a truck pulled up
out front. Yolanda made it her business to know everything that
happened on our street.

"Aiden, um... just... you know..." My laugh was a mess of
noise plagued by more nerves. "He gave me a ride home."

Yolanda blew a thin line of smoke into the air. "Did he?"

The surprise in her voice only fuelled the flutter in my chest.
"It was nothing," I said.

To most people, it would have been nothing. Five minutes
of silence. Me, biting the inside of my cheek, unsure what to
say. And still, the memory of sitting next to Aiden left my face
burning. A well-read copy of *The Count of Monte Cristo* had
sat on his dashboard. I'd ached to ask him about it. What was

his favourite part? Who was his favourite character? Did he love reading too? And when I'd ducked my head, sneaking a peek at his strong profile, I'd stopped myself from blurting out, "Why do you smell *so* good?"

Thankfully.

I'd embarrassed myself enough for one afternoon.

"So, it was nothing, eh?" Yolanda said.

"Aiden offered." Grimacing, I added, "I needed some help after going a little bit overboard with some online shopping." *Really* overboard.

Receiving my pay was like winning the lottery. *My* money. In *my* account. To spend any way *I* wanted.

I didn't miss the crisp white envelope of money Chris had shoved at me. The small allowance he'd trusted me to manage had barely been enough to cover our food. My stomach had grumbled more than once, and some weeks, I'd been so very grateful there was a complimentary fruit basket at the clinic where I used to work. After paying for everything Chris needed, there had never been much left over for me.

"Nice man, that Aiden McKinnon," Yolanda was saying. "Strong. Proud. Built like a soldier." She took another drag of her cigarette and smirked. "Not much to say for himself, though."

That was true. Aiden rarely said much, but he was always watching. Thoughtful. A blush crept up my neck as I absently traced the neckline of my dress. And those *eyes*. I could drown in his stormy grey eyes.

"Fancy him going out of his way like that," she added.

I spluttered a protest, reassuring her, "It was on his way home."

"No, pet. It's not. He lives up there"—the cigarette cradled in her fingers pointed in the opposite direction of the cottage—"in the hills."

"Oh." My heart fluttered against my ribs. He'd driven me home for no reason other than wanting to?

"Oh, she says." Yolanda smirked. "Easy on the eye, isn't he? A man like him catches the attention of the tourists coming through. He's never shown much interest, though. Prefers keeping to himself, that one."

"Perhaps he enjoys a simple kind of life?"

She croaked a laugh. "A man like him needs a woman. He's rattling around in that big house with no one to share it with. And don't you listen to any stories about Aiden and Ruth Wilks. She's a beauty, make no mistake, but nothing you'll hear is true. They're friends. That's all."

I bit down on my lip. Who was Ruth? One of Yolanda's friends from the church? Someone else I'd wandered past in town and never realised? I'd never seen Aiden talk to anyone except Harry... And he grunted his way through most of those conversations.

"That's...nice," I said.

"Nice, she says." Chuckling, Yolanda blew a puff of smoke into the air.

"I'm sure Aiden will find someone."

That comment got her eyebrow up again, and her steely eyes narrowed on me.

I pressed my lips together, but my chin still trembled. I knew what Yolanda was doing. Matchmaking. *Interfering*. And yet, I could imagine sitting next to Aiden on a hundred drives home without ever growing tired of the comfortable silence.

But whoever that sweet man found to share his big house in the hills wouldn't be me.

Fear stamped a black patch over my new life. Love was out of the question for someone like me. I was flawed. Useless. Too stupid to do anything right. And as much as I tried to blot out the words Chris had roared at me too many times, his cruelty drowned out any whispers of hope when I dared to dream about something more.

And I dared to dream about Aiden more than I should.

· ❤ · ❤ · ❤ · ❤ · ❤ ·

BROOKE FLIPPED THE LOCK on the clinic door. "I thought to-day would *never* end," she moaned. "I'm going home to drown my sorrows in a bubble bath, a glass of the sparkling wine you brought over for our pedicure day, and binge-watch too many episodes of *Soccer Mum Socialites*."

I tugged my tote higher on my shoulder. "Today wasn't *that* bad, was it?"

"Rose Parker almost had a heart attack!"

"She most certainly did not."

Despite Rose declaring her impending doom to the waiting room, my official diagnosis was heartburn from indulging in too much chocolate. A good way to go, if you ask me. After some extra fussing, an antacid, and sharing a cup of ginger tea, she'd pottered out of my room an hour later, as good as new.

Brooke grinned. "Did she convince you to meet her grandson yet?"

"She may have suggested catching up for a coffee with him."

"He's one of the firefighters in town, you know."

"A fact she reminded me of many times."

"So, what did you say?"

"I politely declined."

"Because?" When I only stammered out some sounds, Brooke's grin widened. "Does your reluctance have something to do with a certain cabinetmaker, perhaps?"

"No..."

She snorted a laugh. "Sure thing, Lolly. Well, the next time you just *happen* to bump into Aiden, can you put in a good word for me?" She tossed her hair off her shoulders. "I need all the help I can get with Harry."

"You're interested in him?"

"I've been prancing around for a year trying to get that man's attention."

"No bites?"

"Not even a nibble!"

"I'll see what I can do," I promised. *"If* I happen to bump into Aiden."

After waving goodbye, the fact I headed straight to the store had absolutely nothing to do with tempting fate. No. That wasn't my plan at all.

The basket clutched in my hand swung empty as I wandered around the aisles, my mind lost, imagining how bristly Aiden's beard would feel against my skin if he kissed me. It was a silly fantasy that plagued my thoughts more and more. Stopping in front of the baking section, my fingertips brushed over my bottom lip, a spark rippling over my skin.

I decided kissing Aiden would feel *wonderful.*

Still distracted, I tossed a bag of flour into my basket and turned the corner—only to halt, my heart stuttering to a stop just as I collided with a broad chest blocking my path.

I pushed my glasses up my nose. "I—I'm so s-sorry."

"It's okay."

The rich rumble of Aiden's voice rolled over me. I almost dropped my basket. "H-hi," I said.

He squared his shoulders and tugged the buttons of his flannel shirt as if he were trying to make sure they were extra straight. "Evening, Lola. You, um..." He stuffed his hand in his pocket. "Is that one of your new outfits?"

Nodding, I suddenly became self-conscious, twisting my fingers in the belt of the floral dress. "It's a little...much..."

"No. It's nice. Pretty."

"Thanks." The word whooshed out of me. *Nice. Pretty.* I couldn't remember the last time a man had complimented my outfit. My chest filled with a warmth as soft and satisfying as fresh pancakes out of the pan. "And thank you. For yesterday."

His shoulder lifted. "No big deal."

My heart would have sunk if his cheeks hadn't darkened to a hot pink under his beard. Maybe it *was* a big deal.

"I, um... I noticed your book," I said. "In your car. I didn't mean to peek. It was on your dashboard. *The Count of Monte Cristo.*" I nibbled on my bottom lip to stop the rambling.

"I like reading."

"Me too! I haven't read that one yet. I'm making my way through all the classics now that..." *I'm allowed to waste time reading.* I couldn't say that, though. I hoped the smile I managed didn't look forced. "I have more spare time for reading these days."

"It's a good book. Long, though."

"What do you like about it?"

Aiden's head tilted, thinking over my question. "It's just... sort of... timeless." His eyes crinkled at the corners when he smiled. "Most people assume it's only about revenge, but I think it's about redemption. Finding hope where there shouldn't be any. Finding...love."

"O-oh."

"Sorry." He rubbed the back of his neck. "That's a bit heavy after a long day at work."

"No! Not at all. It sounds brilliant."

He smiled. "I picked up some vintage hardbacks at an antique store in the city a few years back. Five volumes. Illustrated. Real leather binding. Gold embossed trim."

Impressed, my mouth dropped open.

He chuckled. "Yeah. Nice, right? I'll let you borrow them sometime if, um..." His shoulder went up again. "If you'd like that?"

"I'd love that." Pressing my palm against my chest didn't calm the frantic thump underneath. "I promise I'll take such good care of your books." The slow way his eyes noticed that movement and locked there only made my heart pound harder.

"You would," he said. "What wouldn't be safe in your little hands, Lola?"

Aiden's tone was gentle. He wasn't flirting. Why would he be? But the naughtiest thoughts popped into my head.

None of him would be safe from my hands.

I wanted to tear open the neat buttons of his flannel and run my hands over the white T-shirt he wore underneath. He looked so strong. His body would be magnificent. *Masculine.* I'd beg him to let me crawl into his lap so I could pet him everywhere... Run my fingers through his beard... Kiss him...

Dazed, I stared up at Aiden. "Caramel," I sighed, twirling a strand of hair around my finger.

A confused chuckle rumbled from deep in his chest. "Sorry?"

I shook myself from the fog of my embarrassing daydream with a nervous laugh. "Caramel is the one thing I can't cook," I explained. "I never get it quite right. The sugar always burns."

I quickly turned away and sucked in an enormous breath, trying to regain some composure. It didn't work. Nerves slipped out in a humiliating giggle.

Balls.

My palm landed on my forehead. Panic smothered the giddy feeling of imagining a future with the man standing in front of me with a blank look on his face.

I'd promised myself I'd be stronger this time.

"You okay, lov—Lola?"

"Y-yeah! Yeah!" I wheezed. "Totally...totally fine!"

The hopeless romantic still foolishly lurking inside me wanted to pin my unfulfilled dreams of true love on Aiden. Why? The answer wasn't hard to find. His rough charm and strong arms would shield me from old ghosts—sure, that certainly didn't hurt. But deeper, beneath all that, I knew it was because Aiden was the first man who'd shown me genuine kindness in a very long time.

I wouldn't find what I needed rolling in my sheets with this gentle beast—if he'd even have me. I needed to live my life for myself. On my terms. Just...

On my own.

"Well... I guess I'd better, um..." I held up my shopping basket. Yes, it was definitely time to go. "It was lovely catching up with you, Aiden. Thank you again for last night."

If he said goodbye, I didn't hear him.

Like a coward, I scurried past, dropped the basket of groceries by the door, and bolted out of the store.

4

He Didn't See the Possibility

Aiden

THE TOWN HALL WAS a furnace.

Bargain hunters crowded stalls selling everything from rusty old junk to dinky jars of handcrafted strawberry jam. Who the hell bought those? Two scrapes on a bit of toast, and you'd need another trip to the village markets. No thanks.

Then again, no one else was stumbling around, tugging at their collar, pretending sweat wasn't dribbling down their neck, and searching for the nearest exit. That honour was mine alone. The other shoppers milling around the stalls looked happy. *Normal.*

How had Ruth talked me into this?

Saturday morning stuck at the village markets was my worst nightmare. Too many people. Too much noise. My mind played tricks on me in crowds like that. Like every other week, the faces blurred, but I clenched my jaw and pushed on, shoving one foot ahead of the other. Thankfully, the cardboard box filled quickly with everything on Ruth's list.

Harry shot from nowhere, weaving through the horde like a pro rugby player, a box of jam drop biscuits tucked under his arm. He dodged. Sidestepped. He only missed the woman shuffling behind a walking frame by the skin of his teeth, but he was all smiles when he pulled up to a stop in front of me.

"Got 'em!" he panted. "Miss Ruthie's favourite." Triumphantly, he held the box of biscuits over his head and chanted, "Harry! Harry! Harry!"

I'd done a damn good job shielding him from my problems over the years. He had no idea about the mess going on inside my head in situations like this, and I wasn't about to start freaking him out now. The thumping in my chest—yeah, I ignored it. The spiralling thoughts warning me that one noise might set me off got pushed away, too.

I forced a smile and mumbled, "Thanks."

"That's all I get?" Harry scoffed. "That sorry excuse for a smile and *thanks*?" His lip curled. "I had to sweet-talk Yolanda for these. A group of tourists cleaned out their whole stall. This was the last box, you know!"

"Thank you *very much*."

Harry waved at me to keep going with better praise for his effort. If he hadn't saved me from an interrogation by the old crows from the church, I would've told him to shove it.

"Thank you very much, *Your Majesty*." I hooked the box of groceries under my arm, and with a flourish of my free hand, I bowed.

Harry tipped his head back and laughed. "That's more like it." He dropped the biscuits onto the bunch of celery sticking out of the box but tapped the top, giving me a hard look. "I want credit for these. You tell Miss Ruthie I got 'em for her."

"You're not coming to lunch today?"

"Nah, better not. Mum..." He shrugged.

Suddenly, his sneakers needed a thorough inspection, and he was done talking. I didn't push him. Harry's mum had good days and bad. Depression was like that. She plummeted quickly, and when she hit rock bottom, she stayed down in the dark for days. He shouldered a lot of weight that shouldn't have been his at only twenty-two.

"If you need a break, come up to my place," I said, making the offer sound like no big deal. It was easier for him that way. "You can crash in my spare room if you want."

"Thanks. I might drive up later." He still refused to meet my eyes. "I should probably"—he jerked a thumb over his shoulder—"head off."

"Drive safe, kid." I slapped a friendly hand on his back before he disappeared in the crowd.

Digging Ruth's shopping list out of my pocket, I scanned the items and tallied everything in the box. All the fruit, most of the vegetables... I squinted. The words shook. I closed my eyes and tried to block out the noise. My hand tugged at my collar, but I still struggled to force down a breath.

Soft fingers touched my arm. "Aiden?" Her voice was soft too.

My eyes snapped open.

The nightmare had somehow become my favourite dream.

Lola's hair was pinned back, a hint of makeup warming her cheeks and lips. I would've thought she was the most beautiful creature in the world—except for the frown she aimed straight at me.

"You doing okay?" she asked. "You look..." Her hand squeezed my arm as she scanned my face with slightly narrowed eyes—doctor's eyes. "Can I help?"

"Uh, n-no—" I cleared my throat. "It's just a bit crowded here."

Lola's nod was firm, as if she knew exactly how I felt about being squashed half to death in the cramped hall.

"Doing some shopping?" I asked her, desperate to get my thoughts on anything but the ricochet of dread shooting up my spine.

I snuck another look at her. A pile of books was stuck under her arm, and her slender fingers wrapped around a jar.

My brows shot up. "You bought the jam?"

"Rose makes and bottles it herself." She twirled the dainty blob of glass and pressed it against her cheek. "Isn't this the dearest little jar?"

"Little" being the key word. I'd demolish every last drop in one bite. My eyes lingered too long on the freckles dotted along Lola's collarbone that disappeared under the strap of her dress. I'd demolish *her* in one bite.

"I actually came here hunting for eggs." Lola huffed enough to blow one of the loose tendrils off her cheek. "Did you know the village store can run out? Ashley said there might be some eggs here, but they sold out, too. *Hours* ago, apparently."

"You need eggs?" Maybe I'd finally have an excuse to drop by her place...

"I *always* need eggs. It's the hazard of being an amateur baker and gluing my eyeballs to too many inspirational videos when I *should* be doing my laundry." She laughed. "It's so easy for me to get sidetracked these days."

I wasn't blinking. My mouth had fallen open. I was staring at her. I *knew* I was, but I couldn't stop myself even when her hand fluttered to her throat and the corners of her lips tugged up in a nervous smile.

This woman.

When she wasn't so guarded... When she was just...*her*...

She was...so...so...

Beautiful.

If I were a normal man, that would have been the moment I got all nervous, stuffed my hands in my pockets, and bumbled my way through asking Lola on a date.

I'd never been on a date. Well, maybe as a teenager, but certainly not by the time I was in the police force. Duty, small towns, and relationships didn't mix. I'd had enough female company to get by. Relationships had never mattered as much as my career in those days.

Where would I take Lola? The bar?

My skin prickled in a cold sweat when I imagined sitting across from her in a claustrophobic corner with no escape. Too noisy. Too many variables I couldn't control. Nope.

Maybe I could ask her over to my place...

The back deck still needed a coat of paint, but it had views over the Coal River Valley and no tourists or interfering church ladies to distract me from my girl. I'd cook Lola dinner, pour her a glass of wine, and fuss over her. The fireplace would crackle in the background. I could risk some music and ask her for a waltz under the stars. Before it got too late, I'd walk her to the door and lay one of those TV kisses on her that looked all sweet and innocent, even though the thoughts running through my head would be anything but.

Maybe Lola thought it was the moment I was going to ask her out, too.

A blush crept up her neck, and she only darted her eyes up every so often to peek at me. She had the prettiest smile on her lips—pink like the roses I'd hand her if she came over for dinner. I'd bet those lips were softer than a petal. I wanted to run my thumb along the crease and feel all that sweetness before I kissed her.

The question waited to tumble out of my mouth. *Join me for dinner?* I just needed to spit it out.

"I'd better..." I lifted the box. "Yeah..."

"Oh, of course." Even I could see the smile Lola plastered on her face took some effort. "I didn't mean to keep you. I just wanted to make sure you were okay. And because..."

She couldn't leave me hanging there. "Because?"

"I like talking to you."

I like talking to you too.

No.

I love talking to you. I can't get enough of looking at you. I'd give anything to call you mine. Come over. Now. Tonight. Tomorrow. Every night. Please.

Instead of saying any of the thoughts desperate to spill out of my mouth, I nodded goodbye like it didn't tear at my guts to walk away from her.

No question. No date. No goodnight kiss.

Impossible dreams weren't meant for men like me.

· ♥ · ♥ · ♥ · ♥ · ♥ ·

"Ruth?"

It was the second time I'd knocked on the yellow door, but only silence answered. There was no flurry in the house or uneven steps to greet me. The box of groceries balanced on my hip dug into my skin when I knocked again.

Still no answer.

Fear gripped around my throat, but I shook my head, urging myself to calm down. I always overreacted when it came to Ruth. No need to panic. She was probably working in the garden and didn't hear me. It wouldn't be the first time.

I hauled the box under my arm and barrelled my way off the porch and down the stairs.

Everything's fine.

My boots crunched in quick steps down the gravel path, and rusty hinges squealed when I pushed through the gate. I added it to the mental list of things I needed to fix.

"Ruth?"

A floppy straw hat popped above the wall of pea shoots edging the vegetable patch.

"Aiden!" Ruth's good hand clutched around the small trowel that she waved at me across the yard. "Is it that late already? I must have lost track of time."

I made my way over, crouching beside a mound of fresh soil, the box of groceries balanced awkwardly on my knee.

"How's the veggie patch coming along?" I asked her.

Most of Ruth's face stayed hidden under the shadow of her hat until her chin tipped up. Her familiar crooked grin flashed my way. "Good." She huffed with frustration as she stabbed her trowel upright in the soil, done with her gardening for now. "But some days, I feel like I'm growing an all-you-can-eat buffet for my archnemesis."

"Paulie the Possum's struck again, huh?"

Ruth pointed at a row of mangled tomato bushes. "That bloody terror ate my whole crop!"

"We can put up some netting if you want."

"I'm willing to try anything at this point. We'll figure out a day around your work next week. But right now, forget it. I'm starving!" Her fingers fumbled in the dirt. "Where the heck—" Her hand froze. "Aha! Found it!"

Her cane popped out from under the pumpkin vine in a rain of soil, and she anchored it into the path and pushed up to her feet. She wobbled, always a little unsteady at first, and when a grimace tugged at her lips, my hand shot out, ready.

Her face stayed hidden under her hat, but I didn't need to see her eyes to know she was glaring at me. "Don't you dare," she hissed. "I can do it myself."

It took a few shaky steps for Ruth to get started down the path, but once she had a good rhythm, her pace quickened. Her chin tipped up with another crooked grin—a silent *"I told you so"* I'd seen a thousand times. She was gloating, but I didn't mind. Not one bit. She was walking. And as I followed Ruth into the kitchen, the sight of the jagged scars carved into her legs reminded me how much rehab she'd pushed herself through to be walking at all.

With a wave of her cane and a shout over her shoulder to "Make yourself comfortable!" she disappeared to the bathroom to wash up.

Comfortable?

I snorted, and the box of groceries hit the countertop with a thud. The last ten years of my life had been like the shirt I'd shrunk in the dryer. A size too small. Suffocating. Worse than a straitjacket. Make myself comfortable? Yeah, right.

I just had to keep moving. My mind couldn't start spinning fairytales again. If the sweet woman twirling that damn scam jam in her fingers hadn't landed in town, the idea of me settling down would still be dead and buried—where it belonged.

I unpacked the fruit and vegetables from the box, arranging everything in Ruth's neatly labelled containers in the fridge. A flip of the switch and the kettle was on. Out came the coffee pot. What next? Maybe I should start on some sandwiches...

"Aiden?"

The uneven pad of feet slowed through the kitchen doorway. I glanced up. Ruth's dark hair dripped in thin, wet strings down her back. The corners of her mouth drooped lower and lower as her eyes flicked between the coffee and mugs before landing on the snacks cluttering the wooden dining table.

Grumbling, Ruth said, "I could've helped with some of that." Her cane nudged out a chair, and I was careful not to offer my hand when she eased down. "I'm disappointed Harry couldn't make it today. I feel like the two of us haven't been able to gang up on you in weeks." Grinning, she grabbed a jam drop from the box.

"His mum's not doing well at the moment." Nothing more needed to be said about that. Ruth understood. "But he ran the gauntlet to get you those biscuits. He wanted to be sure he got credit for them."

"He was at the markets?"

"Yeah."

"Who else was there this morning?"

My hand paused, floating over the sandwich on my plate. The smile flashing my way might have looked innocent to anyone else, but I'd known this woman for thirty years. The mischievous glint in her dark eyes was as clear as day to me. She was up to something.

Still all innocence, Ruth asked, "Did you run into anyone interesting?"

"Like who?"

"I dunno." She nibbled her biscuit. "The lovely Dr. Hughes, perhaps?"

"Have you been gossiping with one of your *friends* from the church?"

"Maybe."

"So... yes."

She grinned. "I'm sure Yolanda will have an interesting update about what's been happening in town when she stops by for a coffee tomorrow."

"It'll be a quick update. I talked to Lo—*Dr. Hughes* for all of one minute."

"What did you talk about?"

"Jam."

"Sure." Ruth scoffed a laugh. *"Jam."*

Frustrated by the direction the conversation was heading in, I dragged my palm down my face. "Look, Lola bought one of those tiny bloody jars Rose sells at the markets. Strawberry, if I remember correctly."

"Uh-huh."

"She did."

"Are we *really* still pretending you haven't been raving about this woman for weeks?"

I grunted. Yeah, we were going to keep pretending that. Hunching over the table, I picked up my sandwich and took a huge bite. The more occupied my mouth was, the less likely I was to admit something stupid.

"Let's see." Ruth tapped her chin as she listed all the dumb things I must have gushed without realising. "Lola loves reading. She cooks. Bakes. Oh, but *not* caramel. She's interested in growing her own herbs. And she must love the colour pink because she wears it so often."

I swallowed a hunk of sandwich and ground out, "That proves nothing."

"And when I asked you if she was pretty—"

"I didn't say one damn word."

"You didn't need to. Your face did *all* the talking. Your ears were redder than a fire truck!"

I sank lower on the chair as heat boiled up my neck. I had a feeling my face—and my stupid ears—had betrayed me all over again.

"Have you asked her out yet?" Ruth nudged.

"No."

"When—"

"Never."

"Aiden—"

"This conversation is over, Ruthie girl. I love you. I do. But please don't interfere in this. Tell your friends from the church to back off, too. Lola and me..."

Ruth's good hand reached across the table and clasped mine. "You could be perfect. *Together.*"

"I don't do relationships. You know that."

"Only because you hadn't met the right person."

Shaking my head, I squeezed Ruth's hand before shifting mine out of her reach. "Leave it, okay?"

Ruth gave me a lopsided smile, but the scheming behind her eyes was impossible to miss. She had no plan to drop her quest.

If anything, her coffee catch-up with Yolanda would only stir up more drama. And honestly? I didn't mind. If the universe was determined to throw Lola in my path, I wasn't about to waste a single second I could spend with her.

But I'd keep my distance.

I refused to ruin her too.

5

She Didn't See History Repeating

Lola

THE *W* ON THE welcome mat at my front door was missing. A pink wooden box replaced it.

"Where did you come from?" I whispered.

Bending over, I picked up the box, twisting and turning it to examine each perfectly crafted corner. My fingertip bumped over the tiny chicks and daisy chains carved in a border around the lid before I flicked the golden latch. Inside, six eggs lay cradled in a wooden nest with a note.

> I KNOW YOU'LL PUT THESE TO EGG-CEL-
> LENT USE.

An enormous grin spread across my face. I didn't recognise the neat block capitals, but I knew the gift was from Aiden. It *had* to be. The pink box shimmered, and I lifted my glasses to swipe away tears, hugging the gift close to my heart.

Aiden *made* this. For *me*. And it was so *darling*.

A week passed.

Another Sunday morning rolled around. Shrugging on my cardigan, ready to head into town, I hauled open the front door to find a plain carton of eggs waiting toe-to-toe with my sneakers.

GET EGG-CITED. FRESH FOR YOUR BOX.

I glanced up.

Yolanda stood at the edge of the white picket fence, her gardening shears snipping at the roses in quick, easy swipes. A satisfied smirk danced on her lips.

"You might be right about Aiden finding someone," she said.

My cheeks heated, and stammering some weak excuse about breakfast burning on the stove, I snagged the fresh carton of eggs off the mat and fled into the cottage.

Another week passed.

My alarm clock beeped extra early that Sunday morning, but I was already out of bed, tiptoeing to the kitchen. I was a woman on a stealth mission. A baking ninja. There was absolutely no need for me to creep through the cottage in the dark. I lived alone. No one would see. But the anticipation added to the fun.

I slipped the cake container off the dining table and scurried back through the blackened maze of furniture, nearly tripping over the couch as I headed for the hallway. Worn hinges creaked when I pried open the front door to peek outside. Clouds smudged the moon, and except for the streetlight glowing above number four, the rest of the town still slept.

I glanced at the doormat.

Empty. No eggs yet.

I bent down and placed a surprise chocolate cake over the *W* with my own note tied on top with a pink ribbon.

I'M NOT A WHISK-TAKER. CHOCOLATE IS ALWAYS A WINNER. ENJOY xo

Chittering a wicked laugh, I raced back to the bedroom, dove under the covers, and tucked them under my chin. I wriggled in the warm sheets, too excited—or was that *egg-cited*—to sleep. But as the dull chirp of birds sang and the sun climbed over the mountains, my eyes drooped, and I fell back asleep.

A few hours later, as I padded to the kitchen, a yawn caught in my throat as I reached for the kettle.

Wait!

I dashed to the front door and cracked it open.

More eggs. And my cake was gone.

I sagged against the wood, my hand pressed over my racing heart, the silliest grin on my face.

Aiden.

Oh, I hope he liked the cake! I wished I could watch him take his first bite. My imagination spun out of control, a tingle rippling over my skin at the thought of the gruff thank you he'd murmur before pressing a kiss to my cheek...

Almost giddy, my head fell back against the door with a sigh. Would I have enough Sundays and different recipes to make that dream a reality?

Please.

♥ • ♥ • ♥ • ♥ • ♥

BY THE FOLLOWING SATURDAY, I still hadn't settled on my next creation to surprise Aiden.

Brooke bounced along beside me as I wandered around the market stalls. I only half-listened to her recap the latest episode of her favourite TV show, my fingertips absently skimming the edge of each table we passed, lost in thought.

Lemon... Carrot... Maybe Aiden would enjoy something unexpected like a brown butter cheesecake...

Distracted, barely glancing at the covers, I reached for another pile of books.

Brooke snatched the top one from the stack already in my hands, her eyes narrowing as she read the title. *"Learn to knit."* Her nose scrunched. "Knitting!" She shoved the book back at me. "Of all the hobbies in the world, why would you choose knitting? On *purpose?*"

I handed the money for the books to the stall owner with an awkward smile.

Brooke arched her eyebrow, waiting for an explanation she wasn't going to be satisfied with. She soared through life with complete confidence. Her idea of a good time was talking, going out, and...*dancing*. I loved catching up with her for brunch. I never minded a chat. But there was no way my two left feet were ever stepping into the Thursday night salsa class with her.

"I thought learning to knit might be fun," I said.

More than fun. Me, huddled on my couch, the fireplace roaring while I crafted cute things. Realistically, I was probably going to end up with a drawer stuffed full of wonky scarves and beanies with off-centre pom-poms on top, but practice made perfect. I couldn't be as hopeless at knitting as I was at pottery. *Surely*.

Brooke tossed a dubious look in my direction. "Will knitting be as fun as the jigsaw you bought last weekend?"

A little defensively, I said, "I happen to like jigsaws."

"We *need* to get you a TV. Do you have any hobbies that aren't like a cranky old nana?" Her lip curled. "Oh! I know!" She bounced on her toes and clapped her hands. "An adult ballet class is starting here in a couple of weeks. Wanna come with me?"

"I paid enough penance in ballet classes in my childhood. Why would I willingly subject myself to more torture?"

"I dunno." Her grin turned sly. "An even hotter bod might help convince a certain *someone* to ask you out." She rolled her eyes. "Finally."

I walked faster along the row of stalls. "I have no idea who you're talking about."

"Tall, dark, always wearing flannel—"

"I really can't date anyone right now."

"Got someone waiting for you back in the city?"

Fear shot down my spine, locking every muscle in place. I froze. Gripping the edge of the cake stall, I pulled in a trembling breath, shoving the memory of Chris's palm stinging against my cheek to the darkest corner of my mind so it couldn't claw its way back out.

Brooke slipped in beside me, shielding my panic from the eager eyes of the church ladies who'd crowded the end of the stall. "Lolly, I'm sorry. I didn't...didn't...mean to..." Her pretty features crumpled.

My hand was on her arm in an instant. I should have been better prepared for questions like that. "It's not your fault," I said. "You didn't know. There was...*someone*. He wasn't..."

Who I thought he was. Who he pretended to be.

Shaking my head, I finished simply by saying, "It didn't end well."

"I'm hearing you," she said, dropping her voice too low for anyone else to hear. "Forget I said anything. Take your time. Men come and go. A good one will wait until you've recovered from the last loser." She pressed against me in a quick hug. "The only person you need to worry about is you, okay?"

"Thanks."

"Anytime! Now..." Her grin was back. "If ballet is off the list... Did you hear the gallery is starting a candle-making class?"

"I'm in."

"Really?" she squealed.

"I can't guarantee my candles will stay upright, but I'd love to learn how to make my own..."

·♥ · ♥ · ♥ · ♥ · ♥ ·

BY THE TIME I dropped by the village store on my way home, I was still overwhelmed by too many cake options.

The trolley rattled as I rounded the next aisle. I glanced at my list. Half the items I'd stacked next to all the junk I'd bought at the markets weren't written on the scrap of paper I'd torn off my pink notepad. The vanilla ice cream was an impulse purchase. The hair treatments and face masks on the shelf in front of me weren't on the list, either.

Another little treat won't hurt...

I snatched one of each, dumped them on top of too many tubs of cream cheese, and kept pushing. The trolley jangled around the corner, but I pulled it back to a sharp stop.

Aiden stood in front of rows of vegetables, a basket gripped in his big hand. My heart leapt, but with my nerves tangling my feet, I rolled the trolley back.

His head turned. "Lola." His chin dipped down in a nod hello.

"Hi, Aiden."

Dark brows furrowing, his lips pressed together. He was like an ancient computer. Every sentence seemed to catch in spinning wheels and error messages before finally grinding out. I wished I were as careful as he was. My thoughts hurtled full speed to the night before, and a hot flush of shame crept up my neck.

I'd thought about Aiden when I shouldn't have.

Alone in my bedroom, when all the lights were out, I'd imagined he'd hauled me onto his lap. Fantasy Aiden had whispered in my ear, telling me how pretty I looked. And when I'd slipped my hand between my legs, I'd pretended it was his fingers making me feel so good, his gravelly voice an urgent whisper, begging me to come for him. I had. I'd moaned his name into my empty bedroom—the first time I hadn't rushed to get an orgasm over with as quickly as possible in years.

Flustered, my heart beating too fast, I fixed my eyes on my feet. This wasn't the time for fantasies. This was the time to say thank you.

I gathered my courage. I wanted to tell Aiden how much I loved the eggs and the darling little box he'd made for me. He must have spent hours—days, maybe—crafting it.

"Thank you," Aiden said, "for the cake last weekend."

He'd beaten me to it. My eyes snapped up.

A smile tugged at the corner of his lips. "Chocolate is my favourite."

"Mine too."

"Something else we have in common. Other than...reading...and...and..." He stuffed a hand in his pocket and, sighing, added, "Cooking." His lips pressed flat, and he returned to his silent thinking for a few beats until he nodded at my trolley. "How are you getting all this home?"

My shoulders hiked up to my ears. I looked helplessly at too many impulse purchases to carry. "A...taxi?" Was there a taxi in town? Rideshare? In a pinch, I could always call Brooke...

"I'll take you home."

"Aiden, I don't want to trouble you."

"It's on my way."

"Is it...really?"

Now, it was his turn to look at his feet. A shrug followed. Yolanda had been telling the truth.

Feeling braver, I challenged him with a grin. "I'll accept on one condition."

"Name it."

"Stay for lunch."

His eyes widened. "You're inviting me to *your* place?"

"Let me cook for you. I haven't had someone to spoil in such a long time."

That only made his eyes pop open even wider.

Too much, Lola. "I... I mean..." I tugged frantically on the sleeves of my pink cardigan until his hand reached out to stop me.

"I'd like that," he said.

Aiden waited patiently while I finished shopping. Outside, he opened the passenger door and offered his hand to help me into his truck. I was grateful he didn't seem to notice my sharp breath in when his rough palm touched mine.

He tugged my seatbelt to make sure I was safely strapped in. He'd done that last time, too. But now, I swear I didn't imagine that his hand lingered on the buckle a little longer, a wisp of mint sighing near my shoulder.

"Oh!" I said, startling him back in his seat when I arched forward to grab the new book sitting on his dashboard. *"Flowers for Algernon.* I read this one not long ago!"

"Yeah?" He rubbed the back of his neck. "Did you like it?"

"I loved it. I cried for a whole day after I finished."

"A whole day, huh?" He grimaced. "Maybe I should save *Flowers for Algernon* for the weekends then." He flashed a wry smile at me before starting the ignition. "I don't need Harry giving me more crap than he already does. Do you have any lunch-break-appropriate recommendations?"

We talked about books for the short drive home. Well, I gushed on and on about reading, and Aiden sat beside me, his eyes carefully trained to the road, turning to acknowledge my rambling with a nod every so often, but not saying much at all. He never said much.

By the time I fumbled my key into the old lock and kicked my shoes off by the door, excitement tingled all the way down to my bare toes.

Aiden lowered the grocery bags to the wooden floor—*all* of them.

"I can carry some," I'd said, reaching for a bag, only to get a playful swat shooing my hand away.

"I'm sure you can," he'd said, "but I want to do it for you. I like being useful."

He also insisted on taking off his boots before coming inside. Hunched over, his fingers made quick work of the laces, but my eyes had already found the fine strands of silver threading through his dark hair. I traced a finger along my collarbone, wondering how much softer that spot beside his temples would feel. But as my gaze continued to drift over him, fear gripped tight around my throat.

Shoes not lined up. A bag carelessly tossed on the floor. The cardigan I'd thrown on top of the whole mess instead of hanging it in the closet where it belonged.

The icy whisper of Chris's voice curled around my chest.

You know what happens when you're careless, Lola.

My heart slammed against my ribs, but not from the anticipation of inviting Aiden to lunch. No, it pounded in pure terror. Frantic, I fell to my knees beside him, desperate fingers clawing at the mess.

"I-I'm s-sorry," I choked out on a strangled breath.

"For what?" Concern etched Aiden's voice. When his head jerked up, I flew back, flattening myself against the wall like a shadow, the rough brick digging into my spine. "Lola?"

I squeezed my eyes shut, bracing for the worst. "I'm sorry for the mess."

The lightest brush of Aiden's fingers grazed my shoulder before slipping away. "A bit of mess never hurt anyone." A chuckle rumbled in his voice. "Not that there is any."

I dared to lift my eyes. Aiden was lining his boots up next to my shoes, and when he met my gaze, his grey eyes were soft. He wasn't angry. Not at all.

I peeled myself off the wall and offered him a shaky smile. He accepted with a dip of his chin. Something about that simple movement always made my stomach twirl. Actually, everything about this man made my soul sing. My cheeks hot, I dropped my eyes back to our feet.

I clapped my hand over my mouth, trying to trap the laughter threatening to burst out.

Aiden's eyebrows rose.

"Your socks," I wheezed.

"My..." He followed my gaze to his feet. Pink socks with cartoon eggplants, peaches, and water droplets. A deep shade of red burned up his neck all the way to the tips of his ears. "Goddammit. Sorry, Lola. I forgot." He rushed to tug the pink socks off and stuff them into his boots.

My chest shook with laughter. "Where did you get those?"

"Harry." Frowning, he shook his head. "Another one of his *hilarious* Christmas gifts."

"They actually are hilarious, you know."

"Careful. You might end up on his Christmas list." Aiden glanced around the hallway. "Where should I drop your groceries?"

"The kitchen's this way. Follow me."

And he did.

6

He Didn't See Anything but Her

Aiden

Lola tossed a nervous smile over her shoulder as she dashed through her living room. She straightened a pink woollen throw over the threadbare patches on the couch and snatched an empty glass from the only free spot on her coffee table not covered in jigsaw puzzle pieces.

"How'd that get there?" Her laugh was strained. "I promise my place isn't always this messy."

I loomed like an awkward lump in the hallway, but my eyebrows crept up. There was that word again. *Messy.* Lola sure was house-proud.

I'd never seen someone so worried about shoes before. She'd gotten herself all flustered. She still was. Her teeth had found a new home buried in her bottom lip. I'd bet that if she'd planned my visit better, she'd have cleaned every inch of the cottage until it sparkled.

I followed her down the hallway, taking a deep breath before heading into the gloom. Lola's place wasn't built for a man my size. I was a giant smashing through a doll's house. My shoulders brushed close to the exposed brick walls, ancient beams so low I stooped to avoid knocking my head. The faint tick of a clock bouncing somewhere in another room didn't help the anxiety coiled tight in my chest. Too many dark corners and close spaces stirred the ghosts in my mind.

But the tired old bones of the cottage were cosy, thanks to Lola's personal touches. Lots of floral. A hell of a lot of pink. Warm. Welcoming. A lot like her, really.

I snuck a peek through the open door at the end of the hall. Lola's bedroom. It had to be. The white comforter was folded down to reveal perfectly tucked pink sheets. I gulped. I'd had a lot of dishonourable thoughts about what I'd like to do with Lola on those sheets.

"Here's the kitchen," she squeaked.

I looked up, but my jaw dropped. A cooking bomb had gone off. Stacks of bowls and scattered ingredients covered the wooden countertop. A floury handprint marked the fridge.

Lola's shoulders scrunched up to her ears. "I'm a free-spirited cook."

My laugh seemed to ease her nerves. "You don't say." I scanned the chaos for a free spot to leave her groceries. "Busy breakfast this morning?"

"I baked some muffins to take over to Brooke's place."

I plucked a lonesome blob of purple off the chopping board. "Blueberry?" I popped it into my mouth.

"The best kind."

"My favourite is apple."

Grinning, Lola tapped her temple. "I'm filing that information away for later."

I caught my lips curving up as I let my hip rest against the counter, the stiffness draining from my body. She was the sweetest little thing. Innocent, somehow. "Are you going to keep baking for me, love?"

My smile vanished almost as quickly as her pale brows popped over the top of her glasses.

My heart stuttered to a stop in my chest.

Love.

I'd called her *love*.

Not just in my mind. Not just in the shameful moments when my hand had been an efficient but hollow substitute for her. I'd almost slipped up once before but had managed to clumsily smooth it over before she noticed. No, this time, I'd been stupid enough to call her *love* out loud.

I had no business thinking about Lola like that. None. I had even less business talking to her like there was ever any possibility she'd be mine.

Did she know that, too? Was that why she twisted the wooden button of her cardigan?

Unsure how to rewind the term of endearment that had threatened to spill out for weeks, I stammered, "I should, um... Yeah... Wash up...or...or something," and headed for the sink under the window.

Stuck in the cramped kitchen with Lola, my pulse pounded like a jackhammer. A distraction wouldn't hurt. I unbuttoned the cuffs of my shirt and rolled up the sleeves to my elbows. Lola was right beside me. Her tiny blue eyes were glued to my hands, examining the way I worked the soapy lather like she was collecting evidence from a crime scene. Something about that look made me want to tug my collar away from my neck.

Lola shoved a scrunched-up tea towel at me to dry my hands before shuffling to the fridge to rummage around.

"So, who's your egg guy?" Her voice floated from somewhere near the vegetable drawer.

Huh? "Egg guy?" I hung the tea towel back over the oven handle, arranging it—and rearranging it—to make sure the stripes were in a perfect line. I didn't want her worrying any more than she already was.

"People talk a lot about the Hollyoak farm," she said. "Is that where you go?"

"Nah, the eggs are from my place. I've got six chickens."

"Six chickens!" She sounded impressed. "What do you do with all the eggs?" She whipped a look over her shoulder to bless me with a grin. "Other than sharing them with amateur bakers, of course."

There was nothing amateur about Lola's chocolate cake. I'd demolished most of it before lunch that day. Her cake was that damn good. I'd grumbled about sharing a slice with Harry when he'd dropped by but snatched the container away before he could help himself to a second. *My cake.* Made for me by *my girl*.

I shrugged. "Eat them." I took some down to Ruth, but now wasn't the time for a messed-up history lesson. "Cook with them."

Her hands still empty, Lola flicked the fridge shut. "I can't imagine having my own chicken coop. It must be so peaceful to have *space*."

Peaceful? I guess. Isolated. Lonely... "Yeah, I've got a couple of acres."

She pressed a hand to her heart and fell against the fridge. "That must be so... *Wow*."

"You'd like to live in the hills?"

She bobbed her head in an eager nod.

"You think you'll find a bigger place...if..." I swallowed heavily. "If you decide to stay?"

She didn't hesitate before answering, "I'm staying." There was a firmness to her voice I hadn't heard before. "There's nothing for me back on the mainland."

"What about your folks?"

Lola mustered half a smile. "Bruce and Barb retired a few years back and bought themselves a Winnebago bigger than this place."

"Are they doing the whole grey nomad thing around Australia?"

"Yeah. I think they're somewhere in the far north at the moment. And I love my parents, but..."

"You're not close?"

Sighing, Lola shook her head. "I shouldn't be stuck on things that happened thirty years ago... Life's so short... But my mother spent most of my childhood convinced she could cure my shyness." She grimaced. "Let's just say the endless weekends trapped at dancing recitals probably made me worse, not better. Here, I have the freedom to be myself. No history. No reminders. You probably don't get it..."

"No, I do. Honestly. I moved down here about eight years ago. Similar reasons." Well, not that similar. I'd destroyed a lot of lives first. "Sometimes, you need a fresh start without other people's expectations weighing you down."

"Exactly. The cottage suits me for now because..." Lola slid a glance to me from the corner of her eye. "The no-car thing. But soon...maybe... A car's on my list."

"What else is on your list?"

She lifted a shoulder with a small smile. "I'm kind of excited that I don't really know yet. I had years where I felt like every second of my life was dictated by someone else's routine. What they needed. Their happiness." Another glance shifted to me, but that uneasy look disappeared with a wave of her hand and a laugh. "Sorry. That got a bit...much..."

I took a step closer. Maybe it was a step too close. "I'm interested in knowing more about you." Preferably, everything.

"I want to know more about you, too." She fumbled with her button again. "Like... what's your favourite food?"

"Pasta."

"Um..." She frowned at the closed pantry door. "I'm not sure I have any."

"Well, we know you've got flour." Grinning, I ran my fingertip through the dusty white trail sprinkled along her countertop and booped her on the nose. Her giggle just about undid me. "If you've still got a couple of eggs left, I can show you how to make fettuccine."

She blinked up at me. "Seriously?" Her mouth fell open. I nodded.

"I'd love that!" Her excited bounces over to the pantry paused mid-step. She turned to look back at me. "I don't have a pasta maker."

"You don't need one. The dough's easy. Roll it, rest it, fold it, cut it. You don't need anything fancy."

"Does the type of flour matter?"

"If you're an aficionado, sure."

"What about if you're a very keen first-time fettuccine maker?"

"Grab your all-purpose flour." I tidied away some of the clutter while Lola rummaged in her pantry. "This is going to be a little messy. You okay with that?"

Arching an eyebrow, she gestured around the kitchen.

I chuckled. "It's really not *that* bad."

I spritzed some cleaner and wiped a spot clear on the countertop. Lola dropped a container of flour there without much care. But she cradled the egg box I'd made her close to her chest as if it were a precious jewel.

"It really is the most darling little box," Lola whispered, her fingertips skipping over the top. "Did you engrave all the details yourself?"

"Yeah." It took a bloody age to carve out the tiny chicks, but the awe brightening her eyes made it worth the extra effort. "You...like it?"

"I love it. It's probably the most thoughtful gift anyone's ever given me."

The quiet gratitude shining in her smile almost broke me. "I'm glad you like it." I silently vowed to make her a hundred more if she'd smile at me like that again. "Should we get started on your lesson?"

"Let's get cracking!"

Laughing, we got to work.

Lola was a diligent student. Pushing her glasses up, she leant over to watch me make a well in the flour and crack the eggs inside. She edged closer and closer as I walked her through each step, mixing the ingredients, sprinkling in salt, and dribbling just enough water to keep the dough from crumbling.

"You make it look so easy," she said.

"I've had some practice." I turned to give her a smile. "Want to have a go at kneading the dough?"

Lola clasped her hands under her chin. "Can I?"

"Of course."

Her eyes narrowed. She meant business. The tip of her tongue poking out the corner of her mouth, she gently kneaded the dough, flicking a look up at me every so often, seeking my reassurance she was doing it right.

"You're doing good, love," I said.

She smiled so big and bright, I didn't even kick myself for calling her that ridiculous name again.

"How long do I keep this up for?" she asked.

"About ten minutes."

"Ten minutes! Okay." Her hands left a white outline on her apron when she planted them on her hips. She jerked her chin down in a nod. "Yes. I can do it."

My eyes wandered over her as she went back to work, memorising every tiny detail. The way her glasses slid down her nose. How her hair slipped from behind her ear to hide her face. My gaze drifted lower. Painted pink toenails. Bloody hell. Even her toes were pretty.

My mind floated back to my dishonourable thoughts about Lola sprawled on her sheets. That was a mistake. I couldn't concentrate. South of the equator stole the blood from my brain. I grabbed the glass of iced tea Lola had poured me and took a huge gulp. Should I leave? It was the last thing I wanted to do. I glanced out the window. The sun still floated high in a pale blue sky. I had more time...

Lola huffed her adorable grunts of effort for a couple of minutes. "I think the dough's getting softer, but..."

"You need to put a bit more *oomph* in it."

Her lip curled. "I'm putting in the *oomph!*"

"More." Hesitantly, I pressed my palm gently over her hand to guide it deeper into the dough. My eyes closed as air shuddered into my lungs. A simple touch, so innocent, yet it felt like something I shouldn't be doing. "Like this." I rocked my hand with hers. "Feel the difference?"

"O-oh. Y-yes." She gulped. "I do." She glanced up at me from the corner of her eye. "Aiden?"

I inched my other hand to rest on her shoulder. "Yes, Lola?" My fingers were rough like sandpaper. The patch of freckles disappearing under the sleeve of her dress was too precious for hands like mine, but I'd give anything to touch one of those marks on her skin.

"A-are you...?"

Her hair was precious too. "Yes?" I stared, almost spellbound, as I wound the pale rose-gold strands around my finger.

"Are you"—she gulped—"going to...kiss me?"

"Do you want me to?" I heard her little gasp when the tip of my nose nuzzled into the soft hair curled around her ear. I loved that spot. She smelled even better this close.

"Y-yes."

She was right to be cautious of me, but I took what I wanted. I pressed soft lips to her forehead. "Was that okay, love?"

"Yes."

I ghosted a featherlight kiss to the edge of her smile. "And that?"

"Very yes."

"What about a longer kiss?" I ran my thumb over her bottom lip. "Here."

Lola nodded.

"But what if..." I bent forward but didn't kiss her mouth. Not yet. I pressed my lips to her cheek again instead. "Lola, I'm not a good man." If I were, I wouldn't have accepted her invitation. I should've walked away weeks ago and never started any of this. "I'm not." The tip of my nose grazed hers. "I can't make you happy."

"Now is enough, Aiden," she said. "And I'm happy now."

Me too.

I wanted to tell her that I treasured our awkward conversations and all the quiet moments we'd spent together. But Lola didn't know about the shadows roped around my mind and the noisy, unpredictable destruction that kept me teetering so close to the edge. I couldn't bear to see rejection in her pretty blue eyes if she found out the truth about me.

Lola brushed the back of her fingers over my cheek. Was she trying not to get flour in my beard? A shiver of longing rippled down my spine. She could coat me in flour if she kept touching me like that. I hadn't let a woman get this close in years. Maybe ever. No one was as sweet as Lola.

"I like your little hands on me," I murmured into her hair.

"Please, Aiden."

Chasing her needy whisper, I dipped my head, my lips finally brushing against hers. Lola was bolder than I'd imagined in my fantasies. She was confident sharing affection—almost eager—and her kiss, so seductive and fearless, was just as demanding as mine.

"Very, very yes," she whispered.

She clung to me, her slender arms wrapped around my neck, letting me know she was mine to hold, to savour, as I deepened the kiss. The groan of pleasure that rumbled in my chest couldn't be stopped. I wanted her to hear the way her lips made me feel. Reborn. *Undone.* I ignored all the warnings—the clock ticking louder in the background, past sins gnawing at the edges of my thoughts...

"Goddamn, Lola... I..." I couldn't breathe. Did I even want to? I wanted Lola in my bones. I wanted to trap her memory, every detail of her, in my soul.

"I feel the same way," she said before capturing my mouth for another kiss.

But I hadn't said anything. How could she know?

I'd been dancing around Lola for weeks, and then, suddenly, I was in her kitchen. She was in my arms. I knew the way her breath hitched when her body melted against mine. I'd tasted her sweet lips, and I knew the tongue she poked out of her mouth when she concentrated tasted even better when sensually tangled with mine.

But I should have ended it. I should have acted like a gentleman. Told her the truth.

In the brief moments our kisses stopped, after we finished making the pasta, ate lunch, and finally, when she walked me to the front door hours later, I should have reminded Lola I wasn't the man for her.

And when her fingers untangled from mine and she asked, "Would you like to come for dinner tomorrow night?" I should have said no.

Nights were always worse.

Instead, I buried it all.

"Yes, love." I trailed my fingers along Lola's jaw, tipping her chin up so I could kiss her goodbye. "I'd like that."

And I pretended life was perfect—finally worth living—even though I knew...

I was going to ruin her.

7

She Didn't See Any Red Flags

Lola

THE KNOCK ON THE door finally came just after six.

Anticipation thrummed in my chest. After a final twirl in front of the mirror to check my floral dress from every angle, I stumbled out of the bedroom, almost tripping over my feet.

A pause behind the front door. A deep breath in. My heart only raced faster.

"Calm down," I mumbled to myself.

But I couldn't. I'd overdone it. The chicken roasting in the oven. The apple pie baking below it. My make-up. The dress. The sheer blush-pink underwear I'd painstakingly chosen to slip on underneath. It was too much. All of it. Everything.

I clutched the doorknob, my fingers unsteady on the cold brass. Fear stopped me from opening my life to a new possibility.

I'd asked Aiden to come for dinner, but...

Was it wrong to crave his compliments? *More?* It had been three months since I'd escaped Sydney. Should I wait longer before inviting Aiden into my bed? I ached for closeness, for *honest* love, but was he searching for that, too? Maybe not. He'd warned me he wasn't a good man...

I squeezed my eyes shut and let my mind float back to the day before. Aiden's cautious touches. So many incredible kisses. His sighs and the reluctant way he'd eased away from me, his grey eyes lingering. He always seemed as though he was about to say something but never did.

Did he want to whisper that everything was happening too fast?

I didn't trust my instincts. How could I? I was too needy. Too clingy. Too... *Lola*. But I hadn't imagined Aiden's tenderness. He'd called me *love*. I could trust that.

After one more deep breath in, I opened the door.

Aiden waited on the other side, a frown locked on the darkening sky before he turned to me. My stomach tumbled in a somersault. Words weren't possible yet. Not when he looked so handsome and rough all at once. He'd made an extra effort, too. His dark hair was combed but had a damp shine as if he'd just showered, and he wore a white Henley and dark pants instead of his usual flannel and jeans.

I hugged the door to keep myself steady. "H-hello," I said.

No hello in response. Aiden thrust a bottle of wine and a posy wrapped in pink paper at me instead.

"The lavender is from my place," he said. "It grows like a weed up in the hills." Almost groaning, his chest deflated. "I'm not...giving you weeds..." His throat bobbed on a heavy swallow. "It smells good."

"Thank you."

Fighting the tremble in my chin, I reached for the gifts and savoured the delicate fragrance of his hand-picked flowers. Aiden's simple gestures touched my heart in a way Chris's gifts never had. His guilty conscience had showered me with endless diamond baubles—lavish apologies for his busy hands and his wandering eye.

Chris thought I didn't know about the other women. For a long time, I'd cried quietly in the shower, stung by my failure to keep him happy. For an even longer time, I'd sighed with relief when he'd slunk home smelling like another woman's perfume…or worse. Those nights had been quiet.

I arched on my tiptoes to kiss Aiden's cheek. "And thank you for coming."

But my lips never landed. In a blur, he pulled me against his chest, the lavender squashing between us, his mouth melting into mine. Oh, I loved his fierce kisses. I cupped his cheek, drawing him closer in a heated, sensual frenzy.

A groan rumbled in his chest. "Lola…" He untangled himself and stepped back to put some distance between us. "I promised myself I'd be a gentleman… Treat you right… Not…" He raked a hand through his hair, jaw tight as he exhaled. "Tonight's just dinner."

"O-oh." I forced a shaky smile onto my face. "Just, um… *Dinner.*" My dilemma about waiting had been answered for me, but I was too embarrassed to look anywhere but at my feet. "I'm roasting a chicken…and…and some vegetables… And I'm baking an apple pie." I fumbled with the belt on my dress to make sure it was cinched extra tight.

"I love apple pie."

I'd hoped he'd say that, but I still couldn't force my eyes up. "It won't take long. Please." I gestured for him to come inside. "Take a seat in the living room. I'll pop the lavender into some water and pour us a drink. We can try your wine…or… I made some old-fashioned lemonade." A nervous laugh tumbled out. "Fresh lemons. Yolanda has a tree out back. She, um…" She'd handed me a bowl full and offered plenty of unsolicited tips about how to lure a man through his stomach. "Yeah."

Calloused fingertips touched my chin. "I'd like to try your lemonade." Aiden's eyes crinkled with a soft smile.

This time, when he headed for the couch, no panic flooded over me. The cottage was spotless. My half-finished jigsaw had been cleared off the coffee table. No glasses were where they shouldn't be. Every surface had been wiped over, and the floors vacuumed. Twice.

I disappeared into the kitchen. My hand still shook when I poured the lemonade.

"Hold yourself together," I hissed at myself in a frantic pep talk. "It's *just* dinner."

Pale yellow liquid sloshed around in frosted glasses when I walked down the hallway.

Just dinner.

After I carefully placed the drinks on the coffee table, the couch groaned as I squeezed into the narrow space beside Aiden's enormous frame. I gasped. My thighs were flush against rigid muscles. I sat up taller, trying not to take up more room, but there was no avoiding how close we were.

"I'm sorry about the couch," I said. "This place came mostly furnished. I'm not complaining. It was helpful because, um... I travelled light." One suitcase was light. It wasn't a lie. "But a lot of what was left here is quite old." I gulped. "And small." Far too small to be comfortable for a man his size.

"It's cosy. It's you."

Just dinner.

"Try the lemonade," I squeaked.

"Lola..."

Cautiously, I looked up. The eyes waiting for me didn't look like they were interested in tasting my homemade drink. No, those stormy grey eyes looked hungry for something...more.

Just dinner.

"I wasn't totally honest with you before," Aiden said.

"Y-you weren't?"

He shook his head. The muted musk of his cologne curled around me when he edged closer. He tucked my hair behind my ear and ghosted a kiss on the spot just beside it. Bristly beard and warm breath lingered on my neck.

"I want to make love to you," he whispered.

Longing sighed through me, the ache twisting a confession from my lips. "I want that."

"Do you?" He seemed to like nuzzling the spot beside my glasses. "Have you thought about us? Don't be shy. Tell me."

"Y-yes."

"I've thought about you."

"You have?"

He groaned against my skin. "Too many times..."

Dinner was almost impossible.

Our knees knocked together under the tiny table. My nervous chatter about books was pointless, and neither of us seemed interested in eating. Every time my fork rattled against the plate, and I darted up a look, Aiden's eyes were already waiting. He insisted on helping me wash up, murmuring his appreciation in my ear more than once. But I was the one who laced our fingers together and led him to the bedroom.

Antique brass creaked as I sank onto the bed. The scent of fresh linen and the slide of cool cotton along my thighs did nothing to settle my nerves.

This *wasn't* just dinner.

The mattress dipped, and a soft kiss found my cheek.

"Let's take these off..." Aiden murmured, slipping off my glasses and carefully placing them on the nightstand.

The world blurred, just out of focus, but it didn't matter. When Aiden's lips found mine, I followed without thinking, only feeling. *More*—that was what I needed. An insistent grab of his shirt and his weight pressed me into the sheets.

Aiden chuckled. "I'm not sure if this bed is made for someone my size."

No, it wasn't. The leg he hadn't thrown over mine dangled off the edge.

"Do you want to try somewhere else—"

"God, no," he said. "I've dreamed about you on these pink sheets. We're staying right here."

Smiling, I arched up, capturing his lips for more of his kisses. My heart couldn't keep up with so many new sensations. I loved being with Aiden—kissing him, the warmth of his big body stretched out against mine, holding me close but far less greedy with his touches than I was.

I knew the names of all the muscles and tendons bunched under my fingertips, but medicine was the furthest thing from my mind. I trailed my hand down his chest, lower... lower... My fingertips snuck under the bumpy white cotton, hitching it up just a little. He sighed against my cheek but took the hint. He'd barely peeled off his shirt and tossed it on the floor before I got my hands on his bare chest.

"Oh," I sighed. "You're so..."

Perfect.

Aiden was broad, so strong, but he wasn't like the guys obsessed with going to the gym. My fingers brushed over his defined shoulders and solid arms, the rugged ridges of muscle on his chest, all covered with a bit of extra padding—he did seem to love his food—and patches of dark, crinkly fuzz in just the right places.

"I like your little hands on me," he whispered.

Good.

My hands still had so many places—so much *man*—to explore for the first time. And he liked it. A lot.

Aiden never talked much, but there was no restraint in how he expressed pleasure. Deep groans of approval rumbled in his chest, and slow kisses turned hungry, his touches deliberate, intentionally sensual, a desperate heat throbbing between my thighs...

Until he captured my hand and pinned my wrist to the bed.

I froze.

The wooden beams of the ceiling shifted from swirling in light and shadow to pitch black. Fear locked my eyes shut even when a tentative kiss grazed my cheek.

"Lola?" The heaviness of him eased off my body, but I still didn't dare breathe. "I did something wrong."

My world stayed dark. "Please don't be rough with me," I pleaded.

Aiden released my wrist. "You want me to be gentle, love?" He kissed the skin in a silent apology. "I can."

Another piece of my shattered heart glued back together. He didn't question why I asked; he simply listened.

I opened my eyes to a soft smile.

"There's my girl," he said. "Can I see the rest of you now, too?"

After waiting for my nod, he unknotted the belt around my waist. But before his fingers plucked open any buttons, I eased off the sheets, a little unsteady when I stood up.

I took a step away. "I'll just turn out the light—"

"No." Aiden snagged my hand, and, sliding to the edge of the bed, he coaxed me to stand between his knees. "Leave the light on."

"But I'm..." Not much. Ordinary. Too... *Lola*.

"You're beautiful."

A glimpse of his hooded eyes and flushed cheeks reassured me that he was telling the truth. He flicked off each button of my dress, starting at the very top, and nudged it open to reveal pale skin.

"God, yes. See?" His palm slid up my thigh, pulling me close enough to sigh into the bare curve of my stomach. "So beautiful. What can I do to show you? What do you like?"

Feeling braver, I swept off one shoulder of my dress, then the other, silk pooling at my feet. "I'd like it if, um..." My hands twisted behind my back, and my bra was unhooked, too.

"Tell me," Aiden pleaded, calloused fingers finding their way under lace straps to slip my bra down my arms and to the floor. "Whisper it if you're shy."

I gnawed on my bottom lip. Why was this part so hard? I was already utterly exposed, wearing nothing but sheer pink knickers and a shaky smile. But my fear wasn't just about him seeing my body; it was about all my insecurities and hopes as well.

I needed to keep being brave.

A whisper was all I could manage in the end. "I'd like it if you could use your mouth, please."

"Such sweet manners." Goosebumps sparked under bare-ly-there fingertips over my breast, my stomach, my belly button, and ended with a whisper of pressure to the already damp lace between my legs. "Here, love? You want my mouth here?"

I nodded.

"God, yes," he said. "Let me do that. Come here."

A guiding hand brought me back to the bed, and his mouth landed on mine in a deep kiss. His belt buckle clinked. A zipper whispered open. Fabric rustled, and his pants were down, off, on the floor, with only thin layers of cotton and lace left between us.

But there was still no rush.

We melted into slow, lingering kisses, exploring each oth-er again with unhurried care. Even the fantasies I'd barely let myself believe hadn't prepared me for the intensity of his gaze or just how much I loved curling my fingers into the ridges of muscle along his naked back.

Breaths ragged, Aiden's lips hovered above mine. "Do you like how I kiss you, Lola from the City?"

"I hate when people call me that," I huffed.

"Oh?" His thoughtful hum rumbled along my ribs before his lips teased my breasts. "How about... Luscious Lola?"

I laughed. "Absolutely not."

"Still no?" A shiver skated over my skin when his fingers curled around the waistband of my pretty pink underwear. "Do you like it when I call you *love*?"

"That's my favourite."

"Mine too." He slipped the lace down my hips and kissed my ankle as the delicate fabric disappeared somewhere on the floor with the rest of our clothes. "I've called you that in my mind for weeks." His teeth grazed along the inside of my thighs, little teasing bites that made my heart race.

"I call you a big brute in mine..." I sighed.

His shoulders shook as he laughed, but I couldn't see his smile. He buried his face between my legs, and the first erotic lick—*heaven*.

"You boss me around." Oh, his voice was so husky. He *liked* doing this for me. "Don't be shy."

"O-okay."

My stammered instructions gave way to something bolder when he obeyed, only drawn out more by his hot, wet mouth on my clit, the scrape of his beard on my thighs, and the low, guttural sound he made when I tugged at his hair.

Embarrassed, I lifted my head from the pillow and whispered, "S-sorry." He made it so easy to get carried away.

Aiden's eyes found mine. Still no smile, but something gentle lingered in his expression. "You're so sweet and quiet. You keep digging those little fingers into me, so I know you feel good."

I stroked his bristly cheek. "I feel incredible."

"Then let me keep going..."

I never wanted those moments with Aiden to end—but at the same time, I so desperately did. I chased the knot of pleasure burning inside me, feeling it wind tighter and tighter as his mouth eagerly brought me closer to the edge. Then, everything blurred, a spark rushed from my toes and exploded through me, tumbling me into a dreamy abyss.

Dazed, I could only stare at the ceiling and listen to the contented sighs that rumbled in Aiden's chest every time my body shuddered with the aftershocks of the kisses he pressed to my thighs, my stomach, my breasts, my throat...

He stood, pushing his underwear down. My tongue darted out to wet my lips, and lust distracted me from focusing on anything except the manly body in front of me. His eyes hooded, one of his big hands lazily stroked up and down his hard length, the other tracing the curve of my hip.

The groan that followed didn't sound sexy, though. It sounded annoyed.

"I don't have anything," he said.

"Hmm?" I dragged my eyes away from all that delicious, rugged man to blink up at him.

"A, um... Yeah. I don't have one. I know some guys carry one around in their wallet, but... I honestly didn't think we'd get this far tonight." His eyes slid to the nightstand. "Do...you?"

It was sweet that he was shy about asking for condoms. "Bottom drawer."

There were more than enough options for him to choose from, next to the tissues and a random tube of lip gloss. Hopefully, the pharmacist didn't gossip as much as the church ladies... Nothing else of interest was in that drawer. The items I needed to feel safe—the pepper spray and the knife—were hidden in the one above. I'd never tell Aiden that, though.

I pushed old memories and fears away. Tonight was about him. Us. And Aiden was a master at distracting me with kisses.

The bed dipped, and his mouth found mine, leaving me no chance to think. And I didn't need to. My aching body knew exactly where I needed him. I reached for Aiden, guiding him over me, his weight sinking me into the sheets as his hips settled between my thighs.

"I want you," I whispered.

"Do you?"

"Yes. Very yes."

"Even though I'm a big brute?"

"Especially for that reason. Can..." I tentatively reached a hand between my legs. "I don't want to be greedy, but can I... when we...?"

"God, yes."

The slow, wet swirl of my fingers over my clit was bliss. More than anything, I loved the way he watched me. That intense scowl. The serious, sexy frown. Like he couldn't quite believe it. *Awed.* I only paused my own pleasure to feel it fully—that moment, the first time—when Aiden's restraint finally gave way and he slid his cock inside me on a broken, shuddering moan.

"See," he murmured, trailing light fingers along my hip. "Nice and gentle."

I gasped in breath after breath. Those first thrusts didn't feel gentle. They felt deep and too full, but the painful, longing ache to be close to someone had finally been soothed. Aiden was inside me. *With* me. My nails carved into his skin, and with every muffled cry against his neck, I clung tighter, desperate to keep him there.

"Still those quiet little moans," he murmured, moving in a slow, deliberate rhythm. "Just for me to hear, isn't that right?"

"Yes." I arched my back, my nipples aching and hard against the crinkly hair on his chest. He needed to be closer. "Just for you." My legs parted wider, my hips grinding against him, pushing my hand firmer to my clit.

He moaned his praise between kisses and the steady rhythm of his body moving with mine. He liked it when I touched him, so I touched him everywhere. One hand kept busy between my legs, but my other hand was free to roam. I loved running my fingers along the smooth muscles of his strong arms more than anything else, and his deep, manly grunts of pleasure only made the ache for another release twist tighter inside me.

"Lola, I had no idea…" A light sheen of sweat glistened on his bare skin, his muscles straining, fighting to hold back. "It shouldn't be this good. I can wait—"

"I want you to come."

"God." Aiden's rhythm faltered, his hips driving into me. "Not—*God,* not yet."

Sweat slicked my thighs against the pretty pink sheets, the bed squeaking almost enough to be distracting, but he anchored me back in the moment. His palm cradled my cheek, holding me close as I worked my fingers over the desperate ache between my legs until I shattered again, moaning a sigh into the space between us.

His restraint broke with it.

"Lola… My Lola…" He kissed me as if he couldn't bear to stop, only pulling back to murmur, "Why would you want me?"

Our foreheads touched as a deep, broken moan slipped from his lips, and he finally gave in. I held him close, his ragged breaths catching in my hair, his heartbeat thudding against my flushed, naked skin. I didn't want to let go. Not yet.

A moment like that was rare. Precious. Worth remembering.

And I let myself believe Aiden felt the same because he kissed me so tenderly and whispered, "This is the best night of my life."

8

He Didn't See Past the Nightmare

Aiden

MY EYES SNAPPED OPEN.

Reality was hazy. Inky shadows drowned the room, plunging me back into the choking waves of a nightmare I never quite woke up from.

Where am I?

Lost. Stuck. My heart hammered in my chest. A scratchy, broken reel of images played over and over, and even with my eyes forced open, raindrops danced in the slow swirls of red and blue lights over a silent highway.

Nights were always worse.

I pressed my hand to my chest, forcing myself to swallow the rock blocking my throat. The squeal of ancient springs under my weight speared through my temple.

Get up.

I sucked in another breath and tried to move, but my body stayed tangled in sheets and the pale, delicate limbs of...*a woman?* I squinted through the shadows. No, not just any sheets. Pink sheets. A fist squeezed around my heart.

Lola.

I eased my leg out from between soft thighs, and my hand slipped away from the gentle curve of her belly.

Lola grumbled in a sleepy protest.

"Shh," I soothed, stroking trembling fingers along her hip, wild eyes scanning the room. "It's okay, love."

It wasn't. Not at all. I'd stayed too long. I'd never meant to fall asleep. I—

The steady, unforgiving click of a clock filled the gloom.

I screwed my eyes shut. Every *tick, tick, tick* was like brittle nails hammering into a fragile skull. There were no clocks in my house. I couldn't risk it—and I was about to make damn sure there wasn't a clock in Lola's cottage, either. I'd hunt that thing down and smash it into a thousand pieces.

I pushed off the bed, but a sleepy hand gripped my side.

"Where...you...?" Lola's voice was groggy and still on the edge of dreams.

"Go back to sleep, love." My hand shook when I smoothed back her hair. I kissed the spot on her shoulder dotted with freckles. "I'm just going to the bathroom."

All I had to do was stick to the routine.

I'd done it a thousand times before. Find the bathroom. Splash some water on my face. Force my mind out of a tortured past back to the present. I could stop the panic before it spiralled out of control if I just followed the routine.

"Mmm 'kay... That way..." Lola's finger pointed to the hall-way before she smooshed her face back into the pillow.

I reached blindly over the side of the bed, fingers sweeping the floor for my clothes. Lola's lacy knickers. Her pretty dress. My underwear underneath. That would do. I tugged up the black cotton as I stood.

Tick.

Tick.

Tick.

My body forgot how to keep me upright. I sank to the floor. The room disappeared into blackness—just like the road that night when raindrops danced in the fog of headlights swirling white, then blue, then red.

"Not real." I screwed my eyes shut, but my heart thumped even faster. *"Not real."*

Shuddering in a long, slow breath, I clenched my fist. I could stop it. Just this once. For Lola. I wouldn't make it to the bathroom, so I needed to skip ahead and follow the rest of the steps.

What can I see?

I swivelled my head, a shaky smile on my face when I curled my finger around Lola's pinkie dangling off the side of the bed. I could see her. My sweet girl. The pink sheet twisted around her legs to hide her bare skin, and her hair fanned over the pillow. Beautiful.

The hammering of my heart slowed.

What can I smell?

Sex. Patchouli. Before I'd made love to Lola the second time, she'd wriggled away from me to light one of her candles. She'd told me the scent was patchouli. Never heard of it. Smelled like clean laundry. Smelled like Lola.

The rasps of my breath evened out.

What can I hear?

Lola. Her quiet snuffles.

Tick.

Tick—

Unforgiving hands pressed over my ears. The clock. I couldn't hear anything but that damn clock.

The scratchy, broken reel of images started spinning again—faster and faster—coming together in one long horror movie. The highway. The steady beat of the indicator as

I cruised along the road. The blur of headlights where they shouldn't be. The swirl of red and blue.

Vomit raced up my throat, but I fought to keep it down. Frantic, I yanked on my pants and stuffed my arms in my shirt sleeves before pulling it over my head. I had to get out of that cottage. Away from that clock. Just...

Away.

I'd stayed too long.

My mind was a haze of reality and a past I never forgot as I stumbled down the narrow hallway, grabbed my boots, and launched out the front door. The second the cold night air hit me outside, I collapsed to my knees and then lurched forward, hurling my guts up behind the untamed hedges near Lola's front door.

"You weak fucking bastard." I punched my fist against my thigh. "Get the fuck up."

Shaking, my eyes focused on nothing but my truck, I got up, forcing one foot in front of the other. Down the path. Out the gate. I slumped against the front tyre of my truck.

My keys dug into my skin through the pocket, but I knew I wouldn't need them. I rarely drove at night and *never* this close to the edge. I sure as hell didn't want some poor cop getting called out of bed to scrape my car off a tree.

I lifted my head just enough to glance back at the cottage. I sure as hell wasn't going back in there, either. What other options did I have? Sleep in my truck? The gossips would love that. Yolanda had probably already alerted half the town about the fact I'd been parked out front for hours.

Looks like I'll be walking back to my workshop.

I jammed my feet into my stupid socks. Boots next. A dog perked up at the sound of my heavy, uneven footsteps cracking along the road, and if I saw the flutter of Yolanda's front curtains as I passed, I ignored it.

It was easy to ignore everything when guilt crushed my chest.

Lola wasn't the type for something casual. I certainly hadn't given her the impression I was, but I'd never planned to stay. My promise to treat her like a gentleman? Yeah, that had lasted for about twenty seconds after I saw her standing there, hugging the door, looking so goddamn beautiful.

That woman made me so weak, but I could never let my guard down around her again.

What life could she possibly have with me? Constantly walking on eggshells, waiting for me to snap? She deserved better. And what would she say if she found out the truth of why I'd ended up this way?

No.

No fucking way.

Lola and I were never happening.

I'd make sure of it.

·♥·♥·♥·♥·♥·

HARRY'S BOOTS SCUFFED ALONG the workshop floor. The sound was the first thing that dragged my attention away from the vanity drawers I'd been crafting for most of the morning.

"Hey, old man."

I scowled when he dumped his cooler on the concrete, his tool belt dropping on top a second later. He aimed his empty iced coffee bottle for the bin like a pro basketballer. Turns out, he was a shit shot. The bottle hit the wall and bounced along the ground.

"You gonna pick that up?" I grumbled.

Harry shrugged. "Later."

I wedged the chisel into the wood, flicking my eyes up at him before my attention went back to my work. "How is it that ninety percent of this place is mine, but a hundred percent of the mess is yours?"

"A little thing I like to call *teamwork*."

I grunted and went back to the dovetail joints.

Harry's hip slanted against the bench beside me. "You in one of your *moods* again?" The fact I ignored him only made him laugh. "That's a yes. Come on, it's ten thirty. Let's hit the road for the coffee shop."

And risk seeing Lola in town? Hell no. "Not today."

"What about your whole morning routine?"

I flattened my lips and refused to say a word. My morning routine had gone out the window when I'd abandoned the woman of my dreams and spent the rest of the night pretending I could fall asleep in the back room of the workshop instead. Then, I'd crept back under the cover of dawn like a coward to pick up my car. Yeah, it was safe to say my well-worn routine had gone out the window.

Harry's eyes narrowed. "You're acting sus. You're usually a drill sergeant. Monday. Ten thirty sharp. Coffee. Right?"

I put my tools down. Truthfully, I was tired as shit, and my back was killing me after being stuck on the pull-out cot. Caffeine sounded good. Maybe Lola wouldn't be at the coffee shop. She wasn't there every day. Not like the store...

"Okay," I muttered.

Wrong call.

Brooke and Lola were wandering towards the coffee shop just as I pulled into the parking space out front. I almost took out a tourist because my eyes were too busy staring at the sweet girl clutching a bright pink container instead of focusing on the road.

Harry was out of the truck in a flash. "Hey, Lola from the City!"

Lola shrank back. She really hated that nickname. Not that Harry noticed. Grinning, he waved to her and then bounded into the coffee shop. Brooke tottered after him.

I would've followed, too, but Lola blocked my way. Café tables and the metal bin trapped me on both sides. I couldn't dodge her.

Her eyes dropped to the pink container clutched against her stomach. "Hi," she whispered.

I said nothing.

"We didn't get to say goodbye this morning." Lola hesitated, taking a breath that made her shoulders hike up. "You, um... probably had a big job to get started on...or...something?" Her blue eyes lifted, misty, and she buried her teeth in her lip.

My heart twisted. I'd done that. Hurt her. I could've made some flimsy excuse and softened the blow, but we couldn't risk another night together.

"No," I said, flat.

Her eyebrows pinched together. "Oh." She pushed her glasses up, an uncertain smile on her pretty lips. "We never got to dessert after, um..." She held out the container. "It's a piece of the apple pie."

Lola was so damn sweet and perfect. I wanted to sink to my knees and confess everything. Beg her to forgive me and give me another chance. Take her home to my bed and show her how sorry I was.

I didn't. I stood there. Silent.

Unsettled by the stone wall glaring back at her, Lola's eyes darted around the street. "Apple is your favourite, right?"

"Don't need it."

Another smile cracked through her confusion. "Well, no one *needs* apple pie." She laughed nervously. "But here"—she thrust the container at me—"it's home-baked and so yummy. I tried some for br—"

Lola's words died in her throat when my palm landed flat against the container. I pushed it back at her.

"Don't *want* it," I said.

The water pooling in the corners of her eyes disappeared with rapid blinks, but she pulled the pink container protectively into her chest. "Aiden, did I do something wr—"

"It's busy in there today!" Harry bounded up with a laugh. "Oh!" His eyes landed on the container. "What you got there, Lola from the City?"

Lola winced. That name again. "Apple pie." She looked nervously between Harry and me. "Would you like it?"

"Oh, hells yeah! You're a great cook, right?" Harry grinned as he balanced our coffee cups on top of each other to free up a hand. "Gimme that."

My gaze narrowed on Harry's grubby paw wrapping around my gift. Lola had packed that for me. I clenched my jaw. If I didn't get to have it, he sure as hell wasn't. I snatched the pink container from him and whipped around to glare at Lola. She shuffled a step backwards.

My voice was low, nothing but ice, when I said, "Take the hint, Lola."

I dumped the container into the bin beside her.

Harry's eyebrows shot up his forehead. "Why the f—"

"We're going," I snapped at him.

I stormed back to the car and ignored Harry's whispered questions about what the hell was happening. None of his business, that was what I told him. He wouldn't get a word out of me, but people would be talking around town soon enough.

Lola stood there, frozen, her head bent, arms hanging limply at her sides. She wouldn't stop staring at that bin. Her eyes only lifted to catch mine just as I opened the door to my truck. A tear slid down her cheek.

I was such a selfish fucking bastard.

The devastation on her face shattered my heart, but pretending that treating her like that didn't destroy me, like it didn't bother me at all, I turned my back on her and left.

9

She Didn't See Him as a Protector

Lola

"Nope. No way." Brooke stripped her blouse over her head and tossed it on her bed. "You can't go out wearing *that*." She waved an accusing finger in my direction.

I glanced down. "What's wrong with this?" The faded black turtleneck was old, but it was functional and fit my mood. I didn't feel like wearing my pretty new clothes anymore.

Brooke's nose wrinkled. "Your skirt has baby puke all over it."

Did it? I thought I'd wiped it off. I took another look. Oh. The milky streak caked between the pleats was barely visible. Sort of. The little boy with his tumble of golden curls had felt a lot better after he'd sprayed his upset tummy all over me. His mother had been mortified, but I wasn't bothered.

I shrugged. "Occupational hazard."

Brooke unzipped her skirt and shimmied it down her hips. She tossed it at the hamper, but it missed and landed on the floor beside the bed. It was the only thing out of place in her bedroom. From the colour-coded clothes hangers in her wardrobe to the labels stuck on every box of neatly stacked shoes, everything in Brooke's house was perfectly organised.

She glanced at me over her shoulder as she slipped off her bra. "Did you remember to bring a change of clothes?"

I blinked. Aiden had tangled my mind into a hundred balls of wool. All the threads that held me together were so jumbled that I could barely remember to put on one set of clothes. There was no way I'd remember to pack a second.

"Sorry," I said weakly. "I forgot."

"Lolly!"

"You said we were going out for a couple of drinks to unwind," I reminded her. "What's the big deal?"

"It's Friday night!"

"So?"

"Half the town will be at the Old Cellar. You need to look hot."

Frowning, I sagged against the doorframe. "I'm not sure I've ever looked *hot* in my entire life."

"What are you going on about? Of course you have! You just need to stop hiding under all those layers. And what if *he's* there tonight?" she teased with a sly grin. "You know, a certain cabinetmaker who dresses a bit like a lumberjack?"

My stomach plunged to my loafers. I didn't want to see Aiden.

I *couldn't*.

The humiliation of his rejection outside the coffee shop was the new shadow stalking my steps. Busy days at work and nights spent with Brooke had distracted me. No one waited for me in the village store anymore. My welcome mat hadn't received any gifts or a solemn visitor offering an apology.

But late at night, in my bed, the memories of Aiden hadn't been dulled by the days that had slipped past.

I could still hear his whispers, still feel the tingle on my skin of him kissing each of the freckles along my collarbone. My heart hadn't forgotten how he sighed, the softest sound, when my finger had traced the trimmed edges of his beard, his eyes locked on mine like I meant something to him. There hadn't been a single sign Aiden was about to rip my heart out.

"That certain cabinetmaker has never been at the bar before," I pointed out. His notable absence on our previous girls' nights had been a big factor in why I agreed to this terrible idea.

"Yeah, but the game's on tonight. All the guys come into town. At least, that's what I'm counting on." Grinning, Brooke grabbed a scrap of red satin off the bed. "I've got a dress even Harry can't ignore."

"I'm sure he's not ignoring you on purpose."

She tossed me a dubious look. "Has Aiden said anything?"

"Uh, no..."

"Lame." Brooke jiggled her hips to slide the tight satin over her bottom. "If Aiden *is* there tonight, you need to look your best. Oh! I know just the thing!" She clapped her hands as she bounced on her toes. "Makeover!"

"No." I held up my palm before her latest idea went any further. "Absolutely not."

Brooke's face fell. "But—"

"No way. This isn't a teen movie montage where you dress me up, take off my glasses, and suddenly all the guys in town notice me."

Brooke pouted. "Will you at least change into something not covered in stinky milk puke? I'm sure I've got something you can wear. You're taller, but we're probably about the same size. Well, except for the boobs." She grinned. "Here." Metal squeaked as she ran clothing hangers along the rails. "*This* would look great on you." She held up an emerald dress.

I wrinkled my nose. Sequins. Lots of them. "It's, um... shiny?"

"Everyone can do with a bit of extra sparkle."

I shook my head. No way was I wearing sequins.

Brooke turned back to her wardrobe, hands on her hips. "Oh! *This* one." She slipped a hanger off the railing and held out a simple black shift dress for me to inspect. "Modest and boring, and it's in the funeral colours you've liked so much this week. We could pair it with a cute belt or a necklace or something."

After a few more half-hearted refusals from me and a lot more pleading from Brooke, I caved. With the modesty of an awkward teenager stuck undressing in a school locker room, I peeled off my turtleneck and skirt and slipped the dress over my head.

Brooke stood back, looking me over as she tapped her chin. "You need a little something more. I know just the thing!" She held out a cropped denim jacket. "Chic. Laid-back. Perfect for the bar."

"Sold." Anything to get this over with. "Can we go now?"

"Almost..."

Brooke grumbled bitterly when I only agreed to a touch-up of the powder on my face and a fresh swipe of lipstick. The cloud of perfume she spritzed made me sneeze. Finally, she launched a fresh attack, approaching me with a curling iron and a hopeful smile.

Folding my arms, I glared at her. "Nope."

"But—"

"Double nope." I let my frustration melt away with a warm smile. "Makeover complete. Let's go..."

·♥·♥·♥·♥·♥·

THE OLD CELLAR WAS a formidable building at night. Like a scene torn from a gothic horror film, two storeys of sandstone and black trim loomed behind gnarled trees shaking loose autumn leaves.

People swarmed the top balcony and the gardens outside.

I twisted the cuffs of the denim jacket in nervous fingers. Brooke wasn't kidding. This place was packed. But before I could stammer an excuse to leave, she grabbed my hand and pulled me inside.

"Hey, do you see Harry?" she asked as she dragged me through the crowd. "I hope I haven't wasted my new dress on a bunch of crusty old pervs."

Almost tripping trying to keep up with Brooke, I scanned the bar. A herd of men clustered together, eyes glued to the game playing on the screens lining the back wall. Harry's familiar crop of red hair was nowhere to be seen, but I recognised some of the faces. A couple of the firefighters. The butcher who'd sliced through his finger and needed two stitches, and—God help me—Evan Barnes.

Fear zipped down my spine, speeding my loafers silently across the floor. Putting distance between me and Evan was the only thing that mattered.

In my rush to get away, I almost missed seeing the man who nodded at me as we passed. He had the kind of face that coaxed me to smile back, even though I had no idea who he was. Dimples softened his weathered skin, and his dusty blond hair gave him a boyish sort of charm.

"Brooke, who's that—" My words died in my throat.

The mystery man nudged the figure hunched beside him at the bar—broad shoulders, dark hair, and a red-checked flannel shirt.

No, no, no.

"Aiden's here!" Brooke breathed, her fingernails digging into my arm. "I told you he would be!"

The man in question flicked a glance over his shoulder. He saw me. I *know* he saw me. His jaw clenched so hard that a muscle popped near his temple. He ignored the mystery man and turned his back. At least he was consistent in his hatred for me.

I tugged Brooke's hand in the direction of the doors. "Can we go—"

"Free seats!"

She tightened her grip on my hand and ploughed ahead, dragging me to the two free stools at the end of the bar. Her hand shot up. The bartender ignored her completely, but she just grinned, unfazed.

"Just so you know, Aiden's looking at you," she said.

I snorted a laugh. Not likely. "Who's that with him?" I asked, carefully trying to steer the conversation somewhere—*anywhere*—other than Aiden.

"Who?" Brooke's voice pitched with interest, and she craned her neck, getting a good look in all directions. "Oh. Him." She sat back, disappointed, and waved her hand as if his presence were a giant waste of time. "Ryan Hollyoak."

"One of *the* Hollyoaks, huh? I haven't seen him in town before."

"He's quiet. He breeds stinky cows and stuff. The church ladies rave about him, but..." Brooke shrugged. "I don't see the big deal."

"What? Too...blond?"

"No."

"Too ruggedly handsome?"

Brooke rolled her eyes. "Hardly."

"Too...not Harry?"

Instead of the smile I was expecting, she sighed. "I really thought he'd be here tonight." Her confidence seeped away, and she sank lower on the stool.

I tried distracting Brooke by asking her about the new reality show she was hooked on. That chatter amused her for about two minutes until her fingernails started tapping impatiently on her knee. She hiked her chin and not-so-subtly peered down the bar.

"Oh!" Brooke's hand shot out to grab my arm. "Aiden looked again."

This time, I didn't stamp down the flicker of hope fluttering in my chest. "Really?"

She squeezed my arm tighter. "He's heading over to order. Quick! Go get drinks for us, okay? It's the perfect excuse to say hi. We aren't getting much love from the bartender anyway."

I edged off the stool. "I'm not sure—"

"Go!"

She shooed me off with an encouraging smile, but my stomach twisted into a lump of knots.

Why did this feel like a terrible idea?

Aiden stood hunched over by the cash register, his finger tracing the trees on the coaster in front of him. His mind seemed lost somewhere else. When I slipped into the empty space, my shoulder accidentally brushed his, and his finger paused, tension locking his body still, but he still didn't acknowledge me.

"Hi... Aiden."

Scowling grey eyes slowly turned. "And what do you want"—his tone was even icier—"Lola from the City?"

Hearing that name was like a slap across the face. The memories of our night together were becoming more muddled, but I hadn't imagined all the times he'd called me *love*.

"You know I hate when people call me that." I couldn't make my voice any louder than a whisper. His words cut almost as deeply as when he'd thrown away the apple pie I'd baked for him.

Aiden's attention returned to the coaster. "I know a lot of things about you I wish I could forget."

Another sharp blow splintered through the protective armour I'd patched around my heart. The wounds I'd carefully hidden by keeping busy were now dangerously close to splitting my heart in two.

"Aiden, what did I do wrong?"

He said nothing.

Did he think I wasn't even worth a response?

Confused, more pathetic words spilled out of my mouth before I could stop them. "Am I too messy? I can be tidier." My fingers fidgeted with the denim cuff. "Did I do something wrong...in...?" I bit down on my lip. Maybe I was *too vanilla* in bed, like Chris had always complained? Not pretty enough? Too... *Lola?* "I thought... I mean... You seemed to like being with me—"

A low whistle crawled up my skin.

Evan sauntered up to the bar, men crowded by his side, the stench of alcohol reeking from his pores. The smirk on his face spread like venom as his unwanted eyes slithered down my body.

"Well, look who it is. Lola from the City." His laugh was loud and obnoxious. "Who knew the dorky mouse was hidin' a pair of legs like that? Almost makes up for the flat chest, right?"

A peal of laughter rippled through the group. Like a broken animal cornered by a predator, I inched back. The edge of the bar dug into my spine. No escape.

"That was mean," I said, blinking back tears as I searched for Aiden.

Why did I bother? He still stood there, but his face was stone. He wasn't going to help. He'd abandoned me again.

"Aww." Evan's pout was only mocking. "City girl havin' a cry?"

My chin trembled. Yes. I was. "L-leave m-me alone," I choked out. The humiliating dribble of tears down my cheek only made me want to cry more.

Ryan Hollyoak's bronze hand braced against Evan's chest to stop him from taking another step. "That's enough, mate," the farmer warned.

Evan shrugged him off. "I'll say when she's heard enough. She needs to know she don't belong here."

An eerie silence fell over the bar, and the only jumbled words making it to my ears were from the game blaring in the background. My arm hugged protectively across my belly, but I didn't dare say anything. I was shutting down, just as I had a hundred times before. I thought I'd left those days behind me in Sydney. Men like Evan—like Chris—wanted to see the tears. They liked it.

Evan bared his teeth at me in a horrifying smile. "You think you're better than me? Better than us?" He gestured at his friends. "Nothin' but a useless woman with a high-and-mighty city attitude. I know your type and just how to deal with you."

The threat hollowed my chest. I desperately searched for the man who'd been so very careful and gentle with me only nights before. He'd protect me.

Our eyes met.

Please.

Aiden held my gaze.

Please.

"Aiden?" I pleaded.

Something haunted flickered across his face, but he shook his head and turned away.

A furious click of heels and Brooke wedged herself next to me like a blonde shield of fury. She propped her fists on her hips. "You got something to say to my girl, Evan Barnes?"

"Piss off, Goldilocks," Evan seethed. "This ain't any of your business."

"Like hell it isn't." Completely unbothered, Brooke flipped her hair over her shoulder. "You still sore because I wouldn't bounce around on your floppy dick last Christmas? That's why your old lady left, right?" She smiled sweetly. "Or was it because she realised you're a worthless piece of shit?"

Anger rolled off Evan in waves. His eyes narrowed, and his muscles bunched like he'd launch for her throat. "You little sl—"

But before he could take his first step towards Brooke, Ryan's hand shoved him back.

"I said that's enough, mate." There was an icy hint of menace to Ryan's voice this time. One of the farmhands stepped up beside him. "You can't keep starting fights. You're going to regret carrying on at the ladies like this again when the booze wears off."

Brooke paid no attention to the drama unfolding around her. She had a new target in her crosshairs. Her gaze snapped to Aiden.

"And *you!*" Her finger jabbed the air in his direction. "Are you really going to let Evan talk to your girl like that?"

Aiden squared his shoulders. He ignored Brooke to look me dead in the eye. "She's not my girl."

"Like hell she isn't," Brooke fumed. "Like you haven't been—"

"Didn't take the hint, did you, Lola?" His mouth flattened into a grim frown. "You listening now? Stay the hell away from me."

Brooke's mouth dropped open in complete shock.

Mine didn't.

Somehow, even though my knees wobbled and my nerves crackled from the threat of confrontation, I still stood tall. I wasn't the same woman who'd run away three months ago. That Lola had cowered from the constant threat of Chris's brutal words and merciless hands.

But I was brave now. I'd survived hell. I'd risked everything and escaped.

I was free.

I had *friends*.

Brooke stood proud and defiant. That blonde ball of fury didn't hesitate to fight for me against a whole pack of men. Even the mysterious Ryan Hollyoak had my back. And when I glanced around the bar, I saw more faces looking on with concern—with sympathy—for me.

I wasn't alone. Not anymore.

I turned to Aiden, straightening my spine and squaring my shoulders, just like he had when he'd humiliated me outside the coffee shop. Any affection I'd had for him was gone. All I had left was a glare.

"It will be my pleasure to stay as far away from you as possible, Mr. McKinnon." My voice was firm. It never wavered. "Life is so precious. I deserve better than wasting a single second of it on someone as two-faced and cruel as you."

And with my friend's arm hugged around my shoulders, I left the Old Cellar with new strength fortifying my veins. I wouldn't settle for being made to feel small. No one would ever treat me like I didn't matter again.

Not Aiden.

Not anyone.

10

He Saw the Signs of Her Past

Aiden

RICHMOND WAS A GREY ghost.

Fog swallowed the hills, and only the tufted peaks of the tallest trees escaped its chokehold over the valley. There was no hint of the town. Not even a twinkle of lights. Usually, I'd welcome the isolation, but after last night's disaster, the silence unsettled me.

I dragged the sandpaper along the raw edge of the porch railing. The slow, constant scratch was the only distraction from my thoughts. I'd paint it next. Nothing fancy. Midnight blue to match the rest of the trim. But it was another job to keep me busy. If I stopped, if I paused for a second, the guilt would rush into the cracks in my chest like quicksand and bury me alive.

I should be happy. I'd gotten what I wanted, hadn't I?

Lola hated me. I'd stayed silent when I should've spoken up. I'd discarded her like trash and watched as the vultures tore her apart.

The sandpaper stopped. I screwed my eyes shut, slouched against the railing, and forced air into my lungs. The darkness wasn't forgiving. The memory of Lola's eyes always pleaded for me to save her. That look would haunt me for the rest of my life.

Had I ever been...*good?* Honourable? Not even the shadow of the man in uniform seemed to exist anymore. Why had I been so heartless? So...so...*savage?*

Why?

The hum of tyres drifted through the valley. I cocked my head, listening, making sure my mind wasn't playing tricks on me. The rumble grew louder. Someone was coming up the driveway.

I sighed, pinching the fingertips of my glove, yanking it off, and hanging it over the railing next to the full coffee mug. When did I make that? I couldn't remember. It was probably cold now, anyway.

Hands shoved in my pockets, I headed out front just as the silver car skidded to a stop at the top of the driveway. Harry had snuck up the mountain in his mum's old junker. The car door slammed shut, and his sneakers pounded the concrete. Speeding up. Getting closer. A second later, I saw him, his cheeks red and his mouth set in a snarl.

All he sneered was, *"You."*

His fist flew straight for my face.

Forgotten instincts kicked in. Time slowed down. Harry swung. I dodged. With nothing to hit, his arm flailed, and the momentum of the lost blow threw him forward, his feet twisting, whirling him around like a tornado.

I waited.

The blur of his fist reared back, his legs pumping as he charged forward, ready to take a second shot. I dropped my shoulder, and pain exploded across my chest when he barrelled into me. But he was clumsy and untrained and hit me like a car slamming into a brick wall. Flying backwards, he landed with a thud on the concrete.

Spread-eagled on his back, Harry coughed, his chest heaving. I stooped over him. Defiant eyes glared up at me, and when I offered my hand to help him up, he slapped it away.

His gaze was wary. "Where'd you learn those frigging ninja moves?"

I lifted a shoulder. "Nowhere." I hadn't shared much about my past, and now certainly wasn't the time to skip down memory lane. "You want to tell me what's going on?"

"You know *exactly* what's going on." He scrambled to his feet, his body twitchy, still ready to fight. "This is about *Lola.*"

I flinched. Harry knew. It shouldn't have surprised me. Gossip spread like venom in this town. I'd bet his phone blew up with every sordid detail the second he drove back in range.

"Mate—"

"Don't you *dare* call me that," he spat. "I looked up to you. Like a *brother*. Like a"—emotion cracked his voice—"like a *father*. And what are you? Huh? Nothing but a *coward!*"

"You don't understand…" The words were weak even to my ears.

"No. I don't. Everyone in this town thinks I'm as dumb as a bag of rocks. Maybe I am. I never finished high school. I don't read *books* like you do. But I'm smart enough to know what you did to Lola was wrong."

I kicked a bit of gravel with the toe of my boot. "I was protecting her."

"Protecting her?" Harry's eyes bulged. *"Protecting* her? Do you hear yourself?" He snorted with disgust. "I suppose you were protecting Lola when you threw her pie in the bin, too? And when that asshole Evan Barnes said all that ugly shit to her? Sure. And then you have the damn balls to tell *her* to stay away from *you!*"

My eyes snapped up, and he scoffed a laugh.

"Yeah, that's right. Hollyoak told me everything. You weren't protecting Lola." His hand landed flat on my shoulder, and he shoved me hard, but I didn't budge. "You were protecting *yourself*."

I took a steadying breath and dropped my gaze to my feet. Harry saw more than he should have. But he was right. I'd convinced myself the reason I'd ripped Lola's heart out and squashed it beneath my boot was because I couldn't let her get too attached to me. But that wasn't it at all, was it? I'd been scared that I was already too attached to her. I had been since the second I'd laid eyes on her.

"Say something, you coward!" Harry demanded.

"There's nothing to say."

"Gutless!"

I nodded. Yeah. I was.

"Why are you doing this?"

"Me... Lola... It's just not..." I rubbed my hand over the ache throbbing deep in my chest. "It can't happen."

"But you like her."

The ache gnawed deeper. I *did*. Too much. If I lingered in my fantasies too long and let Lola's sweet smile lure me into believing I was worth being loved, I'd break her beyond repair. I wasn't...*right*. My mind was a prison, but I'd lost the keys years ago. Escape was impossible. I couldn't risk hurting her any more than I already had.

"I don't like her," I lied.

Harry rolled his eyes. "Piss off. Yeah, you do. Who are you trying to convince? Yourself?" He snorted. "You aren't fooling me, old man. It's been six years since you saved my dumb butt by giving me a job, and I've never seen you act like this over a woman."

"Like *this*? I'm not like...anything."

"How much denial are you in? Your eyes never leave Lola. And if they aren't on her, they're searching for her. I even saw your lips curl up once." He raised his eyebrows with a challenging grin. "You know, just at the corners... As if you can actually smile or something."

I grunted.

"You *like* Lola."

"No."

Harry huffed with frustration. "Yeah. You do. And I'll bet you coffee for a month that you like Lola *a lot*." He paused, eyes on the sky, thinking something through. "I've seen tourists make those flirty eyes at you, but you never smile back. And people can whisper about you and Miss Ruthie all they want. I know nothing is going on between you two." He grimaced. "Not like *that*."

"No, nothing like that." I held back a laugh. I could imagine Ruth recoiling in horror if she ever heard *that* accusation.

"So, keep standing there in denial, pretending it's not different with Lola. Other people haven't realised because you're still grumpy as hell, but I know you." A pained expression scrunched up his face. "At least... I *thought* I knew you."

I shook my head. No one knew me. Not really. Not even Ruth.

Lola had pried open a tiny crack in my chest and burrowed inside. But I'd come too close to tipping over the edge. That night could have gone so much worse. I speared my fingers through my hair, took a deep breath, and flooded the chasm aching in my chest with more air. It didn't help.

Harry sighed. "I just don't get it. Why didn't you stand up for her? How could you let Evan say those things? Man, it's *Lola*. She's like... She's..." Harry braced his hands on the railing and stared out over the valley. He was quiet for a long time. Just thinking. "You ever notice her, Aiden?" He turned back to me with a faint smile. *"Really* noticed her?"

I leant my hip against the railing next to him. "Yeah, kid," I admitted in a low voice. "I have." Right down to the tiny freckles dotted on her shoulder.

"You sure? Watch her again. Lola seems okay around you, but any other man looks in her direction, and she's a nervous wreck. She won't even look at 'em. She spooks like a roo if someone starts hollering in the coffee shop. Otherwise, she keeps herself curled up tight." Harry's voice dropped to a whisper. "Just like Mum."

My eyes rounded. "No... That's not..." Harry's father was a bastard. He was gone before my time, but the rumours still lingered. That man beat his wife. His son. My father had been a hard man, not an ounce of compassion in him. Still, he'd probably been like puppies and cotton candy compared to Harry's dad. "Lola's not like your mum."

"Mum's been scared like that since Dad left. She still is some days. Most days, even." Harry turned his gaze back to the valley. "Lola's the same. Someone didn't treat her good."

My hand shot out and gripped the railing, my knuckles turning white. "But... Lola..."

But...*what?*

Lola was all sweetness, shy smiles, and loving touches, but Harry was right. Signs screamed everywhere. She'd landed in town with nothing except the clothes on her back and been over the moon about her first pay as if she'd never earned a dollar. She'd panicked over a tiny mess. When I'd held her on her pink sheets, she'd pleaded with me not to treat her rough, and after I'd abandoned her, she'd begged me to tell her what she'd done wrong because she'd probably always heard everything was her fault.

I slumped lower against the railing.

And what had I done? Kicked her in her soft, broken belly when she was already curled up on the ground with no one to protect her.

"But...she's..." I choked on the knot lodged in my throat. "She's...so...smart. She's...a doctor."

I was grasping for excuses. Why? In my other life—when I'd still been someone—how many call-outs had I attended? How many women had I seen beaten black and blue who'd lied and said they'd fallen? My chest tightened. Not my Lola. I needed to pretend some bastard had never put his hands on my shy girl with her too-big glasses. I needed to pretend I wasn't like *him*—whoever *he* was.

"Does that make a difference?" Harry asked. "Mum was whip-smart, too. Now look at her. She can't work. She can't leave the house some days. She never saw him coming." His sigh was heavy. "Do you ever, though? Evil people hide in plain sight. They're everywhere. Even the smartest person can't always see the wolf hiding in sheep's clothing."

I couldn't pretend anymore.

I was the wolf.

I wanted. I took. But Lola paid the price.

And she never saw me coming.

11

She Saw the Wild Mare Unleashed

Lola

My knees ached. I'd been crouched on the laundry room floor too long.

The glass door of the washing machine hung open. The pink sheets had been stripped off my bed and stuffed inside, but one pillowcase stayed balled in my fist. I couldn't bring myself to toss it in and snap the door shut.

Stop being so stupid. Forget him.

My heart twisted. I couldn't. Not completely. A trace of Aiden's cologne lingered in the pink fabric, barely more than a whisper, but it was my only proof of the night we shared. The hollow place inside me clung to that memory. I didn't want to let it go.

Sighing, I rose to my feet, flicked the washing machine door closed, and pressed "Go." A chirp, and the cycle started. My thoughts swirled faster than the water tumbling with the sheets inside.

Maybe Aiden wasn't really what I struggled to let go of. Maybe it was losing the *hope* of him. I was fine alone, but *just* fine. Was it selfish to want more?

My parents had a beautiful marriage. My sister was a train wreck, but her marriage was strong, too. I was nothing like my sister. I was cobbled together from the bits of junk left over after my parents created something wonderful the first time around. Broken Lola only chose broken men. Aiden. Chris. All the boyfriends before them who'd put me last, even though I'd only ever begged them to love me.

My relationships were just like all the dolls and stuffed bears I'd owned as a little girl. I'd tended to them so tenderly, healing all their imaginary booboos, but never received a kiss or a whispered thank you. I'd known my future—to love but never be loved back.

Sweet, simple, *stupid* Lola.

With the pillowcase still scrunched in my fist, I wandered through the back door and inside the cottage, not quite sure what to do next. I found myself in front of my wardrobe, staring at the battered suitcase on the top shelf.

I almost laughed. I'd been so naive. I'd thought my days of hiding secrets were over. Not yet. I had one more.

I dragged the suitcase down, dropped it on the bed, unzipped it, and after taking a deep breath, flipped it open. I lifted the binder of my personal papers and pushed away old photographs and mementos. The faded pink pillowcase was still tucked underneath. My fingertips traced the worn fabric. No money from my escape fund was left, but the bump of the engagement ring with its teardrop diamond was still hidden inside. Carefully, I slipped Aiden's pillowcase on top. What a strange pair they made. Old hopes—*failures*—mixed with new.

"No more," I said out loud.

If no one was going to put me first, I needed to put *myself* first. The change had to start with me. *Inside* me.

I'd proven to myself that I could be brave. I'd risked every-thing for a chance to be something more than Chris's disap-pointment and my parents' *other* daughter when I'd moved to Richmond. I'd quietly quit my job and disappeared.

But I was done hiding.

My gaze shifted to the nightstand. A new book waited for me—*The Scars That Don't Show: Rebuilding Your Life After Domestic Violence*. I'd start reading it later. More self-help books were on the way. An appointment with an online therapist was booked, too.

My phone blinked on the nightstand. I bent over. A new message from my mother.

Mum

> No more of this nonsense. Come stay with us. We miss you.

My father had sent one too.

Dad

> What do you call a deer with no eyes?

My lips twitched. My parents tried. Despite my bitterness, I knew they loved me in their own way, but taking the next step in my life was up to me.

I reached for my phone and tapped messages to both of them. The first were for Mum.

Lola

> I'm getting stronger every day, Mum. My friend even asked me to join a dance class with her.

> Love you.

The fact that I hadn't agreed to the dance class made no difference. Mum would be stoked—dancing and a friend. Finally, I wouldn't be the social outcast she'd always feared. But there would be no more false promises to call. My boundaries were just as important as her happiness.

The next messages were for my dad.

Lola

No eye deer, Dad.

Hope the caravan is holding up to the punishment of the outback roads. Miss you.

A quick shove sent my suitcase back to the top shelf of the wardrobe. I peeled off my daggy jeans and T-shirt, tossed them on the bed, and ran my fingers over the clothes hangers. So many pretty new dresses. I could buy whatever I liked and wear what I wanted now. It was a simple pleasure most people took for granted, but one that still made my heart sing.

A gingham sundress yanked over my head, sandals slipped on, and a light sweep of makeup—I was ready. My tiny cottage was my refuge, but I couldn't waste my new life hiding behind the safety of four walls. I knew how quickly freedom could be snatched away.

I grabbed my bag off the hook by the door, marched outside, and headed for town.

It was time to be brave again.

·❤·❤·❤·❤·❤·

THE CROWD AT THE village markets swarmed around me. I weaved through the people, smiling and nodding, saying hello, pretending I was fine.

Totally fine.

I stopped at a stall to sniff the handmade candles, and at another, I sifted through the piles of second-hand books. My bag filled up quickly. A patient I'd seen once or twice sidled up to me as I thumbed through some knitting patterns. Her white powder puff dog yapped at my feet.

"How are you, dear?" she asked, patting my arm.

Brooke had warned me that word travelled fast in a small town, but I wasn't prepared for *this*. Interest. Sympathy. I'd never missed the anonymity of the city more.

"I'm good." I forced a cheerful bubble in my voice with sheer willpower. "The weather's nice today."

She tutted me gently. "Talking about the weather." Her lips stretched in a pitying smile. "Brave girl."

I slipped my arm free from her grip, offered a weak goodbye, and disappeared back into a crowd. But not for long. Other women stopped to say hello. More gentle nudges of encouragement.

Then came the tip of a wide-brimmed leather hat and a smile creasing a bronze, weathered face. Ryan Hollyoak.

"Morning, Dr. Hughes," he said.

"Hello." I owed Ryan more than a simple hello for stepping in, but overwhelming the poor man by throwing my arms around him would be too much. "Thank you...for..." A rush of nerves made me break out with a smile before I could finish thanking him properly. I wasn't used to talking to men outside of work. "Well, thank you...for...that."

Ryan's smile widened as he dipped his chin. "An honour, ma'am."

"I..." An *honour*?

"I s'pose everyone's trying to bend your ear today?"

"I do seem to have found myself the topic of conversation." I looked helplessly around the crowded hall. "I really wish I weren't."

"Small towns." He chuckled. "Living here's a bit like the rain. You can't fight it. You've just gotta make it through the downpour, and then you're all good. Everyone will move on to the next thing soon enough."

"I hope so."

"Just don't let a small-minded fool like Evan Barnes get under your skin. He doesn't speak for all of us. It'd be a sorry day if we lost a good doctor because of the likes of him."

The mention of Evan's name made my heart thud faster, but I tightened my grip on my bag, determined to stay strong. "I'm not going anywhere," I reassured Ryan. "You're all stuck with me."

"Glad to hear it." Smiling, he tipped his hat to say goodbye.

My steps slowed to a shuffle between the next stalls. When I heard Rose's shrill voice call out my name, I wanted to lift the red tablecloth skirting the cake stall, crawl underneath, and never be seen again.

"Yoohoo!" Rose wasn't giving up. "Dr. Hughes!" Gnarled hands shot out, clutching around my arm to snatch me from the crowd.

The church ladies fenced me in so I couldn't escape. Rose in her prim navy-blue suit. Enid, beside her, flustered, fingers fussing with her white hair. Yolanda, silent and still, hovered behind the wall of cakes and biscuits, her steely eyes fixed on me.

I straightened my spine, ready. *Inquisition incoming*. I could feel it.

Rose kept a tight hold of my arm. "You seemed to be having a *very* friendly conversation with the young Hollyoak."

"A nice boy," Edith added.

Rose snorted. *"Boy."* She wiggled her eyebrows. "Oh, honey, he's *all* man now."

Edith squealed a laugh. "Oh, you wicked thing!"

Rose turned to me. "Ryan is a respectable man. His family owns the cattle station outside town. Did you know?" I had no idea, but she didn't wait for me to answer. "Five generations in these parts." She smiled sweetly. "He'd make a wonderful husband."

My cheeks heated. Rose was about as subtle as a sledgehammer in a room full of delicate porcelain plates. I shot down any talk of dating by saying, "I'm *really* not looking—"

"Ryan's always talked about wanting a family of his own," Edith interrupted.

Rose nodded in agreement. "And you can hardly blame him. Stuck out there in the valley with only his father and a bunch of hairy cows for company! That homestead has been too long without a woman's touch. He was only a boy when he lost his sweet mother."

Edith angled herself closer and whispered, "Ovarian cancer."

I forced a tight smile. Those were Ryan's secrets to share, not something to be discussed in front of a stranger. My gaze searched for Yolanda. What did she make of all this gossiping? Her eyes narrowed, watching the exchange—*me*—with intense interest.

"And didn't Ryan prove himself the gallant hero last night!" Rose continued. "Standing up for you against that brute! What's his name again?"

"Evan Barnes," Edith added helpfully.

"Yes," Rose said. "That's the one. A toad of a man. Were you terribly frightened?" She patted my arm. "I heard the things he said to you. They're not fit for repeating!"

"An absolute villain," Edith agreed.

"But I suppose it's hardly a surprise about Evan," Rose continued, oblivious to anything but the sound of her own voice. "Not after he harassed the little blonde one. What's her name again?"

"Brooke," Edith confirmed.

"That's the one," Rose said. "Dreadful business last Christmas. Fancy making a *sexual advance* on a woman young enough to be your *granddaughter!*" Indignant, she stuck her pointy nose in the air. "Unlucky for him, she's got a bite to her. A little pit bull, that one!"

Edith squealed another laugh. "Oh, you're terrible!"

Yolanda finally spoke. "Evan's lucky Aiden wasn't there," she said. "I can't imagine what would have happened if he'd seen—"

"He was there." My voice came out in a low, shaky whisper.

Yolanda's lips pressed into a grim line. "Impossible."

"He was." Pain seared through my chest. I squeezed my eyes shut. Just for a second. Just long enough for me to gather the strength for no one to misunderstand how little Aiden cared about me. "He stood there and did *nothing*."

"That doesn't sound like Aiden, pet."

I flinched. I'd heard that before. It was always my imagination. *My fault.* No one believed me. I was so tired of it. No. I was *exhausted*. If Yolanda wanted to fool herself into thinking Aiden couldn't watch a pig like Evan tear me apart, then she was no friend of mine.

"If you'll excuse me..." I said.

Lifting my glasses, I dashed the tears stinging my eyes, searching for an escape route. I wanted to be anywhere in the world other than the hall. I ignored Yolanda's frantic apology, but before I could disappear into the crowd, the universe had one more test for my new strength.

Aiden stood behind me.

He was rooted to the ground like a proud oak, his shoulders squaring up, a box full of fruits and vegetables hooked under his arm. But his perfect posture lied. The buttons on his shirt hadn't been done up right. The one in the middle was notched in the wrong hole, and his white T-shirt peeked through the gap. His hair was mussed and untidy, and dark circles bruised under his eyes. If someone told me he hadn't slept, I'd believe them.

And then I'd smile.

Good.

Quiet rage burned inside me so fiercely I balled my fist. *Good!*

Aiden stared down at me. I glared straight back. Only a few feet separated us, but the space yawned wider than a canyon. People darted through the gap. I didn't see them. Only him. His eyebrows furrowed, but those grey eyes stayed locked on mine, even as his lips disappeared into a scowl hidden by his beard.

Would he say something? Did I want him to? An apology? An explanation? If he fell to his knees and pleaded for my forgiveness, would my resolve weaken?

No.

This moment was bound to happen. Richmond was a small town. Leading up to the night we'd spent together, we'd bumped into each other everywhere. After that night, we would too. It was inevitable.

I pressed my fist into my chest. The emptiness inside me still echoed.

But Aiden never had my heart. We were never...*anything*. I'd had a crush on a handsome man who'd opened the car door for me and left me a few thoughtful gifts. Two lonely people could have sex, and it only be about...sex. If he'd been honest about us only being a one-time thing, I would've cried, but I would've been okay.

No, the sting in my chest wasn't heartbreak. It was humiliation. It was the shame of allowing myself to fall into the same tired patterns of desperately wanting to love someone and hoping that maybe, just maybe, they might love me back.

Outside the coffee shop, at the bar, Aiden had turned his back on me.

This time was different.

This time, I refused to hide. Chris had kept me locked away from the world and stolen years from me. I'd learned my lesson. I'd fought for a new life. And I'd keep fighting.

I never gave Aiden the satisfaction of seeing any more weakness. The timid mouse was gone. I squared my shoulders like him, lifted my chin, and spun on my heel with all the defiance of a wild mare.

This time, I turned my back on him.

12

He Saw His Only Chance

Aiden

My boot had barely touched the bottom step when Ruth's front door swung open.

"About time you got here," she said.

"I'm five minutes early." I kept heading up but then paused, my foot hovering above the next step. Ruth's smile was big. *Too* big. "What's going on?" My final steps were cautious.

"Oh, nothing," she sang, twirling her cane before floating inside.

My eyes slitted. "Is anyone else coming for lunch today?"

"Nope. It's just you and me, big guy."

Relief deflated my chest. Ruth had an unfortunate habit of thinking she knew what was best for me. For one agonising second, I'd expected to stoop through the front door and see Lola waiting on the other side. Nothing could prepare me for that. A week ago, her blue eyes had stared up at me, a sigh on her lips, welcoming me inside her. Today, the same woman had turned her back on me with unrestrained anger.

But even though Ruth's living room was empty, my eyes widened. "Hey." I nodded at the crooked line of watercolour canvases on the back wall. "You finally hung up some of your landscapes."

"Yeah, I put them up last night." Ruth lifted her good shoulder. "Life's been feeling... I don't know... Kind of different lately. It got me thinking about what you said. The house probably does need a bit more colour."

She made it sound like the paintings were no big deal. It was. But her eyes didn't linger on the watercolours as mine did, and her unsteady steps disappeared into the kitchen. My gaze flicked back to the wall.

Despite the new splashes of colour, a hush settled over the house when Ruth stepped out of the room. It wasn't like her old place on the mainland, where every wall had hummed with life—ribbons and trophies from her equestrian days, Matthew's swimming medals gleaming in neat rows, framed glimpses of horses, and the smiles they wore when they got engaged and said, "I do."

Those memories were lost, every last one of them erased. Ruth had made sure of that.

We never talked about the night of the accident ten years ago. We never spoke about the night of the storm the year after, either. Somehow, that night was almost worse.

Horrified, I'd watched Ruth rip every last reminder of her old life off the walls and hurl them onto the soaked ground outside.

"I have nothing left, Aiden," she'd screamed. "Nothing!"

Even as I'd collected every broken keepsake off the grass, the rain pelting my back like a whip for my sins while Ruth sobbed in a broken ball on her kitchen floor, I'd known I should've done more to stop her. Matthew had abandoned her. She'd needed me. But I'd barely been holding myself together. I hadn't known what to do or how to help.

Most days, I still didn't.

The distraction of packing away the box of groceries under my arm did nothing to stop the ghosts of shattered glass and splintered wood from stabbing my chest as if it were happening all over again.

Just once, I wish I hadn't failed the important people in my life.

"Leave all that," Ruth hurried me along. "Come." She patted the empty chair beside her. "Sit down with me. Tell me about your week. How's Harry?"

My eyebrow lifted, but I sank into the chair. This wasn't where I thought the conversation would go.

"He was on the road a lot this week," I said with an uneasy shrug. "I think he wants to spend some extra time with his mum to make up for it."

None of that was a lie. I'd conveniently left out a hell of a lot of the truth, but it wasn't a lie. Harry and I had parted on speaking terms, and his fist stayed in his pocket instead of having another crack at my face, but things were strained between us. My actions had dredged up too much of his past. He'd said as much.

Ruth was none the wiser. "Oh, I thought you might have asked him not to come. Perhaps because you have something to share with me," she said, her voice far too sunny. "Something...*private*...reserved only for very best friends."

My palms suddenly clammy, I roughed my hands along my jeans. Yeah, this was where I thought we were headed, and I still wasn't prepared. "Uh—what?"

Ruth lifted her coffee mug. "Is there something you want to tell me?" A strange little smile twisted around the rim as she took a sip. "About a certain *doctor,* perhaps?"

"I, uh..." I cleared my throat. "Don't know who you mean."

"Oh, I think you know *exactly* who I mean." Ruth's smile turned smugger than the last time she'd beaten me at Scrabble.

In other words, pretty damn smug. "Tell me about what happened last Sunday night."

My eyes narrowed. Someone had been blabbing, and I had a good idea who it was. "Yolanda Briggs stop by for your weekly coffee catch-up, did she?"

"Yolanda doesn't just stop by for coffee. She fills me in on the town gossip, too. *All* the gossip. Times. Details. *Everything.*"

I tugged at the collar of my shirt. "I, um…" Why did the kitchen suddenly feel like a furnace?

"Spill. Last Sunday."

"There's nothing to spill. Sunday was nothing. I stopped by Lola's…for…dinner." I almost groaned out loud.

What a way to make it obvious, moron.

"Dinner, huh?" Ruth snorted. Yeah, she definitely wasn't buying that bullcrap answer.

I scrubbed a hand down my face. "What exactly did Yolanda say?"

Ruth was only too happy to tease me with every embarrassing detail. "I believe her *exact* words were that you were grunting and groaning and not giving that poor woman's body a moment of peace as you ravished her for hours."

My shoulders slumped, and I propped my elbows on the table, palms pressed against my eyes. This was… *Goddammit.* This conversation was nothing short of a train wreck.

"For *hours*," Ruth repeated with far too much glee for my liking.

"I think Yolanda's exaggerating a bit on the *hours* part."

Ruth's eyes lit up. "But it's true?" A squeal erupted that almost shot me out of the chair. "You and Lola—finally? You're together?"

I shook my head. I hadn't just shattered the fragile bond between me and Lola. I'd smashed through it like a wrecking ball to make sure we were the furthest thing from *together*.

Ruth must have missed my reaction because her excited chatter lit up the room. "Aiden! Yes! This is so wonderful. As soon as you told me about how you met, I knew you were perfect for each other. I can't believe you found some poor woman to talk about all your dusty old books and your stupid chickens. You should invite Lola over here—"

"Ruthie girl." I held up my hand for her to stop. "Lola won't be coming over."

She sucked in a sharp breath. "Are you...?" She glared at the hand sitting limply in her lap. "Are you ashamed of—"

"Never." I didn't let her finish that rubbish train of thought. My palm covered her hand. She couldn't feel it, but I gave her a reassuring squeeze anyway. "Don't ever say that, you hear me? I'm prouder of you than anyone on this whole damn planet. If I were taking Lola anywhere, your place would be the first on the list, understand?"

"But...then...why?"

"Lola and I aren't together."

Ruth's smile was confused. "But you... The two of you... Right?"

"I screwed it up." I choked on the words as my head dropped into my hands. "Ruth, I screwed it up so bad."

"I'm sure it's not as bad as you think."

I let out a pained laugh. "It's so much fucking *worse.*"

"So, tell her you're sorry. Explain—"

"No." Regret sliced through me, and I kept my gaze pinned to my mug. "The things I said... What I did... Ruth, I was so..." I pressed my fist into that bruised spot in my chest. "I was so fucking *horrible* to Lola... I was just so..."

"Scared?"

I couldn't answer. I didn't want to admit it to myself. Scared? I was terrified. There had never been anyone before Lola. Life before Richmond had only been about duty—making my father proud and climbing the ranks to become a sergeant. Life after was full of shadows too dark to inflict on anyone. I never should have gone there with Lola.

Never.

Ruth's good arm wrapped around me, her head resting on my shoulder. "You pushed Lola away?"

"Yeah."

"On purpose?"

I jerked my chin down in a nod.

"Oh, Aiden. *Why?*" The disappointment in her voice was the last thing I needed to hear. "You deserve to be happy—"

"No, I don't! I fucking *don't!*" I shrugged off Ruth's arm, the chair scraping against the wooden floor when I pushed up. Standing by the sink was safer. "I have no fucking right to *ever* be happy after..." Shaking my head, I dragged in a steadying breath. "Not after what happened."

Ruth twisted in her chair to face me. "After what happened with Lola?" Emotion choked her usually bold voice. "Or...before that?"

"All of it."

"Aiden—"

"Don't. Just...*don't,* okay?"

"The accident wasn't your fault—"

"Don't!"

Ruth's mouth pressed into a grim line, and she stared at me, not blinking. "You have to stop doing this." She sighed. "The world already lost three people that night. You have to stop drifting through life like you died with them."

My head dropped, my chin falling to my chest so I had nowhere to look but my feet. I didn't want to hear that. Not a single word. Not from Ruth, of all people.

"Lola is so good for you," she said. "You've been different since you met her. You've been *happy.*"

I grunted. "I've been delusional."

"Because you finally found a woman worth caring about? Because you can see a future, and you're shit scared of actually letting yourself be loved?"

"Ruth, none of this matters. It's done. Over. Lola will never speak to me again."

"What exactly did you say to her?"

I glared at Ruth with my mouth clamped shut.

"That good, huh?" Her mug clunked down on the table. "You know I'm going to find out anyway, right?"

"I'm sure Yolanda will have plenty of interesting stories about how much of a bastard I am when she next stops by for a coffee. I'm not speeding up the process."

"Can I use my former police skills to guess?"

"I'd prefer you didn't."

"Because you don't think I can?"

"Because I don't want you to know!" I raked a hand through my hair. "Fuck, Ruth. You're the one person I've got left on this earth."

"You've got Harry."

"After what I did, his friendship is still very much touch-and-go at this point."

Even more disappointment clouded her dark eyes. "Aiden..."

"Don't you go getting all soft on me now, Ruthie girl. I fucked up with Lola. I deserve what's coming for me. Your hatred is next."

"In your dreams, big guy. Try pushing me away and see how far you get. Maybe that worked on Lola. Maybe you did say all kinds of terrible things to her. But I know you better than anyone. That's *not* who you are deep down. You and me—we're fighters."

"Are you still fighting?"

"I..." She glared down at her hand again. "I'm here, aren't I?"

"Not like you used to be." When she frowned, I nudged a little harder with my next question. "Why don't you come into town anymore?"

"I just..." She shrugged her good shoulder. "It's hard to keep pushing sometimes. The looks. All the whispers. No one even bothers trying to set me up on dates. Who wants the weird disabled girl for their daughter-in-law, right? Maybe some all-knowing being up in the heavens gave me another shot despite the odds, but time's slipping away."

I rushed back to the table and crouched in front of her. "You've got time." I did my best to give her a smile, but she only shook her head.

"Look at us, Aiden. We're getting older. You're thirty-seven now. I'm just about to turn thirty-five. Our chances of having families of our own are running out. Is *this* all life will be for us? Alone? Forever?"

My gut clenched. "Ruth—"

"You have a chance for something better. Something amazing. You can act like a total butthead and say you don't deserve it, but you do. Lola's *your* chance."

"Ruth, I have to let her go."

"That's horse poop, and you know it. Everyone in our families deserted us after the accident, but you and I—*we* don't abandon the people we care about. I know you sure as hell don't."

"I hurt Lola. I did it on purpose."

"Then you better figure out a way to make it right."

"It's too late for that."

"If Lola's worth it, if you truly care about her, you'll fight to earn her forgiveness even if it *is* too late."

I didn't have to think about it.

Lola was worth it.

13

She Saw No Effort in His Apology

Lola

BROOKE SLUNG HER BAG over her shoulder. "Are you sure you want me to come over for dinner?" She stuck her key in the clinic door and flipped the lock.

The day was officially over.

Finally.

"Yes," I said. Instantly. No pause. The last thing I needed was more time on my own. "After today..." I grimaced.

"The joys of living in a small town. Did you see any patients who *didn't* mention what happened on Friday night?"

"One. I think the mother with the projectile-vomiting toddler had bigger problems to worry about."

"You have a special talent for attracting the pukers." Brooke grinned. "How about I wash up, get out of this uniform, and drop 'round in about an hour?"

"Sounds great."

"I'll come with wine and this face." Her features crumpled into a serious frown, and she nodded, tapping her chin.

I laughed. "That's one heck of a listening face."

"Yup! I take my friend duties very seriously."

I waved goodbye and wandered down the street to the village store, my eyes glued to my phone. I needed to look busy—way too busy to stop and talk to anyone still itching to ask me about last Friday night. I saved my only smile for Ryan Hollyoak, who spared me an awkward conversation and simply tipped his hat and held the door open for me as I stepped into the store.

I grabbed a metal shopping basket off the pile and ran through the list of ingredients to host another lonely girls' dinner and drinks. This wasn't the night for moderation. I stumbled around the shelves like a zombie. Yeast to make pizza dough? *Get in my basket.* Extra cheese? *I'm sprinkling the whole bag, and it still won't be enough.*

The dairy fridge was tucked away at the back of the store. My final stop. My fingers curled around the silver handle, ready to pull open the door.

I froze.

No. Not today of all days. Line after line of cold, lonely shelves. All empty.

No milk.

This couldn't be happening. I bounced up and down on my toes, eyes scouring the bare shelves of the fridge. Nothing.

A heavy sigh caved in my chest as I trudged to the register.

Ashley's eyebrow arched.

I dropped the cheese on the counter. "I don't suppose you have any milk hidden out back?" I knew the answer was no, but I was a glutton for punishment. It seemed like the day for it. "I'll pay you a hundred dollars."

Ashley's smile was sympathetic. "Our dairy restock got held up outside Hobart. An accident on the road. We've been running low all day," she explained as she scanned my groceries. "We might have some milk powder left on the shelves."

I wrinkled my nose. Yuck. That stuff tasted like chalk. "No thanks."

Sighing, I lined up the last of my groceries. A carton of milk slid behind it.

Huh?

I darted a look over my shoulder. A big, broad chest stuffed inside a black Henley... A beard...

Well, wasn't that just *peachy?*

Aiden was the last person I wanted to see. I glared up at him. His face was grim, and even darker circles bruised under tired grey eyes. *Good!* A lifetime of bad sleep was the least of what he deserved after the way he'd treated me.

He said nothing, but he dipped his chin. His way of saying hello. Or maybe he was silently pleading with me to accept his peace offering. Yeah, right. He could take his carton of milk and shove it where the sun didn't shine.

I stared him dead in the eye and pushed the carton away from my pile of groceries.

"Don't need it," I said.

Aiden's face gave nothing away. If he knew I was imitating the way he'd spoken to me outside the coffee shop, he didn't show it. The man was a stone wall.

"You need milk. You just said so. Here." Aiden slid the carton back. "It's the last one. Take it."

My eyebrows scrunched together. I'd never be in debt to that man. *Never.* I pressed the carton back again, but my palm was fuelled by too much anger, and the container toppled over on the counter.

"Don't *want* it," I said.

Aiden's eyes screwed closed. "Lola... I..."

"There is *nothing* you need to say to me." I refused to look at that traitor for another second. Whipping my head around, I scooped up my groceries and shoved the pile to the end of the counter away from his milk.

Ashley let out a laugh tinged with nervousness as she leant over and grabbed the milk, whisking it under the counter. "Well, would you look at that?" The carton reappeared, and she plonked it at the front. "I found some milk out back after all." She winked at me. "But you can keep your hundred dollars."

I folded my arms across my chest and stuck my nose into the air, completely ignoring Aiden while Ashley scanned the last of my groceries.

I couldn't get out of that store fast enough. The second Ashley was done, I tapped my card to pay, muttered a quick, "Sorry for being such a... well... *you know...*" and flew out the door.

My fists clenched so tightly around the handles of my cotton grocery bags that my fingernails dug into my palms. My heart hammered faster when the bell for the grocery store tingled in the background. Boots pounded on the sidewalk behind me.

"Lola!"

I pretended not to hear Aiden calling me. He tried again, but I still ignored him. His footsteps picked up, and moments later, a wall of black Henley blocked my path. I jerked to a stop. My grocery bags kept swinging.

That nasty brute of a man! What did he want?

I stuck my foot out to step around Aiden. His hand reached for me like he wanted to grab my arm, but he quickly pulled back. Instead, he blocked my way past.

I huffed in frustration. "Excuse me, Mr. McKinnon."

Again, I tried to dodge past. Again, he blocked my way, and his hand shot out, then retreated before his fingers skimmed my skin. Why did he keep doing that? Was I so tainted and unlovable that he couldn't even bear to touch me now?

"Lola, can we please talk?"

Maybe if adorable pigs with pink swirly tails soared through the valley. "No."

I pushed past him and charged down the path, but I jolted to a stop as he somehow managed to block my way again. For a big guy, he sure was quick on his feet.

Exhausted, quiet frustration roared out of me. My eyes widened. It had been a very long time since I'd felt comfortable enough to express anger. He really did bring out the worst in me.

"What?" I snapped at him. "What do you want, Aiden?"

He shoved his hands into his pockets. "I wanted to, um"—a deep breath—"to tell you—"

"*What?*"

Aiden's eyes fixed on his boots. "I'm sorry."

I didn't freeze—I just stopped feeling. His apology left me numb. The whole production felt like a kid being forced by his mother to apologise for something he definitely wasn't sorry for. But even though I ignored the hope aching in my bones, my heart softened enough to offer Aiden one final chance.

I hiked up my chin. "For what?"

"Pardon?"

"What are you sorry for?"

"Um..." He eyed me warily. "Everything?"

I couldn't help laughing. *Everything?* He had no idea what he was apologising for or why. He wasn't sorry. Not really. Whatever. I was done with him.

"Oh, well, in that case, you're forgiven." I forced my sweetest smile. "You know, for *everything*."

Aiden's eyebrows lowered in suspicion. "Just like that?"

"Sure." I shrugged. "If you can only be bothered to give me a half-hearted apology, you're most welcome to my very half-hearted forgiveness."

Aiden tossed me a helpless look. "Lola, you know I'm not good with words."

I snorted. "You seemed to have no trouble finding all the words you needed outside the coffee shop."

Aiden flinched.

"And what about your grand speech at the bar? You really outdid yourself on that one." I lowered my voice to mimic his rumbly baritone, but it sounded more like a cranky Santa Claus than Aiden. *"I know a lot of things about you I wish I could forget—"*

"I didn't mean that the way you think—"

"—Take the hint. Stay away from me. Please." I rolled my eyes. "And in case you hadn't noticed, I took your hint. I'm trying to stay away from you. So, if you could please move out of my way—"

"I can't do that. I need to..." He shrugged a shoulder. "Make things right between us... Apologise."

I sighed. "Look, Aiden. If Brooke or Ryan or someone told you to apologise to me, you don't need to. We weren't dating. It was one night. Instead of lying and making up a whole bunch of crap about it being the best night of your life—"

"I meant every word I said that night."

I rolled my eyes. "Whatever. I'm not wasting another minute of my life thinking about you. So, let's pretend nothing happened between us. Okay?"

"I can't pretend nothing happened, Lola. You're here." Aiden knocked his fist against his chest. Right above his heart. "Locked in."

My eyes narrowed. Why was he doing this? A week ago, his words would have melted me into a puddle of forgiveness. I knew better now.

"Do you want to hear a story about the best night of *my* life?" I asked him. "It was when I finally grew a backbone and told a man who treated me worse than poop on his shoes to buzz right off. Guess when that night was?" I held out my grocery bags, gesturing at the darkness starting to smother the valley. "Need any more hints?"

"Please, Lola. Give me a chance."

A sad, broken laugh broke free. "I already did."

And this time, when I charged past Aiden, he didn't try to stop me.

14

He Saw Her Bravery

Aiden

I AVOIDED DRIVING PAST Discount Automotive on my way into town. That place was a bloody eyesore. Always had been.

Years ago, it had been painted fuchsia pink. Evan's wife had chosen the colour. The day she'd left town, he'd climbed his ladder and started slathering an obnoxious yellow over the top. A week later, she'd still been gone, and Discount Automotive was moonlighting as a flat banana instead of just the best place for a tune-up.

I avoided looking at the yellow bricks as I plodded from my truck, boots heavy, my hands stuffed in my pockets, and my eyes on the trouble looming above. Black clouds swelled like ink spilling across the sky, and the wind lashed like an icy whip. A storm was coming—fast.

This would be a quick visit.

Evan sat on a stack of tyres inside the workshop. The coffee mug he lifted to his lips paused midair when he saw me.

"Mornin'," he said.

"Morning."

"Problem with your truck?"

"The truck's fine." Was I going to do this? I dragged back a memory. Lola shaking, terrified out of her mind. Yeah, I was. "I thought we should talk."

"Yeah?" His eyes squinted to nothing but a line. "About what?"

"Lola."

Evan snorted. "The door's that way, big fella." His finger pointed me back to the parking lot. "I ain't got nothin' to say about the doctor."

"You can listen then."

He cocked his head. "It's not like you to stick your nose where it don't belong. You here playin' town hero like Hollyoak?"

"He stopped by?"

"Nope, and he ain't welcome here. He fired two of my mates off his farm when there ain't much work goin' this time of year."

"Maybe your *mates* should've thought about that before standing there watching you tear into a defenceless woman."

Evan's eyebrows popped up. "That's how it is, huh?" He sipped his coffee before sliding the mug on the workbench. He pushed off the tyres and stood tall. "You've changed your tune since last Friday."

"I was a gutless bastard for not stepping in. I'm making it right."

"Makin' it right? For what? Gettin' in her knickers?" Evan scoffed. "She put you up to this?"

"No." I screwed my eyes shut and waited for the anger to pass. Evan mentioning Lola's frilly pink knickers made blood roar in my ears, but losing my shit would achieve nothing. "She didn't ask me to stop by."

"I've seen you two talkin'. Everyone has. You ain't here out of the kindness of your heart."

I took a slow step forward. Evan folded his arms, but his eyes weren't sure where to look. He wasn't half as tough as he pretended to be.

"You don't talk to Lola again," I said. "If I see you or any of your *mates* even looking in her direction—"

"Australia's a free country, ain't it? I can look wherever I damn well want."

"Don't test me." I didn't recognise my own voice. The words came out as a sinister promise, making Evan scramble another step back.

"You ain't got no authority here." Doubt flickered in his eyes. He wasn't so sure. "You ain't a cop no more."

That got a bark of laughter out of me. His remembering a drunken confession about my past wouldn't save him. "What's stopping me from taking care of you then?"

He swallowed. "You're a good man. Everyone says so."

"Not when it comes to Lola. Don't make me pay you a visit after hours. Understand?"

Evan answered with a sharp jerk of his chin. Good enough. Loathing crawled over my skin at the thought of throwing my weight around, but some men didn't respond to chats and gentle reminders to act like decent human beings. I did what needed to be done to protect Lola. I'd still be able to sleep at night...if I ever slept again...

A raindrop plopped on my cheek as I headed back to my truck. I swiped it away and glanced at the sky.

Time to get moving.

I'd only just pulled out of Discount Automotive when the storm hit. Water pelted, and I bent forward, squinting through the deluge pounding the windscreen. The road was empty except for old ghosts barrelling towards me. I was useless driving in this state. Slowing to a stop at the turnoff, I forced down a steadying breath, took one hand off the wheel, flexed my fingers, and shook off the nerves. Then, I did the other hand.

Focus. You can do this, you weak bastard.

The windscreen wipers whipped across the glass, but it was impossible to tell where the rain ended and the road began. Everything was a soggy haze of grey... Except...

Gripping the steering wheel tighter, I narrowed my eyes on the spot of pink on the horizon. The spot grew bigger and bigger until it was a person.

"Goddammit, Lola," I muttered to the empty car. "Why the hell are you out in this rain?"

Her skirt wasn't floating around her knees, tempting me to flick it up. The fabric plastered to her legs like a second skin. I thumped my palm into the steering wheel. The wind was like ice. She'd catch a cold. If a big rig came hurtling down the road, she'd be hit.

I crawled my truck to a stop beside her and put down the window. She didn't stop. She kept on walking.

"Lola!"

Her head turned, golden hair flat against her face. Rain-drops dotted her glasses, hiding her eyes, but her mouth speared down. Shivering, sopping wet, she still hated me. Too bad. I couldn't leave her there.

Worry edged my voice when I barked, "Get in!" She didn't budge. "There's a storm."

"Oh, *really?* I hadn't noticed!" She hiked up her chin, defiant until the end, snapped around on her heel like a soldier, and kept marching down the road.

I dragged my hands down my face. There was no chance she'd get in willingly, but I couldn't let her walk down the road to her death. I pulled the truck off the road, shifted into park, and after rummaging around in the back for what I needed, I took off after her. My boots sloshed through the water as I chased her down the road.

"Lola!"

Hearing my voice catching up behind her only made her walk faster. "Hell will freeze over before I accept help from you, you...you...big beast!"

"You're going to freeze to death. You're already soaked through, and it's ten minutes into town on foot from here!" I planted myself in front of her, blocking her way, and popped a black umbrella open over her head. "Are you going to be difficult about this?"

"Absolutely!" To prove to me just how determined she was to reject my help, she marched on.

"I hope you like company then."

Lola jolted to a stop, her mouth dropping open. "You wouldn't."

"You've got two options. You can get rid of me real quick by letting me drive you home. But if you want to be stubborn and keep going on foot, I'm with you every step of the way."

Her eyes slid past me to where I'd parked off the road. "I'm never getting in your truck."

"I hope you like walking then."

"I *love* it!"

And off she went. Perfect, stubborn, sweet little thing. I would've laughed if I didn't think she'd take a swing at me. Easily keeping pace beside her, making sure the umbrella shielded her from the worst of the rain, I glanced down. Goosebumps prickled her pale skin.

"You're cold," I said.

She stuck her nose higher in the air, but only until I started fumbling with the buttons of my shirt.

"Wha—" Pale eyebrows popped over the top of her glasses. "*What* are you *doing?*"

With one hand gripping the umbrella, I managed to shrug off my flannel, the white T-shirt underneath instantly soaking through. The wind whipped past. Damn, it was cold.

"Making sure you don't catch your death," I said, slinging my flannel over her shoulders. "There." She was nothing but a head and slim legs swamped in blue and green checks. "Better."

Lola swished from side to side. "It's so *warm*," she breathed, her arms hugging the shirt to her body.

I smiled. She looked good in my flannel. I liked how it swallowed her up, and the sleeves hung over her hands. She *was* warm. My smell was all over her.

She blinked up at me. "This changes nothing between us."

"I know."

Nothing could change between us. I wanted Lola's forgiveness, but I couldn't have her. It didn't matter what Ruth said. Every day would be a storm if Lola were stuck with me. She'd live waiting for the wind to pick up, wild, unrelenting, never knowing if the thunder was coming. The darkness inside me would overshadow any sunny days of us cooking and reading together.

And what was the other option? Convincing her to agree to something casual? Parking my boots by her door, touching her sweet body, making her feel good, only to tip my hat at sundown and say goodbye?

Maybe that would work for a few weeks until some other bastard swept her off her feet. He'd be the one to tangle his fingers with hers, kiss her cheek, and say, "I do."

That man couldn't be me, and it almost ripped me in half.

I was grateful the rain poured, and I had an excuse to swipe the tears leaking from my eyes. The thought of Lola being with someone else hurt. Hurt worse than a punch in the gut.

No, she would never be mine, but I wanted her forgiveness just the same.

"Lola, I'm sorry for the way I treated you. Not being honest... Leaving... Throwing out your pie... The bar... All of it."

Her lip curled, and she said nothing. My apologies never did much to sway her sympathy.

"I guessed early on something wasn't quite right with you," I said. "I acted like a selfish bastard. I know someone hurt you, and I ignored the signs and went there anyway."

Lola's head slowly turned. I'd hoped to see some glimmer of forgiveness, but the eyes that lifted were narrowed to a murderous line.

"Something's not *right* about me?" she snapped. "So, I'm damaged goods, is that it? You would've saved yourself all this regret and avoided sleeping with me if you'd known someone used to hit me?"

Someone used to... The air strangled out of my lungs. I stopped dead on the roadside. "Lola..." My legs almost buckled, but I kept myself upright. I'd suspected this, but somehow, hearing her say the words was worse.

Lola's tiny fist balled by her side. "Should I have told you how he never let me have my own money? That he controlled what I wore and where I went?" Her voice pitched higher and higher. "That he locked me outside on the balcony for hours to teach me a lesson after I forgot to pick up his dry cleaning?"

Her words punched a crack in my chest. "Lola..."

"Or did you need to know he slapped me across the face for embarrassing him at his birthday party? Or the fact that it wasn't the first time? Or even the worst of what he did to me? Would telling you *that* have saved you from making such a terrible choice?"

The crack in my chest split wide open, breaths tearing in and out, but I couldn't seem to keep any air in my lungs. Lola was the kindest little creature in the world. The idea that someone could hurt her like that destroyed me. What could I do? Track the bastard down on the mainland and give him a taste of his own medicine? Fuck, I *wanted* to do that.

"Lola... Bloody hell... That's not..." Shaking my head, I swallowed to force the lump from my throat and get out the words I needed to say. "I didn't mean it like that. I wanted to spare *you*. I should have protected you. You're a victim."

"I'm not a victim!"

"No... You're...a *survivor*."

"I'm a *person,* Aiden! You *hurt* me! Or do you think the only way you can hurt someone is with your hands? Your words were just as cruel. All your manufactured kindness to get a quick fuck and then desert me like I was disposable cut just as deep!" She croaked a bitter laugh at the storm clouds. "You know, if you only wanted a one-night thing, you should've just been honest. I was so lonely, I probably would have said yes anyway. That's the pathetic part."

"That night... It wasn't just a quick *fuck*, Lola. You know that. That night was perfect."

The fury in her eyes dimmed. "Then why did you leave without saying goodbye?"

"Because *I'm* not right. Inside me..." I pressed a fist over my heart. "I'm no good."

She stepped closer, hugging the shirt around her body. "You can talk to me, Aiden."

Her voice was barely a whisper, yet it slammed into me like a sledgehammer. Could I talk to her? The words threatened to spill out. I wanted to confess all my sins. Fall to my knees and beg for her forgiveness. But some truths were too painful to share. It wouldn't make things better between us, only worse.

I shook my head.

Lola's soft expression hardened, her eyes narrowing the longer I stayed silent. When I pushed back my shoulders and stood taller, she understood there would never be a conversation about all the things wrong with me. I wasn't talking.

"Coward!" She wrestled the umbrella from my hand. "You'll get no forgiveness from me! Find some other way to ease your guilty conscience, Aiden."

She almost smacked me in the face with the umbrella when she spun on her heel.

And off she marched.

I should have collapsed on the road, a broken shell of a man, but the sight of my brave girl charging ahead with the black umbrella bobbing above her kept my spine straight. And when I saw her snuggle deeper into my oversized shirt, warm and sheltered against the wind, I smiled.

15

She Saw Two Endings

Lola

> Did you think I wouldn't find you?

I STOPPED.

My hand stalled mid-air, the white picket gate just out of reach. When I turned, the red door gave nothing away. I couldn't see down the hallway or into the kitchen. A heavy thud echoed in my chest.

Did I lock the back door?

It didn't always catch. I had to flip the deadbolt too, and sometimes, I forgot. My thoughts muddled as I replayed the steps I'd taken that morning—breakfast, a load of laundry, a quick shower, I got dressed... But... Maybe I'd forgotten the deadbolt after hanging the last basket of linen on the washing line?

I clapped a hand over my mouth and squeezed my eyes shut, fear tightening in my lungs.

Breathe, Lola. Just breathe.

I swung my bag onto my shoulder and scurried down the path. Yolanda hovered by the fence. The jet of water gushing from her hose pointed at her rose bushes, and her face stayed hidden behind a puff of smoke, but I knew she was watching me.

Forcing a laugh, I blurted out, "I forgot something."

My hand shook as I stuck the key in the lock. I shoved my shoulder against the front door and barrelled inside, almost tumbling to my knees in the hallway.

My sanctuary had to stay safe. It *had* to.

Dashing from room to room, I checked every window, every door, running my fingers over the catches and double-checking every lock.

I knew this day would come, but I still wasn't prepared. Running away from a man like Chris wasn't like the movies. I couldn't fake my own death or change my identity. I needed to work. I needed to *live*.

Stupidly, I'd hoped this time he'd eventually just...give up. Why did he even want me? He wasn't short of women fawning over him. He was wealthy and successful. People admired him. Me? I did nothing right.

But the other times I'd attempted to escape, he'd hunted for me. A day. A week. He always found me and convinced me to give him another chance by crying promises that he'd change and finally get help. He never did.

I glanced at my phone. The message stared back at me, but my hand had stopped shaking when I hit "Block."

"It's over this time," I said to the screen. "Forever."

After a few swipes of a brush through my hair, a fresh coat of lip gloss, and a big breath, I yanked open the door to start my day again. I turned the key and rattled the knob. *Definitely* locked.

"Is that a new dress?" Yolanda called as I headed back down the path.

"Oh, um... yes..." I smoothed the polka dots, suddenly even more self-conscious under her steely eyes.

"Decided to get pretty for your date with the Hollyoak boy, eh?"

Of *course* she knew about that. Nothing stayed a secret from the church ladies.

"It's not a date," I said.

It wasn't.

I had invited Ryan out for a coffee. The box of muffins stuffed in my bag was simply a polite gesture after he'd insisted on paying for coffee last time. It wasn't like when I'd baked for Aiden. Ryan would talk about farm things I didn't understand. I'd prattle on about books he wouldn't read. The farmer was kind and easy to talk to, but we had nothing in common.

Yolanda croaked a laugh. "Not a date, she says. That won't be what everyone thinks when they see you with him." She blew a puff of smoke into the sky. "That won't be what Aiden thinks."

"Well, I don't really care what Aiden thinks. That big beast can just...just..." Ugh, why did thinking about him always turn me into a raving fool? "He can just shove off!"

"Oh, pet. Give him time."

"To what? Treat me like trash again? No thank you. I'd rather enjoy my very *platonic* coffee with my very *platonic* friend, Ryan."

She smirked. "Maybe I should head into town early to take over the cake stall. When word gets out, I wouldn't mind seeing the reaction of your big beast."

⋅♥⋅♥⋅♥⋅♥⋅♥⋅

"Like clockwork," I muttered.

There he was—the big beast himself.

Every Saturday morning, at precisely 10:20 a.m., Aiden parked his truck a decent hike away from the village markets before heading inside to load up a box of groceries. Sometimes, Harry joined him. Most of the time, he wandered around alone, looking like the cramped, hot hall was the last place on earth he'd rather be.

My plan to wait nearby, casually glancing at my phone—well, there'd been a hiccup to deal with. Aiden might have been on time, but I was behind schedule. My ballet flats scuttled quicker along the uneven stone path.

Panting, I managed to call out, "Aiden!" I waved. "Wait!"

I didn't want him getting any closer to town. Jogging wasn't for me, but some exchanges weren't meant to be seen by the prying eyes of people passing by. I'd be dodging enough questions when people saw me with Ryan. I wasn't about to add Aiden back onto the Person of Interest list, too.

He flicked the car door shut. Furrowed brows and grey eyes turned.

"Hi! Sorry!" I tried to gulp in some air. "Sorry. I wanted to catch you." I unhooked the strap of my bag, took out the box of muffins, and then rummaged through the rest of my junk to find what I needed. *Aha!* There, under the balls of wool. "Here."

Aiden stared at the brown paper package in my hand. "You...bought me a...gift?" The crease between his brows deepened.

I snorted a laugh. "No." In his dreams. "It's your shirt."

He stared at me.

I jiggled the package. Why wasn't he taking it? "I washed and ironed it for you."

"It's...wrapped..."

"I'm learning that certain people in this town are very keen to read into a situation. If they see me give you a shirt... Well, you can imagine." I shoved it at him. "Pretend it's mail. Make up any story you want if someone asks."

"But you washed it."

"*And* ironed it. I know most people hate ironing, but I sort of love it. There's something so satisfying about watching all the creases smooth out. And you can listen to an audiobook or put on some music..." I trailed off with a nervous laugh. There was that *rambling* again. Even when Aiden stood like a blank wall, he coaxed too many words from my mouth. "Your shirt is as good as new!"

His whole face drooped. If I didn't know any better, I'd swear he was devastated. "But your smell won't be in it anymore if you've washed it."

Um... "That's the whole point, isn't it?"

Heaving a sigh, he took the package from me. "What's in the box?" He nodded at my other hand.

"Muffins!" I grinned. "I tried out a new recipe with an apple crumble topping. I baked them for Ryan—"

"You baked apple muffins for Ryan Hollyoak?" His nostrils flared from a deep breath in.

"Yes?"

"Goddammit, Lola. That's..." He dragged a hand through his hair. "I didn't think it would be so soon." When I blinked at him, confused, he added, "You. Moving on."

"It's been months since I left him. That's hardly soon."

"I meant moving on from *us*."

"Was there an *us*?" I tilted my head, thinking about it. My poor lonely heart had wanted there to be an *us*, but Aiden had never promised me that. "We had that weekend, I guess. I know I let my emotions get the better of me the day of the storm." I winced. Secrets meant to stay buried had poured out of me faster than the rain from the sky that day. I'd admitted too much. "I *was* upset about what happened between us, but don't worry. I'm over it now."

"You're...over it..."

I bobbed my head in a nod. "Other people probably fig-ure out their boundaries sooner than me. I've never had a one-night stand before, and I don't think I'll have one again." Part of my brain registered I was back to rambling, and yet my mouth kept going...and going... "I think being with someone is such an intimate chance to spoil them and...and...*connect* with them. The next time I share that part of myself, I want it to be special. I want it to really mean something." I blushed, my teeth gnawing on my bottom lip to stop myself from saying more. That was *way* too much to say on a random Saturday morning.

"We didn't have a one-night stand," he said.

"A half-night stand?"

Aiden scowled. "Lola, you're not hearing me. It wasn't just a one-night thing. It wasn't a *fuck*. I don't... Bloody hell... I don't *do* that kind of thing."

"So, I imagined waking up by myself?"

"That's not what I'm saying."

Wasn't it? It sounded an awful lot like the same old gaslighting I was used to. In the past, I would have smiled and shoved my feelings deep down. Not anymore.

"Aiden, do you know how hard that morning was for me? The sheets were cold. Your stuff was gone. You didn't leave me a note, and then, when I saw you..." I pressed my hand over my heart. The moment he'd tossed out the pie still hurt more than I wanted it to. "Life has taught me so many lessons. I know I never want to be treated that way again. So, as good as our half-night stand was—"

"Please stop calling it that."

I lifted a shoulder. "If you want to pretend it didn't happen at all, that works for me, too." I tucked the muffins safely back in my bag. "Sorry about all that oversharing. I already gave Harry your umbrella when I last saw him. So, now that you have all your stuff back, we can go back to staying away from each other. I'd better head off anyway."

His narrowed gaze dipped over my outfit from head to toe. "You meeting someone?"

"Yeah. Ryan." I patted the outline of the box crammed into my bag. "We're catching up for a coffee. It's becoming a Saturday thing, I think. Breakfast with Brooke. Coffee with Ryan. Pretending I can knit in the afternoon." I laughed. "See ya!"

I got about five steps down the road before I realised I'd hit the mental "block" button on this relationship, too.

16

He Saw the Doctor

Aiden

THE MEMORY OF RYAN Hollyoak touching Lola's shoulder was blistered like a red scar behind my eyes.

It happened in a second. Innocent. Nothing at all, really. He held open the coffee shop door for her. His other hand parked on her shoulder as she slipped past, and when he looked down at her and smiled, she smiled back. It wasn't one of her dreamy smiles, like when nothing existed but the two of us tangled in her pink sheets. But it *was* a smile.

She baked him muffins. *Apple* muffins.

She liked him.

And it burned through me like acid.

I forced in a slow breath, keeping my gaze steady on the knotted lines of wood as I smoothed the sandpaper down the rough edge. Almost a week alone, avoiding the world in my workshop, had done nothing to dull that memory. But Lola had every right to move on. I just had to get used to it.

Harry's boots plodded across the workshop floor. He must have been back from the job at the church. I didn't look up. I wasn't in the mood for small talk.

His butt slumped against the workbench beside me. "Seriously, old man," he said. "What are you doing?"

"Working."

"Hiding."

"Working."

"You're finding an awful lot of work to keep busy these days. I guess you still haven't figured out the answer to your problem?"

I sighed and threw the sandpaper down on the workbench. "No."

"Only you could screw up an apology. You *talked* to Lola, right? You know, actually opened your mouth and didn't just stand there being awkward for once?"

I shot a glare at him. "I *talked* to Lola." My sigh was defeated. "I just keep saying the wrong thing."

That was an understatement. Every time I tried to make things right with Lola, I only made it worse. Frustration coiled around my chest. I needed to do something. Keeping myself busy and burying my problems was a damn good option. I snatched the chisel from the rack and got back to work on the cabinet.

"Did you talk it over with Miss Ruthie?" Harry asked. "Get a woman's perspective?"

"I talked to Ruth."

"And?"

"She told me I need to try a lot damn harder."

Harry laughed. "I think she's probably right."

"I think I probably need better friends."

Another of his laughs erupted in the workshop. Even though I scowled at him, a smile tugged at my lips as I flipped the cabinet. I should have clamped it, but I was distracted, so I steadied the side with my palm and started to square off the joints with the chisel.

"Well, if the rumours are true," Harry said, "you better figure out how to make it right with Lola pretty quick."

"Ignore the rumours, kid. The gossip's all bullshit."

Harry's grin was far too smug for my liking. "But this is *church lady* gossip. The *best* kind. Those ladies know how to bake the yummiest cookies *and* spill the best tea."

I grunted. A sinking feeling blackened the pit of my stomach. Something warned me I didn't want to hear any gossip from those old crows. I pretended to focus on tidying the edges of the cabinet instead.

"Yolanda was singing your praises," Harry said. "No one else was buying it. Word of the crap you pulled at the Old Cellar has put a lot of the ladies offside."

"That's not news."

"True. But I was minding my own business, rewiring the fans in the tearoom, and—whadda ya know—I just happened to hear that true love has blossomed for one lucky couple after all." He fluttered his eyelashes. "Apparently, the lonely farmer will soon take a doctor for a wife."

Jealousy boiled my blood. That split second of distraction was all it took. The chisel slipped. A flash of cold metal sliced through my hand like butter, and even though shock numbed the pain that should have followed, there was no mistaking what I'd done. Blood pooled into the wood, the raw pine blooming an eerie shade of red.

"*Fuck.*" There wasn't much else I could say, really.

Harry made some otherworldly retching sound as if his soul had just been yanked out of his body. He flew back and hit the wall. He didn't blink. His eyes were frozen wide open, and his skin drained to an icy white.

"You not good with blood, kid?"

Harry's mouth opened, but no sound came out.

"Don't look at it, okay?"

First aid training be damned. The first rule of dealing with a cut was to raise the wound to slow the blood flow, but I kept my hand low, out of Harry's line of sight. We didn't need to end up with two casualties.

I called to him over my shoulder as I headed to the sink. "Do me a favour and grab the first-aid kit. Back room. Top shelf."

Harry nodded, sucking in huge gulps of air before staggering away.

I fumbled to turn on the tap, and a deep shudder ran through me when the water hit the open wound. *Goddammit.* That stung. I was so bloody stupid. I knew better. I should have had my mind on the job. The gossip was bullshit—it was only ever half the truth—but Lola and Hollyoak might be a reality I needed to get used to. *Fast.*

"Got the first-aid k—" Harry dry-retched again. His eyes locked on the deep, red gash in my hand. "Wait, is that...? The white bit...?"

His eyelids fluttered.

It only took one step to reach him. I managed to slump him over my shoulder just before he passed out. The first-aid kit crashed to the floor, its lid cracking open, and everything inside tumbled across the concrete. Harry was out cold.

With his skinny body flopped against me like a rag doll, I crouched down, sifted through the mess to find the gauze swab I needed, ripped open the packet, and got it on the cut. Dark red bloomed instantly. Not good. I fumbled another packet open.

Harry's back jolted. He pushed off me but fell to his butt on the floor. "What happened?" He blinked.

"You're not good with blood," I said. "Take a few deep breaths. The feeling will pass in a minute or two."

"How are you okay with that?" Harry nodded at my hand. "The...blood and the...the...seeing the"—he clamped his hand over his mouth as his shoulders heaved in another retch—"the bone bit?"

I shrugged. "Just used to it, I guess."

"*Used* to it?" Harry squeaked. "This is just like your ninja self-defence moves on the mountain. Or that time you hauled the Collins' kid out of the river when he nearly drowned. Are you gonna tell me where you learned all that crap?"

"In another life."

Harry's eyes narrowed. "Were you some kind of secret special-ops commando or something?"

"Nah, that's army shit."

"You going to admit the truth if I keep guessing?"

I shook my head.

"Alright. Keep your secrets. But I'm onto you, old man." He shook his head. "*Used* to it."

I shuffled through the mess on the floor and finally spotted a bandage. "I do need someone to look at this pretty quickly, though." I kept my voice calm and low—nothing to panic about. "Think you can drive?"

"You want me to take you to the clinic?"

"Yeah." I flicked him a glance as I wrapped the bandage around my hand. "I don't think I can drive like this."

"I can't drive you to the clinic."

"Kid, you're fine. It's only five minutes—"

"No. Not the clinic."

"You scared of doctors too?"

"No." He rubbed the back of his neck. "It's, you know... Brooke works there."

"And?" My eyebrow rose. "Look, kid, if something happened between you and the blonde, just sit in the car while the doctor patches me up." I threw him my keys. "But you're driving."

Harry sat silent for most of the drive into town. Restless, never sitting still, his fingers drummed the steering wheel. When we stopped at the last turn coming into town, his gaze flicked to me.

"It's not like that." Harry's voice was strained. "With Brooke, I mean. She's gorgeous, but I'd never, you know... It's not like that with her."

I was on a roll for sticking my foot in it with the people I cared about. "I'm sorry. Heat of the moment. If I assumed the wrong thing—"

"Nah, it's all good. But Brooke...and me..." He shook his head and blew out a slow breath. "Forget it."

Harry's nervous tapping on the wheel continued the rest of the way into town. Something was bothering him. A couple of gentle prods to talk went ignored, and I didn't want to push my luck further. Our friendship was already hanging by a thread.

When he pulled up outside the clinic, he didn't unbuckle his seat belt. His jaw clenched, tense. Poor kid. I clamped a reassuring hand on his shoulder before I hopped out of the truck.

For only the third time ever—which was still three times too many—I walked through the clinic doors.

The waiting room was deserted. Brooke lounged behind the reception desk, one of her bright red heels kicking out as she flipped through a magazine and shoved a bit of muffin into her mouth. My shadow looming over the desk eventually caught her attention. Her eyebrows slowly lifted as if my presence were the biggest inconvenience in the universe.

I held up my bandaged hand. "Workshop accident."

"Just your hand?" Brooke fluttered her eyelashes. "It's a pity you didn't get sliced and diced lower down." She picked up the desk phone and tapped a few buttons. "Doc, I've got a bleeder out here if you're free."

Her red fingernail pointed at a row of chairs. She wanted me to sit my backside down and wait. Too bad. I ignored her and lounged against the wall. I had no intention of getting comfortable. The sooner I was out of that damn clinic, the better.

Every so often, Brooke flashed me an evil smirk over the top of her magazine. I'd bet she was planning how to murder me for the unforgivable way I'd treated her friend. A map of one of the remote wilderness trails was probably hidden in the glossy pages, a big red *X* marked where she planned to bury my body. She was pure type A, that one. She could pull it off without getting caught. No one would know.

The sweetest voice in the world floated down the corridor. "Alright, who have we got...?"

Lola stopped dead in her tracks. Her eyes flew to Brooke, my bandaged hand, and back to Brooke. But before she could protest and refuse to see me, I saved her the effort.

"No." Nerves thumped through me that had nothing to do with my butchered hand. "I need to see the other doctor."

Lola threw her hands up.

Add that to my list of screwups, but there was no way I could be alone in a room with her after everything that had happened between us—the bar, the storm, and *definitely* not after seeing her with Hollyoak. I couldn't face her again until I found a way to fix us.

Brooke smiled at me sweetly. *Too* sweetly. "The other doctor is doing their rounds at the old folks' home this afternoon. Only Dr. Hughes is available."

I looked helplessly at Brooke, pleading for mercy. I'd take murder over the torture of being alone with Lola. "I can't see Dr. Hughes."

Lola shrugged. She was completely done with me. "Whatever. Your choice." She waved me away. "Bleed out in the corridor if you want. There's a warmed-up raspberry muffin and a pile of test results waiting for me." She spun on her heel and headed down the corridor. *"Adios, muchacho!"*

"Hey, hey, hey!" Brooke bent over the reception desk to holler after her. "I don't want the big oaf bleeding out on my nice new carpet!" She pointed her red fingernail at me. "You heard the doctor. Move your butt to the treatment room, *muchacho*."

I trudged down the corridor.

Brooke cackled. "Don't worry," she called after me. "The doctor will take *real* good care of you."

My murder might be on the agenda after all.

17

She Saw the Patient

Lola

A NERVOUS BEAT BOUNCED off the treatment room walls.

Aiden's broad shoulders crowded the corner he'd wedged himself into. He sat on the edge of the bed, his posture stiff, every muscle tight. The constant tapping of his boot hinted at frayed nerves, and wary eyes tracked my every move before sliding to the closed door.

Only one of my patients had bolted for their life from a treatment room. Maybe I was about to see the second.

"This won't take long," I reassured him.

Aiden said nothing. The beat of his boot sped up.

I scoured the shelves, grabbed everything I needed, and with a shove, the metal trolley with all my goodies rumbled across the treatment room. I faltered, wobbling. Aiden's gaze was back on me. Oh, those eyes—wild and grey like a storm over the ocean, yet somehow soft like a big ol' rumpled teddy bear.

My fingers twitched on the cold, steel handle of the trolley, fighting the urge to stroke the hair around his temple and gently, neatly, curl it behind his ear. Every instinct in my body screamed at me to comfort him and promise that everything would be okay.

But he hadn't earned my kindness. Acting detached and professional was the only option to keep me safe from repeating the same mistakes.

I pointed at Aiden's bandaged hand. "How did you do it?"

He grimaced. Did the injury cause him pain, or was it the cold, clinical bite of my voice?

"Chisel," he eventually answered.

I nodded like I had the faintest idea about tools and scooted my stool beside him. It took a stern glare before Aiden presented his hand. Red spots peeked through the heavy layers of gauze. He'd made a real mess of his hand with that chisel thing. I squinted. Even though the bandage was twisted and bunched in some parts, the smooth, neat lines looked professional, as good as some doctors could do—maybe better.

Curious, I tilted my head. "Who dressed your wound?"

"I did."

"One-handed?" My eyebrows popped up. "You did a pretty good job. You've had first-aid training?"

"Something like that."

That man never gave me a straight answer. "Just full of secrets, aren't you?"

The tap of Aiden's boot stopped.

Sighing, I focused on unwrapping the bandage. My mind looped with a steady chant.

I can do this.

I prided myself on being a good doctor, but there were some parts of the job I'd never get used to. Losing someone always hits the hardest. I'd cried myself to sleep almost every night during my oncology rotation at medical school. But worst of all was seeing someone I cared about hurt. Attachment made it harder to separate the patient from the person. It was impossible not to feel their pain under my own skin...

Gulping big breaths, I slowly peeled away more of the bandage. But as the red blot grew wider and wider, familiar prickles of dread spiked down my spine. I screwed my eyes shut and forced in another breath. Time to lift the final layers of gauze. I cracked one eye open and peeked at Aiden's hand. So much blood.

Nope. Not ready.

Gritting my teeth, I pried off the last piece. A retch shuddered through me, but I quickly recovered to pretend I hadn't almost vomited all over the clean, white sheets tucked over the treatment bed.

Aiden chuckled. "You're a bit of a soft touch, Lola."

I narrowed my eyes. Was he insulting me at work? Oh, heck no. This was the one place I refused to be disrespected.

"It's called empathy," I snapped. "Maybe you should learn about it sometime."

Silent, Aiden's head bowed, his gaze falling to the syringe in my green dish of goodies on the trolley. The stoic mask he wore brightened. "I don't want that," he said, pointing at the dish.

"Scared of needles?" I wiggled my eyebrows. When he didn't crack a smile, I sighed. "It's a local anaesthetic. Just a teeny sting to numb the pain."

He pulled his hand back.

"Aiden, I'm not incompetent. I know how to administer it properly."

"I know."

"Okay, so let me—"

"Don't need it."

I rolled my eyes. Not this nonsense again. A typical stubborn man trying to act like a hero. "There are no extra prizes for getting stitches without anaesthetic."

"I want to feel it. Every single stitch."

"Aiden—"

"Do it. Patient autonomy and all that." He sat up tall, pushed his shoulders back, and stuck out his hand. "Take some revenge. I'm ready. No matter how bad this hurts, I know it still won't come close to how I made you feel."

He was wrong—so *wrong*—if he thought I could ever be that cruel to him. "I'm not like you. I don't get any pleasure from hurting people."

"I got no pleasure from the way I treated you. I still lie awake thinking about it most nights."

"I'm sure that's not—"

"Lola, I don't know how to fix what I did or how to prove to you I'm sorry. My apologies come out wrong. I'm scared to overstep my mark by leaving you gifts you don't want. I damn well almost bought you a car after the storm—"

"Please don't!"

Aiden jerked a nod. "I know you wouldn't want that. You're going to be strong and do that all on your own. But I need to do *something*. More than anything, I need to feel your pain. So, if you won't punish me, I'll do it myself."

All my protests were met with his swift refusal. I offered the pain relief again as I sterilised the wound. Another offer was made as I showed him the needle that would stitch him up.

Aiden's answer was always the same: *no*.

The stubborn beast wanted me to punish him? Fine. So be it.

Aiden flinched when the first prick marked his skin. My jaw clenching, I paused, the needle wobbling in my hand.

Get it over with. You're good at this!

Careful and steady, with only the slightest tremble rocking the needle and not one sound uttered by Aiden, I got the job done in record time. My glasses slipped down my nose as I examined his hand. A proud smile spread across my face. Six tiny, neat stitches.

"There we go. All better," I murmured, my index finger absently stroking his hand as my eyes swept a final check over the wound. "You need to be more careful next time, hon."

My brain screeched to a panicked stop. Did he hear that ridiculous endearment tumble out of my mouth? Gnawing on my bottom lip, I lifted my eyes. Aiden dipped his chin with a smile. Yeah, he'd heard me, alright.

I bolted upright and snatched my hand away. A nervous laugh escaped before I could stop it. "I, um, you know... I call everyone *hon*." I waved my hand dismissively. "That didn't mean anything."

"Hearing that meant everything to me."

I ducked my head so he wouldn't see the heat burning my cheeks and tried to distract myself by weaving a fresh bandage around Aiden's palm, but he wasn't having it. His fingers captured mine to stop me, and he leant closer.

"I like your little hands on me," he murmured.

The tenderness in his voice curled around my heart. I wasn't sure if it was the smell of his cologne or the memory of when he'd last whispered those words to me in my cottage, but the gentle tug of them threatened to pull me dangerously closer to him.

I snatched my hand away. "You can't talk to me like that. Not here."

"Lola, I know nothing will take back what I did. I know that." His voice lowered when he touched a cautious hand to my elbow. "If I could turn back time, I'd change everything. I'd never leave your house. I'd never act the way I did outside the coffee shop or let Evan say a single word to you. I'd protect you. Trust you. Please, Lola. If you believe nothing else, believe that."

Aiden always knew pretty words to say. This was no exception. But one promise stood out and screamed for my attention above all the others.

Trust.

My mind latched on to that word and wouldn't let go. Aiden didn't trust me. He avoided questions. He talked in riddles and warnings. But was there more to him? Secrets he kept hidden from the world? Secrets like mine?

My voice trembled as I gave him another chance he didn't deserve. "Tell me where you learned to dress a wound like that."

Aiden's spine went straight. He pushed his shoulders back. I'd seen this defence mechanism before. But just when I thought he was going to shut down again, he surprised me by mumbling, "I wasn't always a cabinetmaker."

"A paramedic?"

"No."

"The army?"

Dark eyebrows went up. "Why does everyone always think I was in the army?"

I shrugged. "You're big and stand around with perfect posture, glaring at everyone."

His chest rumbled with a laugh. "I wasn't in the army. Unless being in Scouts counts?"

"Nope."

"No? It's hard work getting all those badges, you know. I was an ace at bushcraft."

What the heck was *bushcraft?* It sounded terrible—like camping, or worse, actual craft. Anything beyond my sorry attempts at knitting—no thank you, sir.

"Are you going to keep avoiding the question?" I asked him.

His smile fading, he nodded. "I moved here to forget that life. You understand wanting a fresh start."

I did. Oh, how I *did.* "Tell me…" I dug deep for every bit of courage to ask the question that hurt the most. "Tell me why you left that night."

Aiden's fingers dug into the treatment bed, the tips blanching whiter than the sheets. My eyes darted up. His jaw locked, every line of his face drawn tight, and short, sharp breaths heaved in his chest.

"Geez, was I that much of an ogre?" I joked, trying to steer his thoughts away from whatever was short-circuiting in his mind.

Aiden shot me a desperate look. "It wasn't you. It had nothing to do with you. I told you, Lola, I'm not *right*. I wanted—I wish—" He shook his head again as he laboured under breaths that never seemed to reach his lungs. "I wish so much I'd stayed." His hand started to shake, his fingers digging deeper into the sheets.

He was deteriorating into a full-blown panic attack. Any anger in me vanished. I reached for his unbandaged hand and curled my fingers around his.

"I'm here, Aiden," I said in a soft, even voice. "I'm right here. You're safe here with me."

He blinked panicked eyes. My reassuring smile did nothing to calm him. "Lola... Please..." He shifted on the bed, his muscles primed and taut like he was ready to bolt. "I can't..."

"Let's take a big breath and count to ten, okay?"

"Ye-yeah." He squeezed my hand so tight. "Okay."

I was surprised when he followed my lead. Slowly counting to ten wasn't enough. As I counted him through another round and another, my mind never stopped clicking over. Nothing made sense. The same man who'd sat through six stitches and barely flinched had panicked over a memory. He'd told me the truth—something *wasn't* right about him. But it didn't scare me away. Instead, worry swelled in my chest.

By the fifth round of counting, Aiden's breathing returned to normal.

His head hung low. "Sorry."

"Aiden, have you seen someone about the—"

"No." He shook his hand free and hopped off the bed. "Just—*no*. I don't need more doctors."

"You need help."

He grunted some annoyed noise at me and charged for the door.

"Aiden!" I didn't bother hiding the frustration in my voice. My hands went to my hips. "Can you at least wait to get a prescription for antibiotics before you storm off?"

He paused, his grip firm on the door handle.

"Unless, of course, you're happy for your hand to fall off from an infection." I rolled my eyes. "It doesn't bother me either way. I've got both my hands. It'll be your loss."

Aiden refused to look at me, but he hovered by the door long enough for me to scrawl out a prescription. I tore it off the pad and held it out. Before he could grab the piece of paper, I pulled it back.

"Aiden, whatever's wrong... Just know... It doesn't need to define you." Was I saying that more for him? Or me? "You don't need to battle through everything alone."

His eyes closed, but some of the strain left his face, and for a moment, I wondered if it was the first time he realised he didn't always need to be strong. He looked at me, his mouth opening, but there was no time for words. Instead, it was the sickening thud of the door cracking against his shoulder that echoed in the quiet room.

Brooke squealed. "What the...?" She stuck her head through the gap. "Urgent message for the big oaf."

Aiden cocked his head, listening.

"Your ginger sidekick needs rescuing," she said. "He's at the Old Cellar."

"What's he doing there?" Aiden asked.

"How should I know? The message was to tell you to get to the Old Cellar. *Finito.* Message delivered."

"And received." Aiden sighed, turning back to me. "Lola, I... Thanks. For the stitches. For the, um..." He shook his head. He wasn't going to mention the panic attack. "Just thanks."

Exhausted, my shoulders slumping with each slow step, I dragged myself back to my room. I knew parts of Aiden so well. His patience. The gentle touches and sensual kisses. His love of books and the quiet life he lived on the mountain. But there was a side to him I didn't understand. Part of him could be cruel and selfish but also so afraid. Why? The man was a riddle wrapped in red-checked flannel.

I flopped into my chair and jiggled the mouse to turn my computer on. My gaze landed on my phone.

What the heck?

Four missed calls from my father. I snatched my phone and hit redial. The pound of my heart roared in my ears. It was an emergency. It had to be. Dad never called. Was Mum okay? My sister?

When the call connected, I didn't wait to say hello. "Dad!" I shrieked.

"Hey, Lo... It's, uh..." He cleared his throat. "It's real good to hear your voice, bug."

"Dad, what's going on? Are you okay? Is Mum?"

"Oh, yeah. We're just outside of Cairns. We're good. We saw a croc in the water when we went for a walk yesterday afternoon, but he kept his distance. Hey, what's the best way to cook a crocodile?"

I groaned with annoyance. I'd gone from a complete melt-down to being subjected to more of his terrible humour. "*Dad—*"

"In a *croc* pot." He didn't bark his usual laugh. "Yeah..."

"Dad, what's going on?"

He sighed. "Lo... Your mother... She... I think she might've done something stupid."

"What? Not another perm? The curls suit her, but she knows she's allergic to the—"

"She talked to Chris."

Don't freak out.

My fingernails dug into my knees, and I forced air into my lungs. This was fine. I expected he'd reach out to them—he always did—and I'd been extra careful about sharing too many details. No places. No people. Only general chitchat.

"Okay…" I trailed off.

"He's a real charmer, that one. I told her to get off the call. Lo… Did he…" A shaky inhale crackled through the line. "Your mother got herself worked up when she got your message all those months ago, and now you keep changing phone numbers. I know you wouldn't be doing all this for no reason. Was he… Jesus, Lo… Was Chris putting his hands on you?"

A few months ago, I would have denied it. Not anymore. "Yes," I whispered.

Silence, and then a sniffle. "I wish you'd told me, bug. I know we're not around much—"

"You earned your retirement, Dad. I'm an adult."

"Maybe, but you're still my little girl. Always will be. I'm not always great at showing it. And your mother…" He sighed. "She thinks she's helping, Lo… She doesn't understand."

"What did she do, Dad?"

"She gave Chris your new number. He must have been firing questions at her because she was telling him all about the night you rang. Jesus, bug… I'm so sorry. He's looking for you. He told her to tell you. He's looking."

18

He Saw She Wasn't Safe

Aiden

BERNIE WAVED FROM BEHIND the bar when I walked into the Old Cellar.

The place smelled like beer and aged wood, and the bartender's bald head shone under the dimmed lights. He slung a plaid tea towel over his shoulder and pointed to where Harry slumped over the bar.

"He's had a few," Bernie called out to me, shaking his head.

I grunted. A few, huh?

Harry's skinny legs twisted around the wooden stool with a wet coaster stuck under his cheek for good measure. I glanced at the drink in front of him. Droplets of water slithered down the empty beer glass. The kid couldn't handle booze. He rarely touched the stuff out of principle—probably because of the ugly shit he'd lived through with his father—and without an ounce of fat on him, he had zero tolerance.

I rested my bandaged hand on his back.

"Go 'way," Harry grumbled. "Sleeping."

He shrugged my hand off and buried his face deeper into the crook of his arm. I gave him a shake. His muffled groan was easy enough to decipher: *Piss off, old man.*

"Hey, Bernie!" I called.

He lumbered over, the uneven, clunking steps a reminder of his motorcycle accident a few years back. He was lucky he made it.

Bernie cocked his head. "You jumping on the wagon with him, big fella?"

"Nah, nothing for me." I nodded at the empty glass. "How many did he have?"

Bernie chuckled. "I cut him off at two beers. Your boy can't handle his liquor." He pointed to the booth in the corner. A group of women giggled and clinked cocktail glasses. No one looked familiar—probably tourists. "One of those trouble-makers might have snuck him a couple of vodka shots when I wasn't looking."

I scrubbed a hand down my face. Harry was well and truly toasted. I'd be hauling his butt back to my truck and taking him up to my place to sleep it off. His mother wouldn't handle it. She'd sniff the booze on him and drop into a panic attack. Those memories hadn't left her just because her husband had shot through town.

I wrapped an arm around Harry and tried to lift him off the stool. Even drunk, he wriggled more than a worm on a hook. The second I got a firm grip under his armpits, he twisted and slipped out of my grasp to snuggle back on the wood.

"Don't wanna go." Harry's flailing arm stopped me from getting my hands back on him. A wayward palm smacked me on the chin—a lucky hit. "Dreaming 'bout the Sunshine Princess."

Dreaming about the...*what?*

"Kid, come on." I seriously didn't need this. I'd give anything to pop a few painkillers and head to bed. My hand throbbed like hell, and Lola had twisted my heart in a knot I'd never unwind. "Time to go—"

A deep grunt of pain finished my sentence when my side slammed into the edge of the bar.

What the...?

Someone had damn near tackled me. I flashed an annoyed glare over my shoulder, only to be met with panicked eyes behind enormous gold-rimmed glasses.

"S-sorry." Lola's apology was rushed. She had no interest in talking to me. "Hey! Hi! Bernie!" Her breath came in gasps as if she'd sprinted from the clinic. "A white wine, please."

Bernie's lips curled in an amused smile. "I've got a nice Riesling—"

"Anything." Lola waved her hand to hurry the order along. "Just give me whatever you've got."

The creases on Bernie's forehead bunched tighter when his eyebrows rose. Lola didn't notice his surprise—or mine. She was distracted. Her hands fidgeted in the folds of her skirt, and her hair bobbed up and down from the impatient way she bounced nervously on the spot.

When Bernie slid the drink in front of her, she launched on it like lightning. She snatched the glass, tipped it up to her pretty lips, and the wine disappeared in huge gulps.

The empty glass clinked on the bar when Lola plonked it down. "May I please have another—"

"Whoa, whoa, *whoa*." I clamped my hand over the glass. "Give yourself a breather, Lola." I jerked my thumb in Harry's direction. "You don't want to end up like him."

Lola craned her neck to peer around me. "Is he okay?" She straightened her glasses and swept a concerned look over him. "What happened?"

"A few too many." Well, *any* was too many for Harry. "He'll be right once he sleeps it off. He's had a tough day." I was playing with fire, but I couldn't stop my smirk. "He handles cuts almost as well as you do."

"Careful." Lola's eyes narrowed. "I can rip out those stitches quicker than I put them in."

"If it means you're putting your little hands on me, you can do anything you want." I shifted closer to whisper a word that would probably earn me a punch in the gut. *"Hon."*

I teased her. I shouldn't have. But any attention from Lola was better than her pretending I didn't exist. Hearing her say that sweet term of endearment? That had meant the world to a dumb fool like me. It was *hope*. My heart had rocketed into a beat faster than a teenager talking to his first crush.

Lola pushed her glasses up her nose like she was preparing for battle, but her chest deflated. "You always bring out the worst in me."

She huffed a defeated sigh and whirled around. There was nothing to stare at except her back until she flagged Bernie's attention away from the old-timers sitting at the other end of the bar.

He lumbered back with a grin. "Ready for another round, Lola from the City?"

Lola wilted. Bloody hell. She didn't need to hear that crap on top of everything else she was going through.

"Bernie, come on," I said. "Don't call her that."

His eyes flew to me. "Sorry?"

"You heard me. She's a part of this town just like you are."

"Like me? No offence, big fella, but I've been here more than forty years—"

"Maybe, but that doesn't mean she's an outsider. She's part of this place. She patched up your grandson when he came off his bike last week, didn't she?"

Bernie's head bowed. He was eating his words now.

"No more of that Lola from the City crap, understand? You call her Dr. Hughes." I threw a grin in her direction. "Or maybe if she likes you, she'll let you call her Lola."

Bernie mumbled something under his breath. I wasn't sure if it was a reluctant apology to Lola or a giant "Fuck you" to me.

He forced a smile. "So, Doc, you want another?"

A growl rumbled in my chest. Didn't I just warn him?

"Doc's okay!" Bernie's panicked eyes pleaded with Lola. "Doc's okay! Right?"

Lola giggled and swatted my arm, a playful warning for me to back off. "Yeah, Doc's okay."

Mutters trailed behind Bernie on his trip to the old-timers whose necks were about to snap off from all their gawking. I grimaced. Causing a scene hadn't been part of the equation. I flicked a glance behind me. A bar full of eyes stared back. Oh yeah, they'd heard me. I'd made a declaration I was interested in Lola. Was I bothered about the gossip? Nope.

"Aiden." My brain stopped the second Lola's hand touched my arm. "Thank you."

I dipped my chin. She had nothing to thank me for. "I should've made it right a long time ago."

"Yes. You should have."

"I should never have done what I did in the first place."

"Yes."

"I'm going to make it up to you."

She grunted an adorable sound. "I don't think you can."

"What about more eggs? You liked the eggs."

Lola blinked up at me, and the hint of her smile made my breath stick in my throat like glue. My heart started thumping—another one of those panic attacks, but good.

"I did like the eggs," she said. "Opening my door those Sunday mornings was the highlight of my week. I wish..." She trailed off with a reluctant shake of her head.

"You wish we'd had more weeks like that?" I did. If I'd kept my promise and slowed us down, would we still be talking?

"Yeah." A tinge of pink flushed her cheeks.

"What would you have baked next?"

"I was horribly stuck on what to pick, but I think I was *almost* settled on a brown butter cheesecake."

"One step closer to finally mastering caramel, huh?"

"Maybe." She laughed. "Let's not get *too* optimistic. I truly am hopeless with caramel."

"I'm sorry I missed out on tasting your cheesecake. What tipped you over the edge into day drinking?" I waved a hand at the glass. "Land yourself with a patient even more difficult than me?"

Lola almost managed a lopsided smile. "I, um…" She sagged against the bar. "I got some…news…" An uneasy glance shifted to me from the corner of her eye. I'd seen that look before. "I knew it was coming, but I still wasn't ready."

Him. She was talking about *him*. I knew it, but I skirted around the edges to make it easier for her.

"Your family okay?" I asked. "Don't tell me Bruce and Barb encountered a crocodile on their adventures up north?"

Smirking, Lola ran her fingertip around the rim of the glass. "Funnily enough, they did stumble on a crocodile in Cairns. But even a croc wouldn't be game to mess up Bruce and Barb's three-quarter life crisis. It was, um…" She sighed. "Remember the day out in the storm?"

I edged closer, lowering my voice. This wasn't something for anyone else in town to hear. "Is that bastard giving you trouble?" I'd take care of him. Somehow.

"He's…he's looking…for me." She gulped. "I was careful this time, but he got my number."

"He's been messaging you?"

"I blocked him. I even got another number. But Dad called and said Mum had done something stupid. She talked to Chris.

He dazzled her and convinced her to give him my new number. She told him everything we'd talked about. I was careful about what I said to Mum, but... God, Aiden. Chris is so smart. He's got money. It's not a question of *if* he'll find me, but *when*. I just..." She sighed. "I just don't understand *why*."

"Why he's looking for you?"

Her head bobbed up and down. "He hated everything about me. He was never short of other options. Why won't he move on to one of them and leave me alone?"

"Power. Control." Cautious, as gentle as I could be, I rested my palm in the curve of her spine. "Are you safe, Lola?"

"I've never been safe, but I'm stronger here than I was with him. I'll do all the usual things. I'll change my number again. Check my locks. Fix the broken latch on the back door. I'll even hike up my big girl pants and stop by the police station to talk to them. I just wish I could've had more time living my life and not worrying about the minute it's all going to be snatched away, you know?"

I'd had moments with her like that. "I do." The only difference was I'd chosen when to strike the match and blow up what Lola and I might have had.

"Hey!"

Brooke's furious bark rang out across the bar. If there was one set of eyes not already staring at me after telling off the bartender, they were on me now. Guilty, I dropped my hand from Lola's back and stuffed it in my pocket.

Brooke's hair sailed behind her like a war banner as she charged over. "You better not be messing with my girl, you big oaf."

"I'm not causing any trouble, Brooke," I promised.

Harry's head shot up. "Brooke?" He blinked, his eyes wild and darting everywhere. A goofy grin spread over his flushed cheeks when he saw the medical receptionist. He almost fell on his butt as he staggered off the stool.

Brooke's eyes rounded. "What the hell happened to him?"

Harry propped his elbow on the bar. He was probably aiming to look cool, but he slumped over the wood more like a limp fish. "You happened to me, Sunshine Princess." His dopey smile only got dopier.

Brooke's mouth dropped open. Lola's too.

I scrubbed a hand down my face. This was about to turn into a train wreck. Harry was drunk out of his damn mind, but his awkwardness about driving me to the clinic started ringing like an alarm in my ears. I needed to do some damage control before he made a complete fool of himself.

"Come on, kid." I put my hand on Harry's chest and tried to push him away, but he clambered past me, legs flailing like a newborn giraffe, and he latched his arms around Brooke. She squealed.

Harry buried his face against her neck. "Oh, Princess," he cooed. "Your hair is like golden waves of the sweetest honey."

Lola snorted a giggle.

I tried to pry Harry's skinny arms off Brooke. He was squeezing the life out of her. "He's had a bit to drink," I tried explaining as I tugged him away.

Harry sighed as he nuzzled Brooke's hair. "I bet you taste like sunflowers," he told her.

I groaned. "Make that a *lot* to drink."

After I managed to pull his arms off, Harry wobbled side to side, not quite sure where to land, and started dropping to one knee.

Oh—shit!

"Marry m—" he started.

I laughed over the top of his drunken proposal, capturing the collar of his T-shirt before he made it to the ground. "I better get the kid out of here." I flicked my eyes to Brooke. "Can you make sure Lola gets home safe?"

"Wha...?" Brooke's face was frozen in shock. A jab of Lola's elbow snapped her out of her daze. She nodded. "Yeah, of course. Always." She trilled a nervous laugh. "Got your back, lumberjack." She cocked her fingers like a pistol and winked.

Harry batted at me like a tired toddler. He protested nonsense about me ruining his chance at true love with every awkward step it took to haul his drunken backside out of the Old Cellar and down the street. He vomited all over my boots a second later.

I sighed.

Defeated. Exhausted. Damn near ready to give up.

It had been the day from hell. My hand. The kid. I couldn't bear to think about the rest. My heart was already torn to shreds worrying about Lola. She needed to do more than check her locks. I could camp outside a few nights a week... Better yet, every damn night. The only thing stopping me from racing back into the bar was knowing the blonde was looking out for my girl. No one was stupid enough to take on Brooke.

And the day could've been worse.

The kid could've puked in my truck.

19

She Saw His Protective Side

Lola

A STAPLER WHIZZED PAST my open door.

I rocked back in my chair as the red menace crashed to a stop in the corridor. Edith glanced up from her magazine, a white eyebrow arching before she decided the latest celebrity divorce was more interesting than Brooke's tantrum.

I sighed. The growing list of blood results I needed to review would have to wait. Again.

It wasn't my first trip into the lion's den for the day, and if I was lucky enough to make it out alive, I could almost guarantee it wouldn't be my last. After I grabbed the stapler off the floor and took in a big breath—*you've got this, Lola*—I headed into battle.

Brooke was in a frenzy.

The reception desk was buried under a mountain of patient files that she *absolutely, positively* had to reorganise in the Monday-morning rush. Colourful sticky notes were plastered over every other spare inch of the desk. None of the mess both-ered Brooke. Her fingers cracked down on her keyboard at a furious speed, and her eyes glared straight ahead at the monitors.

I plonked the stapler onto the reception desk. "Lose something?" I teased.

Nothing was going to interrupt Brooke. She only paused her typing to jam her hand into the half-empty bag of jelly beans on her lap. She popped a fistful into her mouth.

"That stupid old thing was out of stupid staples," she muttered, the jelly beans jumbling her words.

I bit back a grin. "Throwing it down the corridor does seem the logical way to fix that."

"You being funny with me, Lolly?"

I sighed. "Not working, huh?"

She glowered at me.

I crouched beside her chair. "Brooke, I'm worried about you. If this is about Harry—"

"You just stop right there!" At least, I thought that was what she said because she'd stuffed another handful of jelly beans into her mouth. "We don't mention his name in this clinic. He is *dead* to me."

Yikes.

This was a new development.

I frantically searched my brain for solutions, words of encouragement—anything that would help. But what did I know about men? The situation with Aiden suggested I had no clue. My history before him proved I knew even less. I forced a smile and patted her knee.

Brooke pouted. "Do I look cute today?"

"You look cute every day." Her bottom lip wobbled, so I quickly added, "But you look *extra* cute today."

"Then why is he avoiding me?" she wailed. "It's been three days! Three whole days!"

Brooke didn't need to tell me how many days it'd been. I'd spent all weekend camped out on her couch. I'd relived and analysed Harry's drunken confession more times than a sports commentator had recapped the slow-motion replay of the greatest touchdown of all time.

I forced another smile. "I'm sure Harry's not avoiding you—"

"He is! This morning, you wouldn't believe it if I told you." More jelly beans went into her mouth. "I stopped by the store to grab a few things for the break room. That ginger hunk took one look at me and was out the door. He left a whole bag of groceries behind. Ashley had to chase him down the street!"

I hid my grimace. As tough as Brooke acted, she was a marshmallow of self-doubt on the inside. Harry's actions shook her confidence. Being stuck behind her desk of chaos, overanalysing the universe, probably wasn't helping, either.

I popped back up. "Come on, let's take a break. You've been so busy all morning. It's after ten, and I've got a gap in my appointments. Let's head to the coffee shop early today. Anything you want. My treat."

Brooke folded her arms. "Nope. No way. I'm not going." She shook her head furiously. "*He'll* be there."

That was kind of the point... "Don't you want to see Harry?"

Brooke scoffed like I'd said the dumbest thing in the world. "I've been chasing that man since I moved here a year ago. If he wants me, he knows where to find me." She stuck her nose in the air. "But when you get to the coffee shop, you march right up to him, and you tell him that, okay? And if you're really my friend, you can kick him in the nuts while you're at it."

No amount of coaxing or bribery moved Brooke's bottom off the chair. When she tipped the last of the jelly beans into her mouth before going back to her *very important* typing that looked suspiciously like she was booking a singles cruise, I admitted defeat and headed out.

But I was determined to brighten Brooke's day—somehow.

Kicking Harry in the nuts probably wasn't going to happen, but I could pick out a sticky treat for her at the coffee shop. I'd snag a bunch of flowers on the walk back, too. She'd love a gift like that.

I turned the corner to the coffee shop.

"Mornin', four-eyes."

Evan stood slouched against the chipped white paint, tapping on his phone. He pushed off the brick wall. My heart hammered faster with each plod of his heavy footsteps.

He shoved his phone into the back pocket of his jeans. "Are doctors too important to say hello?"

"H-hello."

Evan's eyes glued to my loafers when I stumbled backwards. His eyes slid back to mine, a smirk tugging the corner of his lips. He liked intimidating me.

"You city girls. One ain't no different from the other," he said. "You think you should get treated *special*. My missus was from the mainland. When times got tough, she fucked off back there." His footsteps pounded closer. "Good riddance to her."

My head sank low, but my eyes darted everywhere. I needed an escape. The coffee shop wasn't far. "I'm s-sorry to hear about your w-wife, Mr. Barnes." The alley was closer. I could run. I could squeeze through. The dumpster with the big red lid was there. I could hide.

He lunged at me, laughing when I cowered into the wall. "Not so brave without your blonde pit bull—"

Evan's words choked to silence. The whites of his eyes bugged so wide they looked like they were about to burst like an overblown balloon. A protective wall of red flannel stood between us.

Aiden's voice was a low growl. "I warned you."

Evan shoved him away. "You think payin' a visit to my garage matters?" He spat out every word as he pushed his T-shirt back into his jeans. "You actually think she's stayin'? She ain't."

"She's staying."

"You hopin' for a turn once Hollyoak is through with her? Is that why you keep stickin' your nose in?" Evan cocked his chin. "What happened to Ruth Wilks? The cripple not good enough for you no more?"

Aiden didn't say a word, but his fist clenched by his side, his knuckles turning white. I dared to peer around his back, desperate to catch a glimpse of his face to make sure he was okay, but I never got the chance.

Evan's beady black eyes locked on me. He lunged forward. His grease-covered fingers snatched my arm, twisted, and a short, sharp scream escaped my mouth. I scurried back, diving through the gap to the alley and scrambling to safety wedged beside the dumpster.

The scuffle between the two men swirled like a dance across the parking lot.

Evan reared back his fist and launched blow after blow. Every one missed. Aiden's eyes narrowed, calculating and timing every move, and at just the right moment, his hand clamped roughly around Evan's collar.

"You don't talk to Lola again. You hear me?" Aiden dragged the flailing man closer. "I know where you work. I know where you live. No more warnings." He shoved Evan hard enough for the mechanic's body to hit the concrete with a heavy thud. "If I hear you're still bothering Lola, I'll be paying you one final visit. Understand?"

Tremors ricocheted through me like bullets bouncing off every muscle. When Evan slunk away, the shaking hadn't stopped. I squeezed my eyes shut and curled myself into a tiny ball next to the brick wall. The stench of damp water didn't even bother me. It was still safer there.

Boots approached on the concrete. Aiden was close. "Lola?"

"I d-don't want a c-coffee any-anymore."

"I know." He crouched on the dusty ground behind me. "Can I..." He scooted a little closer. "Can I touch you?"

My chin trembled as I managed a nod.

Gentle fingers stroked my arm. "It's okay. See?" Aiden's body shielded my humiliation from the eyes of anyone passing, and his big arms wrapped around my shoulders and knees. "I won't hurt you."

"Evan scares me," I admitted in a whisper.

"I'm going to take care of him." The tickly bristles of Aiden's beard rested against my hair as he sheltered me close to his side. "I promise."

"Are you going to hurt him?"

The only sound was the steady thump of his heart under my ear.

"Aiden?"

"It goes against everything I believe in, but..." He sighed. "Yes. I am."

My heart twisted in my chest. After everything I'd been through, I couldn't let that happen. I'd be a hypocrite—as bad as the person who'd turned his fists on me. Violence was never the answer, was it?

"Please, Aiden. Don't."

"Small towns aren't like the city. Sometimes, you've got to take care of things yourself."

"Maybe you could talk to him?"

"I already have. I stopped by his garage after what happened in the bar. Some folks will tell you he hasn't dealt with his wife leaving him, but that doesn't give him an excuse to throw his weight around. I think he'll listen more to my fists than any words that come out of my mouth."

"You said it yourself—acting like that goes against everything you believe in. It goes against what I believe in, too."

"I'm hearing you, Lola, but you deserve to feel safe. You have the right to walk around and not get people commenting to you...or...or..." He puffed out a breath. "Coming at you."

"Please, Aiden."

"Okay." He sighed. "I'll talk to him. No fists. I promise."

I buried my face against the soft cotton of his flannel shirt. We were still huddled in the dusty alley, hidden from the world, but the stolen, quiet moments when his thumb caressed the back of my neck were perfect.

"Aiden, what happened to Ruth? She's your friend, isn't she?"

"More than that. She's like a sister to me." He chuckled. "An annoying one who always knows best."

"You've been friends a long time?"

"Yeah, forever. Since I was seven and she was five. She wanted to ride her bike with me and my friends, but I told her to buzz off and go play with her Barbie dolls. She hated that. She stormed over, punched me in the gut, and then turned around and pushed my brand-new bike into the creek." A soft laugh rumbled against my back. "We've been best friends ever since."

"She sounds tough." Tougher than me. Ruth didn't sound like she'd be the type to cower in an alley if someone stood over her.

"She's as tough as they come."

"And...what Evan said?"

"Don't listen to Evan. The only thing coming out of his mouth is filth. But Ruth..." Aiden's sigh was heavy. "She was in an accident about ten years ago." His arms squeezed me tighter. "I nearly lost her."

My heart twisted until it broke. "Oh—I'm sorry—"

"None of that. You didn't know. Ruth's okay. And even if she weren't, she'd never admit it, stubborn thing that she is."

I grinned against his chest. "Sounds like someone else I know."

"I'm trying, Lola. I want to let you in. I'm getting closer..." Another gentle squeeze tried to convince me. "What about you? Ready to brave the world again?"

"I think so."

Scooting back, Aiden held out his hand, and when I placed my palm in his, he carefully helped me to my feet like I was lighter than air. He fussed, dusting the dirt from my clothes with the gentlest, most careful touches, and then, without any warning, his hands braced my shoulders. I nibbled down on my lower lip, not ready for the faint trace of his fingers brushing my hair behind my ears. My glasses slid off my nose and up onto my head.

"Just a couple of smudges." Aiden's thumb brushed under one eye and then the other. "All better."

My feet stayed glued to the spot. The haze of the alley made his eyes impossible to read, but he dared to stroke my cheek for a second before his palm drifted away. I should have hated that touch, but without thinking, I clapped my hand back over my flushed skin to trap the sweet, soft feeling for a second longer.

Aiden dipped his chin with a smile. "Want to try again to get that coffee?"

"Y-yes." I could do better. I was stronger. I popped my glasses down and straightened them on my nose. "Yes! But can I treat you to say thanks?"

"You have nothing to thank me for."

"Oh, but I will." I wiggled my eyebrows. "I need to ask a favour."

Aiden tilted his head, eyebrows raised. I'd intrigued him.

"If Harry's around," I said, *"apparently,* if I'm a good friend, I'm supposed to kick him in the nuts. Is it a fair trade if you do the honours? You're the one with the fancy fighting skills, after all."

Aiden's chest rumbled with a deep laugh. "Is Brooke losing her mind about what happened last Friday?"

"You don't know the half of it. What the heck is going on between those two?"

"No idea. The kid is playing his cards close to his chest on this one..."

We wandered side by side to the coffee shop, and a short time later, past the florist, and then back to the clinic with enough treats to win over a hundred jilted hearts.

We chatted and brainstormed a thousand ways to get two other people together, but we still weren't ready to deal with the mess that had happened between us.

20

He Saw Justice Delivered

Aiden

I KEPT MY PROMISE to Lola.

Not one finger touched Evan. Ryan Hollyoak bestowed himself with the dubious honour of taking care of that problem.

The scene playing out in front of me in Discount Automotive was like something from a horror movie. A bare bulb hung from a string, murky yellow light dancing up the walls in a slow sway with the wind. Rusted blood clung to the night air. The only sounds were the pained grunts that echoed through the empty garage and the dull crack of Ryan's fist—quick and sharp to Evan's jaw, his face, and once to his stomach.

My back pressed into the rough brick, my arms folded across my chest. The violence turned my gut, but I made myself watch every second of that beating. Evan needed to pay for what he'd done to Lola, and I needed to be there when he did.

The memory of her curled up, shaking, and her face whiter than a ghost haunted me. I'd seen my fair share of ugly shit when I was on the police force, but I'd never seen someone so scared.

Evan had done that. But if I'd stepped in that night at the bar like I should have, she would have been spared what happened in the alley. She would never have felt so scared, so small, lost in that dark place I couldn't help her.

It was all on me in the end. My fault.

Ryan swept a hand over his brow. His chest heaving, he stepped back, straightened his spine, and rolled his shoulders. Punishment delivered. He was done.

Evan was done, too.

The mechanic let his knees buckle, and he collapsed into a sprawled heap on the oil-stained concrete. "Gonna call the cops on you pair." He groaned.

Ryan wasn't worried. He snatched a clean rag from the workbench. "Calling the cops, huh?" He didn't wince when he rubbed the rag over his broken knuckles. The farmer was tougher than he looked. "You're fresh out of luck there, mate. The only patrol on Tuesday nights is the one the sarge begins and ends at the pharmacist's house."

That was news to me. Ruth usually filled me in on everything happening around town—whether I wanted to hear it or not.

"Seriously?" My eyebrows rose. "He's seeing the pharmacist? I thought he was chasing the girl who runs the little antique store."

"Yeah." Ryan balled up the rag and pitched it into the sink, grinning back at me. "He's seeing both of 'em."

"Shit, eh?" I chuckled. "That's going to land him in hot water."

Evan glared at us with the one eye that wasn't swollen shut. "You bitches done gossipin'?" He pressed his palm on the concrete and tried to push himself up. A pained grimace shot across his face, and he collapsed onto his back. "Can one of you at least pass me my phone? I need to call a doctor or somethin'."

Ryan shook his head. "You want to call a doctor?" His gaze flicked to me. "Aiden, who do you reckon is on call tonight?"

"I heard Tuesday is always Lola."

Ryan wandered over to where Evan lay sprawled on the concrete. He put his hands on his hips and looked down. "You sure you want to take your chances with the doctor? Lola's pissed as hell at the big guy here. See those stitches in his hand?" He jerked a nod back at me. "She did 'em raw. No pain relief. Just stabbed 'em right into his skin."

Evan's good eye darted to my hand and then to my face. I nodded. I could have come clean and told him I'd begged Lola to deliver me the punishment I deserved, but my mouth stayed shut.

Evan's skin blanched white.

Small towns were strange places. They had their own rules. After years of working on the right side of the law, if someone had told me I'd spend a Tuesday night beating up some close-minded bastard, I would've laughed in their face. And despite Lola's hesitation because of her past and her heart being too damn soft, vigilante justice was sometimes the only option.

That didn't mean the guilt of betraying her trust wouldn't eat me alive. Good intentions got me nowhere. My list of sins only grew longer.

Ryan's gaze shifted to me. "You reckon we're done here?"

"I reckon so."

His boot nudged the mechanic's side. "You listening to me?"

Evan's lip curled. One annoyed eye glared up at the farmer. He was listening.

"Think of tonight as your awakening," Ryan said. "Your days of harassing the women in this town are over. Understand?"

Evan grunted.

"I don't want to hear any more stories about you hassling the girls at the coffee shop or hitting on the blonde working at the doctor's clinic. That shit ain't right." Ryan sighed. "But my mama always believed everyone deserves a second chance. She thought even the worst man could be redeemed. You don't want to make a liar out of my mama, do you?"

"Your mama's been cold in the ground for more than twenty years."

"And your old lady's been gone for five. If you're still dealing with some raw feelings, get some counselling, you weak bastard."

Ryan dropped Evan's phone onto his chest and was thanked with a pained howl. I followed the farmer into the pitch-black fog of the street outside. His boots ground to a stop on the gravel in the parking lot.

He braced one hand on the top of his truck. "Hopefully that's the end of it. Something should've been done about Evan a long time ago."

"It wasn't our job to sort him out."

"Maybe not, but it shouldn't have come to this. Evan threatening Lola on the street? Bloody bastard." Shaking his head, Ryan clenched the hand on his truck into a fist. If it was to calm his anger, it didn't work. His voice was still etched with disgust when he said, "That never should've happened."

"You're right." Shame haunted me. I doubted I would ever forget the memory of Lola cowering in the alley. "That shouldn't have happened."

"I hope this sends a message to everyone else in town, too," Ryan continued. "I don't like the way people talk to Lola. She's not worth less just because she didn't grow up here. There should be no difference if she comes from the city or a five-generation farming family like mine. She's a good person."

A smile tugged at my lips. "Yeah, she is. Never met anyone better."

"She's nice."

"Too damn nice."

"Kind, even."

"Sweeter than honey."

"Pretty."

"Beautiful," I corrected him.

Ryan cocked his head. He was the one smiling now. "Yeah, I thought you might say something like that." His smile faded, all business again. "At least you decided to get your head out of your arse and help this time. The way you treated Lola at the bar—"

"Ancient history."

Ryan's eyebrow rose. "That's what you're telling yourself? I haven't forgotten. You're lucky I didn't plant you flat on your arse when I was taking care of Evan."

"Reckon you could?"

He scanned me from head to toe, sizing me up. "I reckon I'd have a good crack at it. I'm prepared to fight dirty to get you down." His gaze narrowed. "You ever treat Lola like that again, and I *will* take a crack at you. Understand?"

I jerked a nod. Understood. But he didn't need to worry. "What I did..." I trailed off with a shake of my head. "I wish I could go back in time and smack myself in the face."

"Life doesn't give us those chances. You can't look back. Accept where you stand on the road and keep walking. But you sure dug yourself into one hell of a pothole by acting like you did. And why?" He waited for an answer, but I didn't give him one. He sighed. "She liked you, you know?"

Past tense. That hurt. A lot. "Yeah, I know."

I didn't have much to say after that. Looking up at the night sky didn't give me any answers, either.

Ryan clapped a friendly hand on my back. "We did good tonight. Teamwork. You look like you need some sleep, and I sure as hell know I do. I'm meant to be up in six hours to start the morning run."

The corners of his eyes crinkled in a quick smile to say good-bye. He pulled open the door of his truck.

"Hey, Ryan..."

The farmer turned back, waiting for me to finish.

"I'll be out of town for a week or so. Harry and I have a job in the city. Keep an eye on Lola for me?"

"Yeah, I'll make sure no one bothers her."

"If you run into the sarge at the bar, ask him, too?"

Ryan frowned. He didn't question me. Worry must have been carved on every inch of my face because he nodded with solemn eyes. He understood.

We parted ways from there. Instead of driving into the hills, I drove back into town and pulled to a slow stop to park on the fringe. I had somewhere else I needed to go first.

The cops were useless. I ran my own patrol. Not just on Tuesday nights. Most nights. I made myself suffer through the agonising drive up to my place in the pitch-black because my nerves would be even more rattled if I didn't take a walk across town.

I only made one stop.

Lola's place.

The lights of the tiny cottage burned bright. I kept my eyes low, not trying to peek at Lola, but looking everywhere else for signs of anything out of the ordinary. Her bin was waiting by the gate for collection the next day. The lavender she'd planted along the fence looked pretty as a picture. Everything seemed secure. Nothing was out of place.

The night was cold enough to catch my breath in a misty sigh of relief.

The house next door was dark, but the lacy curtains of the front window edged to the side. I raised my palm and waved to Yolanda like I'd done last night and all the nights before. The shadow of her wrinkled hand waved back before the curtain swished shut.

It was the confirmation I needed to head home.

We were both still watching. Keeping an eye on Lola. Keeping her safe.

21

She Saw His Friend

Lola

THE BAKING SECTION WAS empty.

No flour.

Determination set my jaw. It couldn't be another case of small-town supply issues. I must have been looking in the wrong aisle, my thoughts jumbled, constantly twisting in knots trying to understand Aiden.

What were his secrets? How could he act so heartless and then so kind?

My mind was occupied trying to unravel the riddle in red-checked flannel when I bumped into someone else in the middle of the aisle.

I slid my glasses up my nose. "Sorry—"

My hand clapped over my mouth to hide the shock of seeing Evan's bruised face. Mirrored sunglasses hid his eyes, but not the violent purple lump blooming around the socket. His lip was split, and a sickening shade of green tinged the swelling along his jaw.

Was he...*okay?*

Evan's head snapped left, then right. The shopping basket slipped from his fingers and crashed to the floor. This was a man who'd treated me despicably, but squashing the empathy—the doctor—inside me was impossible.

I reached out a tentative hand. "Mr. Barnes—"

Evan yelped and dodged to the side before I could lay a finger on him. "Sorry, uh... my fault." His sneakers tangled together, and he tripped backwards. "Sorry, Miss—Dr. Lola." He took another step back, and another, until he disappeared around the aisle.

Silence followed for a beat until the bell over the door jingled. Evan had bolted.

Confused, I glanced down, searching for a clue about what had scared him off. My white sundress was cute. My new sandals and freshly painted pink toenails were even more adorable. I channelled a domestic goddess more than a terrifying troll capable of scattering the villagers.

But I knew a grumbling giant with a scowl capable of clearing a room—and it just so happened he had a score to settle with Evan.

Aiden McKinnon was a dead man.

He'd promised he'd only talk to Evan. No fists. No violence. *Promised.*

And he'd lied. Big time.

How long after we'd talked had he waited before inflicting his vigilante justice? A day? Two?

My thoughts were still lost on Aiden on my walk home. I kicked at the loose pebbles littered over the path.

That man drove me crazy. Hot one minute. Ice cold the next. Never anything in between. He sure liked playing the knight in shining armour—when it suited him. Frustration itched at me to march over to his workshop and give him a piece of my mind. Not that I ever would. Or could. When Ryan and I had caught up for coffee, he'd ever-so-casually mentioned that Aiden was out of town for work. What *convenient* timing.

Shops faded to houses, the road grew quieter, the trees bushier, and finally, the hint of fresh rosebuds peeking over Yolanda's fence welcomed me home.

I pushed my shopping bag to the crook of my arm to fish out my keys. After I followed the clinks to dig them out of the bottomless pit, I glanced back at my gate.

A woman wearing a floppy straw hat bent over my fence, fussing with the lavender. I'd bought it from the markets when it was barely clinging to life. Now, it thrived, lanky and out of control against the white picket slats. She plucked a small sprig for a sniff.

Alarm bells rang in the back of my mind. Not because she was a flower thief. I was just never at ease with memories lurking around every corner.

But I forced a smile into my voice and called, "Good morning!"

The woman froze, then wobbled slightly as she turned.

"Morning!" she said, a bright laugh bubbling out.

Most of her face stayed hidden beneath the brim of her enormous hat. She stood tall, her yellow dress floating like sunshine, but something about her was unsteady. A walking cane rested on the fence. That might be the reason. She rolled one shoulder, shifting a woven bag back into place, and a delicate gold charm bracelet slipped down her wrist when she grabbed the cane.

"I dropped by to see Yolanda," she said.

"She left an hour or two ago." I knew this because Yolanda had stopped me on my way to the village store to chat about a certain cabinetmaker. "Yolanda helps out at the church cake stall on Saturday mornings."

"*Does* she? I had *no* idea." The nervous bite of her lip hinted to me that she knew Yolanda wouldn't be home.

I quirked an eyebrow.

"Silly me. I must have my days mixed up," she said. "By the way, it's nice to meet you. I'm Ruth."

"Ruth?" The penny dropped. *Of course.* "Aiden's friend."

"Yes. Sometimes." She muttered under her breath, "When he's not acting like a total butthead."

I laughed. Maybe Ruth and I would get along after all.

"I'm sorry you missed Yolanda," I said. "She won't be back until the afternoon. You're welcome to come in for a cup of tea while you wait... If you like?"

Ruth's head popped up. She accepted my invitation with a sunny smile.

Ancient hinges squeaked when I pushed open my gate, and her floppy hat twisted and turned as she drank in every detail. The only sound was her cane as it clipped on the front path and then on the wooden floor when she followed me inside.

I set my grocery bags onto the kitchen counter and pointed to the empty chairs at the tiny dining table.

"Make yourself comfy," I said.

Ruth tilted her shoulder, her bag slipping down her arm to hang over the back of the chair. She tilted her cane against the table, nudged out the chair to sit down, and off came her enormous hat.

My eyes widened, and my keys tumbled from my hand.

Ruth was beautiful in a way I couldn't describe. *Ethereal* was the closest word that popped into my mind. Her dark hair was swept into a loose bun. Beneath heavy lashes, her owlish eyes blinked slowly, absorbing every detail of the tiny kitchen. Not even the jagged lines of the angry red scars bolted up her neck detracted from delicate features that only looked prettier when she beamed one of her endless smiles.

"Oh!" she exclaimed. "I brought some snacks!"

She fumbled in her bag to pull out a yellow container, her left hand resting daintily but motionless in her lap. I carefully hid a worried frown and kept myself busy putting on the kettle.

Ruth never used her left hand. Aiden had said she was in an accident—he'd warned me it was serious—but a silent heaviness crushed my heart flat to imagine all she must have gone through ten years ago.

After a whirlwind of dashing about, mild panic, and a last-minute delivery of a pink teapot with matching cups to the table, I sagged into the chair.

Ruth shoved the yellow container under my nose. "Would you like to try one?" Her grin shook at the edges, her offering to me as serious as a sacrifice to the gods.

Curious, I peered inside. My heart sank.

The miniature cupcakes were adorable. Strawberry icing swirled around fluffy white cakes with marzipan butterflies dotted on top. Next to them was a stack of honey jumbles with thick pink icing. My eyes narrowed. They were home-made too—just the way I'd told Aiden I loved them the day he'd come for lunch.

This was nothing but another attempt by that infuriating man to earn my forgiveness.

Sighing, I rubbed my temple. "Aiden put you up to this."

"No!" she insisted. "He's actually going to kill me when he finds out I stopped by. He gave me one of his long, boring speeches about not sticking my nose in his business." She rolled her eyes. "I wouldn't have to stick my nose in if he wasn't acting so—you know—like *him*."

I couldn't help laughing. I knew. I nodded at the treats. "So, Aiden just sits around waxing lyrical about my favourite cakes and biscuits?" I lifted the teapot to fill our cups.

"And everything else. He never stops talking about you. He's completely head over heels. I've never seen anything like it."

I stared at Ruth, my jaw on the floor, water gushing from the teapot even though it was dangerously close to spilling over the rim of the frilly pink teacup.

"Sorry!" Ruth waved her right hand at me, frantic, and I quickly pulled back the teapot just in time. "*Sorry.* Aiden told me I *definitely* shouldn't say something like that." She clapped her hand to her forehead. "Am I making this worse?"

"I'm not sure it's possible to make it worse."

"He messed up that bad?"

My shoulders hunched a little more when I sank lower in the chair. Ruth seemed nice, but I barely knew her. How much had Aiden told her? How much sugarcoating had he done to paint himself less like the devil who'd rejected me in front of everyone crammed into the bar?

"That man." Ruth shook her head. "He has no idea. He's never been in a proper relationship before. Or—you know—*any* relationship."

"What?" My eyebrows shot to the ceiling. Aiden was impossible to get to know, full of secrets, but he was gorgeous in all the right ways. Masculine. Strong. Talented. Sometimes, he'd spoiled me with moments of kindness so sweet it made my heart ache. *"Never?"*

Ruth shook her head. "In high school, sports kept him busy. Then, it was work. He was so dedicated to climbing the ranks he had no time for anything else. Not that women didn't fall over themselves when he was around." She lifted her shoulder like the whole idea of it was unthinkable. "I guess there's something about a man in uniform." She grinned. "Even a big dumb one."

My hand stilled, the teacup hovering close to my lips. "Uniform?"

Ruth let out an annoyed sigh. "He didn't tell you, did he?"

"Aiden has a pretty consistent habit of purposefully telling me as little as possible."

Frustrated, Ruth plucked a honey jumble from the pile and stuffed a bite into her mouth. "I hate that Aiden does this. He erases half his life like it never happened. All because..." She trailed off, her eyes locked on the hand frozen in her lap. A beat passed. And another. "Aiden used to be a police officer. A sergeant, actually. He was awarded a bravery medal and everything."

"That makes sense," I told her simply.

Ruth's owlish eyes blinked at me. I forced a tight smile. What else was I supposed to say? Curse Aiden because he'd never trusted me enough to share anything about his old life? Been there, done that, had the scars on my heart to prove it. And it *did* make sense. Aiden fit the bill of a police officer, right down to the way he stood at attention, watching everything, never rattled. Why he needed to keep that a secret, I had no clue, but all the puzzle pieces snapped together perfectly.

"I can't believe he didn't tell you." Ruth finished off her biscuit, chewing, lost in thought. "What else hasn't he told you?"

"I'm guessing... everything?"

A frown dulled Ruth's pretty features. "I shouldn't poke my nose in where it doesn't belong. He'll be furious, but... Lola, he cares about you."

I started to shake my head but froze, surprised when her hand darted across the table to land on mine.

"I know it doesn't seem like it, but he does. He's too hard on himself. He has this idea stuck in his head that he's some terrible person, and nothing I've ever said has convinced him otherwise. But when he met *you*..." A shaky smile spread across her face. "The change in him. Night to day. He's happy for the first time in forever. Lola, you're *so* good for him."

"I'm not here to be good for Aiden. I won't be his emotional punching bag while he figures out how to treat me like an actual person."

"He's not good with words—

"Ruth," I said gently, trying to end this conversation without hurting her feelings.

"I know he's botching everything and making it so much worse, but he *is* sorry. Maybe you could find it in your heart to give him another chance?"

I squeezed Ruth's hand before pulling away. "I know he's your friend, and deep down, I think he's a good person. But the way he treated me..." I pressed my lips together to stop the tremble that always started when I let those memories get the better of me. "Aiden's apologised so many times. I think I've already forgiven him, but it's just too hard to forget. I don't know if I can trust him not to hurt me again."

Ruth nibbled the edge of the biscuit, still and wooden, staring at her hand. She was only trying to be a good friend. Still, if she expected my heart to magically knit itself back together based on nothing more than Aiden's promises—which he was terrible at keeping—I'd only disappoint her.

The silence in the kitchen itched like ants crawling up my spine. I wriggled in my seat. Ruth was my guest. No matter why she'd dropped by, no matter how much I didn't want to hear about Aiden, I wanted her to feel welcome. I could get through this and be the bigger person.

I plastered on a smile. "I don't think I've seen you around town before."

She shook her head. "I don't come in as much these days."

"Do you live nearby?"

"I have a place about ten minutes outside of town. It's nothing special. Probably not much bigger than this place. But I have enough land for a small hobby farm."

"Do you grow anything? I've been trying to get started on my own herbs."

She nodded. "I started with herbs, too. I have a few fruit trees now. A native beehive. Over the last year or two, I've been building up my vegetable patch. *Well.*" Ruth's eyes flipped to the ceiling. "Except for the bits devoured by the possum. Aiden helped me put nets over the all-you-can-eat buffet, but somehow this one fluffy terror still finds a way in to gobble everything up."

I laughed. And as the hours passed, I laughed even more.

Ruth and I got along easily. We chatted about every-thing—cooking, gardening, and silly stories about the locals. Safe territory. She might have scolded Aiden for keeping secrets, but she kept her fair share, too. There was no mention of her life before moving to Richmond or her accident. But by the time the sun's dying flames lit up my kitchen and Ruth stood to say goodbye, it was clear the two friends had never quite recovered from whatever tragedy they'd survived all those years ago.

I propped open the front door so Ruth could slip past. "I'm sorry, I don't have a car to drop you home," I said. It was still on my list. *Soon.* "If you're walking, I'd be happy to keep you company."

Ruth shook her head. "It's okay. I'm going to stay with Har-ry's mum tonight. She worries when the boys are away for work. Any distraction helps, and I have lots of gossip to share." Her eyes widened. "But not about—*you know*—you and that big butthead."

Laughing, I waved goodbye. Ruth started her uneasy journey, her cane clipping along the path, guiding every step.

She paused at the gate. "The bar has a Games Night coming up," she called back. "They run one every six months or so. I haven't been in years, but they're super fun. Silly games, food... If you have a couple of friends, maybe we could pull together a team or something?"

"Sounds like a blast. Sign me up."

Ruth grinned, a twinkle of mischief sparkling in her dark eyes. She was planning something, and it wouldn't take Sher-lock Holmes to guess that one of the people she selected for the team would be tall, dark, and wearing flannel.

22

He Saw It Was Time to Talk

Aiden

HARRY STUMBLED ACROSS THE motel parking lot, duffel bag dragging on the concrete, and his T-shirt riding up as he stretched in a yawn. He carried on like I'd hauled him out of bed at three o'clock in the morning. Too bad it was five in the afternoon.

"Morning, Princess," I said.

"Sorry." Harry's head lolled back in another yawn. "I dozed off in front of the TV. I didn't get much sleep last night."

"Your mum's hit a bit of a rough patch again?"

Harry kicked a rock with the toe of his sneaker. The tiny pebble soared over the oil-stained concrete and dinged against a hubcap, but he didn't hoot about making the shot. "You were listening." He frowned.

"Thin walls, kid." Really thin walls. It wasn't the first night he'd been stuck on the phone for hours. "Look, it's not my place to say anything—"

"Then don't," he said. "I know what you're going to say."

"Think so?" Possible. I'd suggested a few times that he should consider moving out of his mum's place. He was a good kid, but his whole life was passing him by, paying for someone else's mistakes.

"Yup," he said. "You're the king of routine. I could set the clock on my phone by you. You're predictable."

He spat the word *predictable* out like it was a disease. My father had always said the word for what I had—*disorder*—like it was a disease, too.

I squared my shoulders, defensive. "Nah, not really." Who was I kidding? I only functioned because of the routine.

Harry grunted. "Says the man who's eaten the exact same breakfast since we checked in last week."

"Did not."

"The motel owner didn't even bother asking for your order today. She already knew!" To prove his point, Harry held up his hand and started ticking off my breakfast on his fingers. "Four strips of crispy bacon. Two fried eggs. A slice of toast. An apple." He wiggled his thumb. "And a cup of black coffee."

I scowled. And just what was wrong with that? "That's a good breakfast!"

"It's predictable." He cocked his head. His eyes were on the black Henley I'd paired with my jeans. "This shirt, though. I wasn't expecting that."

"Blame Ruth. She sent me a message earlier." Or seven. "I was instructed to dress nice."

Harry snorted. "I don't think that shirt is what she meant when she said that."

"Yeah? What does she mean then, smart arse?"

"Good clothes. You know, something fancy." He tugged at the ribbing around the neck of his T-shirt. "Something with a proper collar. And when Miss Ruthie says *nice,* she definitely doesn't mean *jeans.*"

"You're wearing jeans," I pointed out.

"That's 'cause Miss Ruthie didn't tell *me* to dress *nice*." He grinned. "You're gonna be in so much trouble."

I hauled Harry's bag off the dusty concrete and into the back of my truck. "I'm already in trouble. Ruth's been on my arse all day about being home by six o'clock. Her last message had ten exclamation marks reminding me we should've left an hour ago."

"She got something planned?" Harry's eyes lit up. "Is she doing Fiesta Fridays again? Man, I've been dreaming of her tacos."

"Sorry, mate, no tacos. She's dragging us to the bar."

"Lame."

One hundred percent lame. We were on the same page. It wasn't up to me, though, and standing around gasbagging all afternoon wasn't getting us home any quicker. I pointed for Harry to get moving. He was dawdling to the passenger side when he skidded to a stop.

"Hey, old man," he called over his shoulder. "There's, uh—there's a *tree* in the back of your truck."

No shit. "It's for Lola."

"We *talked* about this, right? When I told you to up your game, I meant you should ask Lola out to dinner or something." He shook his head, dumbfounded, pointing at the stump. "What's she gonna do with that giant hunk of wood?"

"This isn't just a hunk of wood." I ran my fingers over the rugged silver bark. "See this?" His lip curled. Guess not. "This is Tasmanian blackwood. Beautiful timber. A hundred years old."

"Yep. I believe it. It's as grey and wrinkly as Old Ben Shepherd, and he's pushing at least eighty."

"I'm going to build something for Lola."

I tugged at the strapping. Secure. Not going anywhere. My fingertips traced the coarse bark, the chipped edges of the mottled crust barely hinting at the red timber underneath.

A knot tightened in my chest. Maybe that piece of blackwood was like me. Hard and rough on the outside, but a rich golden heartwood waiting on the inside if someone could be bothered to find it. With some patience, even that broken old stump could be turned into something useful—*beautiful*—for Lola.

Because of Lola.

"You good, old man?" Harry grinned. "Need some time alone with your hunk of tree there?"

I shoved him closer to the passenger door. "Save it."

"You're gonna need more than your...*wood*...to get back in Lola's good books." He wiggled his eyebrows. When I didn't burst out laughing at his joke, he rolled his eyes. "You got those messages from Hollyoak, right? Lola's on the warpath!"

I groaned. I didn't need the reminder—and warpath was an understatement.

Hollyoak, his head stuffed with cow feed, had dumped me on top of his manure pile. He'd been too busy fluttering his eyelashes at Lola over *coffee* to turn his brain on and make up a decent excuse to cover our backsides.

Sorry, he'd said. Didn't realise she was so smart, he'd said.

Had Hollyoak paid any attention to Lola at all? She was sweeter than damn sugar but smart as a whip. She'd had him over a barrel, spewing all the details of our meeting with Evan before he even blinked.

My jaw clenched. I dragged the seat belt over my chest, and my eyes locked on the scowl darkening my rearview mirror as I reversed out of the motel parking lot.

I was pissed as hell, but... What was I angry about? Getting caught for dealing with Evan? I wasn't sorry about that. The first time I'd rocked up to his garage, I should have done a better job. I was prepared to wear Lola's wrath if it meant she was safe.

I loathed to admit it, but the thing sticking in my gut was those bloody messages from Hollyoak after his *coffees* with Lola.

She was just peachy, he'd said. No problems to report. My reply? Awesome. Smiley face. He'd treated her to a drink at the bar, too. Cool, hope she had a good time. He'd walked her home. I'd pretended to ignore that message even though my fingers itched to reply with the emoji of a hand flipping the bird and then toss my phone at a wall.

My jaw clenched tighter.

Screw Hollyoak.

Harry craned his neck to peer at me from the passenger seat. "You doing okay there, old man?" He nodded at my white-knuckled grip on the steering wheel. "Are you jealous of the farmer spending time with your woman?"

I grunted. "She's not my woman."

"What's the issue then?"

I wanted to be the one pushing open the coffee shop door for Lola and pulling out the chair so she could sit down. Jealousy didn't even begin to describe the dark, ugly feeling twisting my gut.

"They've been having *coffee* together. Every damn day we've been gone." I threw Harry a helpless look because this was killing me, and I had no idea how to handle it. "Is *coffee* like when Ruth tells me to dress nice? What does *coffee* actually mean?"

"In Ryan's case? It means they drink a coffee."

I relaxed my fingers. Tension eased from my hands as I turned the truck onto the highway. But I still scowled like a grumpy toddler when I mumbled, "Why does he get to have coffee with Lola every day?"

"Have you *asked* Lola to have a coffee with you?"

"Well, uh... I mean..." I sighed. "Not exactly."

"There's your answer."

I blew out a frustrated breath. "Give me some tips, then? How do I talk to her?"

Harry's mouth dropped open. "You're asking *me* for advice?"

"You've had girlfriends, right?"

He spluttered but eventually managed to choke out, "No!"

"Seriously?"

His cheeks flamed redder than his hair. "I mean—I'm not like... I've done...*stuff*." He shifted uncomfortably in the seat. "Haven't *you* had a girlfriend?"

I lifted a shoulder. "Not really. I've never done the whole relationship thing. I'm not even sure if I should try. I'm not...built right."

"Is that why you treated Lola like shit?"

"Harry..."

His lips flattened into a frown. "How does she fit in then?"

"I don't know," I answered honestly. "Maybe the two of us could be friends?" Emptiness filled my chest. The thought of being "just friends" with Lola itched at my brain like a scratchy woollen sweater.

"You don't need my advice to make friends," Harry said. "Dunno how, but you managed to find a couple all by yourself." He cocked his head with a grin.

I tried to smile back, but my mouth was stiff, fighting not to show the tightness gripping around my lungs. "What if I want to be more than friends with Lola? How do I do that? I'm not good at talking to people. You are. Give me some pointers?"

"Just be yourself."

Careful to keep my attention trained on the road, I glanced at Harry from the corner of my eye. My eyebrows were on the roof. Was he serious?

He laughed. "You're overthinking it. Maybe just..." He cleared his throat. "Try acting a bit less... awkward."

He had to be taking the piss. "You know me, right?"

"You're not *that* bad."

"I once told Lola that her freckles were like chips of wood."

I swallowed hard. Harry didn't notice because he was laughing his arse off. But... Lola's freckles. In her bedroom. The second time I'd had her that night, when she was a little braver, moaned a little louder, her hand clawing at the sheets... *Goddamn*. Moments like that were the stuff dreams were made of.

Tears stuck to the crinkles of Harry's eyes as he fought back laughter. "Yeah, okay, you're right. That's pretty bad." He wheezed a few more breaths. "What is it with you and bits of wood? Is this some kinky cabinetmaker thing? You're supposed to tell girls they're pretty, and you love how good they smell."

"Oh, yeah?" I teased. "Something like how her hair's like golden waves of honey?"

Harry sank low in his seat. "Screw you," he grumbled.

"Sounds like something kinky a friend of a cabinetmaker might say."

He laughed.

My hands loosened on the wheel. I'd missed our banter—our friendship. The week away had been good for us. The days were long, and work kept us busy, but Harry had filled every moment of silence with a constant stream of consciousness as we'd worked. We'd finally talked things out and regained some of the ground we'd lost after the way I'd acted.

I glued my eyes back on the highway. "So, what's your excuse, then, smooth talker?" When Harry mumbled a *huh*, I added, "Why are you avoiding Brooke?"

The mood shifted. The inside of the truck chilled frostier than the Antarctic winds that whipped over the valley. No more laughing. He didn't answer.

"She's real sweet on you, kid," I said. "Everyone says so."

Harry turned to blink out the window. The never-ending blur of green zipping past was more important than facing whatever thoughts spun in his head.

"Harry, what's going on? Is it what happened at the bar? You're not the first guy to say something stupid when he's drunk." Or even when dead-cold sober, but no one needed a reminder about my dumb arse.

"It's not that..." Harry sighed. "Well... It's kinda that... But..." Another sigh.

"Brooke likes you. You were down on one knee, so I'm guessing you like her, too. Seems like a no-brainer."

Harry scowled at me, but then his face drooped, and his chin fell against his chest. "I'm like you, I guess. I can't be in a...a...*relationship*."

"Sure you can. You've got the sweet talk figured out." I grinned and added, "You understand the rules about dressing nice."

"But what if..." Harry's voice lowered, strained. "What if I'm like my dad?"

A sucker punch hit me in the chest. That poor damn kid. "You're nothing like your dad."

"But what if I am? I couldn't live with myself if I ever..." Harry's head knocked back against the seat. His eyes squeezed shut. "That day up at your place, my brain got stuck. I couldn't think about anything except..." He shook his head. "It's *in* me, Aiden. I'm capable of thinking like him. I didn't give it a second thought before I came at you."

"With truly the worst right hook I've ever seen, mind you." The joke fell flat. I sighed. "You were sticking up for someone who needed help."

"That doesn't make it right!"

"You wouldn't hurt a fly, mate. You're sure as hell nothing like your father."

"I could be. How would I know? I've never been...you know...in a *couple*. And couples fight all the time!"

"I guess some do. Just 'cause you're sweet on someone doesn't mean you'll always agree about everything. That doesn't mean you'll..." I refused to say the words out loud. There was no chance he was like that. "Your mum pisses you off when she goes off at you about leaving your socks around the house, and you gripe about it, but that's where it ends."

"I can't risk it. Anyway... Not like it matters. Brooke deserves better than some dumb electrician."

"Hey. First off, you're not dumb. High school doesn't mean shit once you head out into the real world. Second, finishing your apprenticeship took hard work. I'll let you talk a lot of crap, but that's something to be damn proud of."

Harry's mouth pressed down to a thin line. He said nothing.

"Maybe you should talk to someone about what's going on in your head?" I suggested.

Harry folded his arms and sank lower in his seat. "Maybe *you* should talk to someone."

"Yeah..." My empty sigh filled the truck. "You're probably right."

His gaze snapped up to stare at me dead on, mouth open.

"I used to, you know?"

He shook his head. Of course he didn't know. No one did. Not even Ruth.

"I used to see a shrink every couple of weeks in the city," I said. "I stopped a few years ago. I figured out a routine and decided I was done trying to get better. What was the point? I was doing okay." My fingers tensed around the steering wheel. "I've been kidding myself for a long time. I'm not okay."

"Do, um... You wanna talk about it?"

I shook my head. "And that's got nothing to do with you, kid. It's just..."

"Hard. Yeah, I know. I don't like talking about...stuff...either." Harry stared out the window, and his frown reflected in the glass. Finally, he asked quietly, "So, you think you will? Talk to someone, I mean?"

"Yeah, I will. I need to." Harry was too old for it, but I stuck my hand out and ruffled his hair. He laughed. "I'll be a better man if I start dealing with what's going on in my head. I can't keep letting my past rule my present."

Or my future...

23

He Saw His True Feelings

Aiden

I WASN'T EXPECTING THE welcome wagon when my truck pulled up outside Ruth's place, but there she was, standing under the porch light as white specks danced around her in the glow.

After a string of ignored messages, a call she ended after snapping at me for not sticking to her schedule, and the follow-up call to Harry where she barked at him for me being late, I was fully expecting Ruth to blow a gasket. Or three.

But when I turned off the ignition, there was no smoke, no fury. Only a crooked, white smile waited for me.

Dread skated across my skin.

Something wasn't right.

Harry hopped out of the truck first. He bounded up the stairs two at a time and smothered Ruth in a hug. Her laughter swirled as he spun her around before dropping her safely back to her feet.

He took a step back. "Look at you all dressed up, Miss Ruthie." He let out a low whistle. "Show me more of this outfit."

"You like?" A little unsteady on her bad leg, she twirled to show off a yellow...dress...thing. What did I know about dresses? It was floaty and way too fancy for a night at the bar. "It's new. What about the hair?" She twisted her neck and fluffed at the dark lump to give Harry a look at the back.

"Oh, yeah," he said. "Ten outta ten."

I slammed the car door shut, suspicious eyes narrowing on Ruth's fashion show. New dress. Hair done up. Enough gold jewellery stacked on her wrists to rival a pirate's stolen treasures. She was dolled up like we were going to be the guests of honour at a royal wedding instead of heading out for a drink.

She was *definitely* up to something—and I'd fallen right into her honey trap.

Once, I'd fallen into her web and taken the fall for a bottle of whisky stashed under the front seat of my parents' car. Another time, she'd tricked me into finding her engagement ring the week before Matthew had planned to propose. The last time was when she'd pulled me into the spare room at her old place and asked about converting it into a nursery. They'd been thinking about trying for a baby. Before the divorce. Before the accident.

A sting of salt blinded my eyes. I dragged my palm down my face, begging those buried memories to disappear into the oblivion of my mind where they belonged. Tonight wasn't the night to get lost in the past. I could hold it together.

I stomped up the stairs to the porch.

Ruth's smile vanished. "And just what do you think you're wearing?"

"Clothes."

"Did you read *any* of my messages?"

Some of them. Lots of exclamation marks. "Yeah."

"Are you sure?" she scoffed. "I distinctly remember telling you to wear something *nice*. And this"—she pointed an accusing finger at my shirt—"is not nice."

"Told you," Harry muttered.

My brows furrowed. I tugged at the black Henley to get a closer look. No stains. Fit good. Nicer than the plaid flannel and jeans I usually wore to the bar. "What's wrong with what I'm wearing?"

Ruth ignored my question and turned to Harry. "I knew he'd do this." Her frustrated huff blew wisps of dark hair off her forehead.

He indulged her with a mournful look and pouted. "We can't take him anywhere, can we, Miss Ruthie?"

"Oh, for fu—" I took a deep breath, saving myself at the last second from ruining Ruth's special night. "We're going to the bar. We're not traipsing down the damn red carpet."

Ruth's cane poked me in my shin. "You won't be going anywhere until you march yourself inside and change."

"Ruth," I pleaded.

"Get marching, mister!" She jabbed her cane at me again. "Tonight's important. This is my first night out in a year!"

I sighed. That *was* a big deal. She'd been cooped up too long. "Okay." I turned to head down the stairs. "I've got some clean clothes in the truck—"

Her cane whipped out and blocked my path. I wasn't taking another step. "And those rags will *stay* in the truck," she said. "I have what you need. Inside. Go, go, go!"

I flicked a desperate look to Harry. Grinning, he flopped onto the porch swing. "Tootles!" he laughed, waving me off as he put his phone to his ear to call his mum.

That little...

Some friend. Zero help. I was marching into the bowels of hell on my own with the smiling devil whipping her stick at my heels. Two steps inside, I spotted my punishment on the dining table. A postage satchel with the logo of some high-end men's store sat torn open.

Nope. Not happening.

I spun around, but Ruth's cane whacked against my shins to stop me in my tracks. Trapped. There was no escaping the horrors awaiting me in that bag. She ripped off the tissue paper and pulled out a blue button-up shirt and a pair of scratchy trousers that looked like something my accountant would wear.

"No." I folded my arms over my chest. "Absolutely not."

"But look how nice this shirt is!" Ruth pressed the fabric against her cheek. "It's made from organic linen. It's so soft. And see, this blue is pretty but masculine and will show off your eyes—"

"No one's looking at my damn eyes."

Ruth shoved the pile of clothes at me. "You're putting these on, and you're going to like it."

"No."

She gritted her teeth. "Put. On. The. Clothes."

I narrowed my eyes. I was deadly serious about those ugly clothes never touching my skin.

Ruth's chin wobbled.

Goddammit.

She blinked slowly to blot crocodile tears down her cheeks. "You want me to suffer? Is that what you want? I thought we were friends!"

"Ruth…"

"Imagine what people must say about me! Oh, that Ruth Wilks. She used to be a top-notch police officer once, but look at her now." She cracked open one tearstained eye to peek at me before continuing to wail. "Nothing but a forgotten spinster. Put her out to pasture. No one will miss her."

"Give me those." I snatched the pile of clothes from her hands. "One day, your wobbly chin won't work on me anymore."

Ruth twittered a laugh. "The wobbly chin never fails. Go!"

I lumbered down the hallway to the bathroom, cursing under my breath and wondering where the hell I went wrong with my life. Was it that time I stuffed the last piece of birthday cake into my mouth at Tommy Winslow's tenth birthday party? That cake was damn good. It had pink frosting and sprinkles. But was it worth it? Was it all downhill from there?

Just when I thought it couldn't get any worse, Ruth called out to me from down the hallway.

"Make sure you have a shower! I don't want you smelling like some seedy motel off the highway for this! There's a nice body wash on the shelf for you. Oh! And fix your hair! Do it nice!" And before I slammed the bathroom door, she yelled a final instruction in case my head wasn't already spinning. "Brush your teeth!"

Harry didn't dare laugh at me when I stomped down the steps, primped and preened to Ruth's satisfaction. My face was a storm. He got the message. He slunk off the porch swing and back to my truck with nothing more than a smirk.

I slid into the driver's seat, dragged on my seat belt, and tugged at the sleeves of that awful shirt to fold them up to my elbows. That fabric was scratchy as shit. It was nearly as bad as the pants.

"Soft, my arse," I muttered.

Ruth snickered in the back seat.

"I heard that," I said.

Harry grinned. "Chin for the win!"

"You're not helping," I warned him.

I glanced in the rearview mirror. Ruth's eyes sparkled like the fairy lights she'd had me twist through the branches of the stunted birch tree out the front of her place. Maybe clothes only fit for the incinerator were worth seeing her smile so big for the first time in years. *Maybe.*

I pulled into the parking lot out the back of the bar, slowing down for the swarm of people milling around. Fridays at the Old Cellar were busy, but this was on a whole new level. I gripped the steering wheel tighter.

You can do it, you weak bastard. Hold it together. It's just one night.

Harry whooped out a cheer. "Games Night! Awesome!" He leant forward, fingers on the dash. He wasn't looking at the crowd with puke lurching in his throat like me. He was excited. "I completely forgot this was on!"

Games Night? More like Hell on Earth Night. Well, if this were hell, at least I was wearing the right outfit.

Harry twisted to grin at Ruth over his shoulder. "Who's on our team?"

Whoa, whoa, *whoa*. *"Team?"* I turned slowly, eyes narrowing on Ruth.

She squirmed in her seat. "You know, just a small team." Her laugh wasn't convincing. "I invited a few friends to fill up the table."

My jaw tensed. A sinking feeling was settling in my gut. *Friends?* If Yolanda Briggs sat at that table, Ruth's chin could wobble until Hollyoak's hairy cows came home, but I'd be out that door faster than she could say *organic linen*. I didn't care if I had to walk the whole damn way up the mountain to get home.

Ruth fumbled open the car door with her good hand, and despite an almost spill that had my heart in my throat, she was out like a shot, her yellow dress lighting up the parking lot as she clipped away from me at an uneven, frantic pace. Guilty as sin, she was.

Inside, she waved Harry away to get us a round of drinks, and I was thankful when she led the way through the laughing hordes to a table in a quieter part of the bar. Water jugs, cups, and coasters were set up for six. A placard with gold lettering sat proudly in the centre.

My fingertips traced the fancy gold swirls spelling out the team's name. *"Taking Care of Quizness?"* A grin crept on my face.

Ruth beamed. "Awesome, right? It was Lola's suggestion."

My smile vanished. "Lola?" Ruth had better be kidding.

She grimaced. "Yeah, um, you know…" Her eyes zipped back and forth. "Lola came up with the name when we brainstormed over lunch today—"

"You had lunch with *Lola?* Today?"

Ruth's eyes darted everywhere. "Well, um, *yes.*" She gulped. "And maybe—*technically*—last week, too."

"Technically, huh?" I pinched the bridge of my nose. "So, even though I specifically asked you not to stick your nose in because I'm so shit scared of making things worse with Lola, you went behind my back and spent two days hanging out with her?"

"Well, *technically* it was three days because she came over for dinner the other night—"

"Ruth!"

Her smile was pleading. "Lola's *real* nice."

That was stating the obvious. "She is."

"We get along like a house on fire."

"I bet."

"You look *so* handsome tonight."

I fought back a laugh, but I lost. "Flattery won't work on me, sister."

"I promise I didn't make it worse. I just want you to be happy." Her good arm went around my waist, and she rested her head on my shoulder. "If you could see the way Lola smiles when I talk about you."

"You talked about me?"

"Only good things!"

"Like?"

"Um..." She was back to those nervous laughs again. "Stop worrying about all that!" She squeezed me against her side. "Lola's going to take one look at you all dressed up tonight and—*bam!* She'll fall head over heels."

"It won't be like that. Maybe one day she might want to be friends, but... more than that..." The shake of my head was slow. "Don't get my hopes up, Ruthie girl."

She hugged me around my waist and whispered, "But Aiden, doesn't Lola look so pretty tonight?"

I snapped my head around to the doors. First came Brooke. She marched at the head of the pack, red dress, red lips, ready to conquer the world. Lola slipped through the gap behind her. Maybe no one else noticed her, but my eyes stuck on that shy girl like glue. A pure goddess, draped in floral, her cheeks flushed pink from the chilled evening air.

I couldn't speak.

My heart thundered in my ears as I grabbed for the back of the chair, desperate for the support. My legs had gone soft beneath me, and I wasn't sure they'd hold me up anymore.

The woman I'd been aching for all week—my whole life—was *right there* at the door. She took off her coat. She headed for my table. My brain registered Hollyoak behind her, his bronzed hand on her shoulder, but I didn't even grit my teeth with thoughts of yanking it off because I was mesmerised by the pretty twist of Lola's lips.

That smile.

Suddenly, it wasn't the crowd of the bar sucking the air from my lungs. I drowned in memories of every time I'd been lucky enough to be with Lola. The ill-fated days in her cottage. Wandering around the grocery store. The night in the bar when I'd become the kind of man I'd vowed never to be. The storm. The two of us in the alley.

Every memory. Good. Bad. But she was always the same. My sweet, perfect Lola, with her wood-chip freckles and the enormous gold-rimmed glasses that slid down her nose.

Ruth's prediction was almost correct. It wasn't Lola who fell. It was me. One look at Lola and—*bam!*—I was head over heels.

Madly. Completely. Utterly hopelessly.

And no matter how many times I reminded myself not to get my hopes up because I had no right to, I finally admitted to myself that I was in love with Lola Hughes.

I had been all along.

24

She Saw a New Beginning

Lola

RUTH SNIFFED MY LAVENDER a week ago.

Since then, I'd discovered she adored horses, was ruthless in her pursuit of winning a game of Scrabble, and was deeply suspicious of any guy sporting a man bun. Something about hipster irony. She wasn't a fan. She was also no criminal mastermind. Her dreams of Aiden and me eloping into the sunset had been twinkling in her eyes since the day we'd met.

So, when I walked into the bar behind Brooke, and my eyes landed on that big brute of a man tugging uncomfortably at the collar of a shirt I was certain Ruth chose for him, I wasn't surprised. I knew he'd be there.

He was more than a bit surprised to see me, though. He bolted up taller, straighter, his eyes wide. The slightly awkward smile I offered him across the crowded room didn't help. Caught off guard, he gripped the chair in front of him with his big hands, and his eyes dropped to his feet and stayed there.

Brooke snatched my arm. "There's your man, Lolly."

I pierced her with an icy glare. "He's not my man," I hissed. "And will you please keep your voice down? I'm pretty sure they heard your wishful thinking in Canada."

Brooke's stride in her high heels was impressive. She charged ahead, not bothered by my rare outburst in the slightest. "You gonna put that grumpy old bastard out of his misery?" She grinned over her shoulder. "Admit how much you missed him?"

"I didn't miss him." I spluttered everywhere. "I certainly haven't forgiven him!"

"Is that so?" Brooke said.

Ryan's chuckle died into a fit of pretend coughs when my dark look speared him next. "Want to know a secret to put you out of *your* misery, Doc?" he asked. "He missed you even more."

My cheeks flamed.

All the rehearsals in front of Brooke's mirror had been for nothing. I was supposed to charge into the bar, all guns blazing, and give Aiden a piece of my mind. If he thought he could waltz around town playing the vigilante hero, he was in for a rude shock. But all my perfectly practiced words fluttered away to leave me with nothing but nerves.

Would anyone notice if I snuck out? My palms stayed clammy even after I rubbed them down the front of my dress. My symptoms could be passed off as an illness. Yeah, that was it. I had the plague...or...something.

I bit down on my lip, eyes on the doors.

My escape route disappeared behind a wall of red. "Don't you even *think* about it, Lolly." Brooke's hands landed on her hips.

"But I'm feeling"—cough—"*so* sick."

"We practiced this! You are strong. You are fearless." When I refused to speak, she tapped her foot impatiently. "Like we practiced. Go."

"I am strong. I am fearless."

"Damn straight. Now, paint on a smile, march yourself over to that table, and give him hell!"

I nodded and slid my glasses up my nose, quaking in my heels but somehow ready. First, I pushed my shoulders back like Aiden did when he was nervous.

I can do this. Strong. Fearless.

I took a deep breath. But before a smile wobbled on my face, an evil twitch kicked Brooke's lips up.

Wait, what—

Brooke shoved me, and I lurched the last few steps to the table.

Balls.

When a hole didn't open in the floor to swallow me up, I held up my palm in an embarrassed wave. "Hi, everyone."

"Lola!" Ruth jerked unsteadily around the table. Her arm pinned me in a warm hug. "Look at you! You look like a dream." She flashed a sly smile at the man avoiding my eyes. "Aiden was *just* telling me how pretty you look tonight."

His eyebrow rose. "You were the one who sa—"

"It was definitely you," Ruth snapped through gritted teeth. She was all sweet smiles again when she turned to me. "It was *definitely* him."

Brooke slung her handbag over the back of a chair and leant over the table to snatch a gold card. "Awesome! Name cards!" She flicked it around for me to see. *"The Sunshine Princess."* She grinned. "I guess this one's my seat."

"Lola and I came up with some fun code names for everyone," Ruth explained. "I'm Rue the Day. Brooke, you're next to the Ginger Ninja. Lola, you're next to the Grumblejack, and I've popped your other friend next to me. Hopefully, she's not running too late. I think they'll kick off the games soon."

"Um... *He*," I corrected.

Ruth's face fell. "He?"

"Yeah, my friend Ryan Hollyoak is here."

Withering under her glare, I flicked my hand, motioning for the farmer to step forward and save me. He didn't appear. Where the heck was he? Sidetracked talking to some guy about Scottish Highland cows? He'd done that before.

"You haven't met Ryan before?" I asked. "His family owns the farm outside town. Cattle, mostly, but their orchard is where I got all those limes for the tart I made you."

Ruth's frown only speared down more with every word out of my mouth.

Where the hell was Ryan?

I twisted around, half-expecting him to be on the other side of the bar, but I jumped, startled, when I found him standing right behind me. He stood frozen, eyes wide and mouth open, like a stunned fish pulled out of the river. I nudged Ryan. Nothing. I threw a helpless look at Brooke. She shrugged. She was as confused as I was.

Ruth's eyes were daggers. "When you came up with the name Hollier Than Thou, I assumed your friend's name was Holly or something. I wasn't expecting a"—her hand waved at Ryan like she was swatting away a hundred annoying flies—"*you know.*"

I carefully hid my smile and played dumb. "A...*farmer?*"

Aiden chuckled.

Ruth's eyes narrowed to an even sharper line, glaring in Ryan's direction. "You." She snapped her fingers. "Ryan Hollyoak, is it?"

The man in question shook off his daze. His hand twitched with nerves as he straightened his shirt. "Uh—yes." His cheeks were stained bright pink. "Yes, ma'am."

"*Ma'am?*" Ruth snorted. "I'm not your granny."

"No, ma'am." His throat dipped on a hard swallow. "You are not."

"Stop with that *ma'am* stuff. You can call me Ruth. Now, scoot yourself over here. Your spot is next to me."

Ryan stumbled around the table and planted himself next to Ruth, eyes on her like a dopey puppy waiting for praise. She covered her surprise with a nervous laugh, and his jaw dropped.

Oh, brother. The man was smitten.

Brooke cocked her hip and arched her eyebrows at Aiden. "So, where's the Ginger Ninja? Still too scared to show his face?"

Aiden smiled. "He's grabbing a round of drinks."

"Well, fancy that. I was just headed to the bar myself." Brooke prepared for battle. She flipped her hair over her shoulders. "I'll bring us back some drinks." She winked at me. "And maybe a side of revenge."

My safety blanket clicked away with vengeful strides. I always knew I'd have to face Aiden alone.

I could do this.

Strong.

Fearless.

There wasn't much space in the crowded bar. I wriggled through the gap, my body skating so close to Aiden that his shirt brushed against my arm. Nerves fluttered in my chest. He was too close. Always too close. I tried to twist out of his way, but there was nowhere to go.

His hand gently cradled my elbow. "Are you mad at me?"

Strong. Fearless. "Yes."

"Because of what happened to Evan?"

"Because you broke your promise. Remember? No fists."

"I didn't—"

I jerked my arm free. "Watching Ryan do your dirty work is just as bad, you know."

I would've dramatically yanked out my chair to sit down if he hadn't already pulled out the chair for me. He sat beside me. I ignored his touch on my knee. My gaze locked on the name card. Ruth had done the lettering. She was artistic. She wouldn't craft a coffee mug that looked like a wonky poop.

"Lola, I'm sorry I broke my promise to you, but I'm not sorry for what I did." And there wasn't a hint of remorse in his voice, either. "Evan was never going to stop hassling people unless we did something."

"That doesn't make it right."

"No, it doesn't. But I'd rather risk you hating me forever than you not feeling safe for even a second. And before you jump on me, I'm fully aware of the hypocrisy of that statement. I know I'm one of the people who didn't make you feel safe. That kills me."

"Uh-huh."

"I want you to feel safer with me than anyone. That's how I feel when I'm with you."

I stared at the hands dancing nervously in my lap. Brooke had painted over where I'd chewed my fingernails to a blunt pink mess. The last week had been so hard. New messages from an unknown number I knew in my heart were from Chris. Every creak in my house made me jump, and ghosts lingered in the shadows that crept up the walls at night. Aiden worried he didn't make me feel safe, and maybe that used to be true. But I couldn't deny that, right now, I felt a lot safer knowing he was nearby.

His eyes locked on my wringing hands. "Lola, if you don't want me here..."

"You have every right to spend time with your friends."

"If Ruth's overstepped—"

"Stop that. She's great. She's been keeping me out of mischief." I thought about it a little longer. "Or getting me into mischief. I'm never sure." I laughed. "We get along really well."

"I've heard. Like a house on fire."

Biting back a smile, I fumbled for a better fidgeting spot in the fabric covering my knees until Aiden's big hand covered mine. A rush of warmth raced to my cheeks.

He leant closer, his voice a gravelly rumble only for me to hear. "I missed seeing you."

"O-oh?"

"I missed not knowing what you're reading. What book has your attention now?"

"I'm not sure how I feel about it yet, but I started *Wide Sargasso Sea* by Jean Rhys."

A smile tugged at his lips. *"Have all beautiful things sad destinies?"* he recited in an achingly gentle voice. My heart soared. He'd read it. "That won't be your fate, pretty Lola."

"I'm n-not pretty."

"No?" His finger lightly traced the hem draped over my knee. "I think you're absolutely stunning."

My heart cracked so hard against my ribs I was sure he could hear it. "Y-you, um, look great, too." I gulped. "I like your shirt."

"You do? It's, uh..." He coughed into his fist, and lowering his voice, his tone almost seductive, he added, "It's organic linen."

I giggled. "It's nice. It suits you." I pushed up my glasses, nerves getting the better of me. "It matches your eyes."

Ruth snorted.

Aiden shot a warning glance over his shoulder. "Ruth, mind your business. Talk to Ryan about his horses."

"What?" Ruth squealed, excited eyes flying back to the farmer. *"Horses?"*

Ryan nodded. "We have three horses on the farm. Well, four, actually. I helped birth a foal this morning. We named her Dolly. She's a real beauty."

"Aiden, did you hear that?" Ruth clapped her hand against her cheek. "Ryan has horses!"

Aiden smirked. "Imagine that."

Ryan turned hopeful eyes to the woman beaming next to him. "Do you like horses, Miss Ruth?"

She scoffed. "Do I like horses..."

She sat on the edge of her seat, lost in a never-ending stream of excited chatter with the farmer. She was like pure sunlight when she was happy, and Ryan basked in the glow with a smile bigger than I'd ever seen on his face.

I bumped my shoulder into Aiden's and whispered, "And Ruth thinks she's the only matchmaker in the room."

Aiden didn't laugh at my joke like I expected. "I truly am sorry about all this. Ruth... Her interfering..." He sighed. "Once she gets an idea in her head..."

"She's determined? Stubborn? Doesn't listen to anyone because she knows best?" I tapped my chin. "This sounds an awful lot like someone else I know."

Aiden grunted.

"So, in your constant battle of wills, which of you backs down first?"

"Me."

"Every time?"

"Every damn time."

"Have you ever beaten Ruth at Scrabble?" A slow grin spread across my face. "Or do you let her win that, too?"

"Let her win? In my dreams. It's a triumph worth crowing over for months when I finally beat her."

Proud, I lifted my chin. "I've beaten her."

Aiden's mouth dropped open. "Bull."

"Four times."

"Lies."

"The secret is blocking all those triple-word scores she likes to get."

"Nah, no way. She's letting you win. It's all part of her plan. She's been lulling you into a false sense of security so she could sneak attack with the matchmaking."

I laughed. I never wanted these silly moments between us to end or for his smile to fade. I wanted to talk about Scrabble and listen to him tell stories about Ruth forever. And it was shallow, and vain, and so very silly... But I wanted him to tell me again how pretty I looked. No, not just pretty. *Stunning,* he'd said.

"Hello..." A tap on a microphone blasted through the speakers, followed by acoustic feedback that screeched loud enough to shatter me to my core. "Hello? Everyone? It's time to get started. Welcome to Games Night!"

My ears still rang. I darted a look at Aiden. No bright smile warmed his face anymore. His head hung low, and white fingertips dug into his knees like he was hanging on for dear life off the edge of a cliff.

"Aiden." I was careful to keep my voice quiet so no one else would hear. "Are you okay?"

"Y-yeah." The answer came out through gritted teeth. "I wasn't expecting the noise, that's all."

"I'm here." I soothed my hand in a circle on his back. "Tell me if you want to take a breather. We can go outside and get some fresh air."

His eyes lifted, wild, like the day at the clinic. My shoulders tensed, waiting for the hit. I expected him to shrug me off, bark that everything was fine, and to mind my own business. But he didn't. His face didn't shutter. No harsh words ever came.

Aiden nodded. "I don't want to ruin tonight for Ruth—or you. Will you count with me? Like you did the other time?"

I started the count, our eyes locked on each other, every beat from one to ten. At six, his hand relaxed, pink returning to his fingertips. At eight, his hand left his knee, fumbling under the table for new comfort. His fingers wove around mine as if it were the most natural thing in the world.

"Almost there," I whispered, starting again at one.

Not just for the count.

For us.

In my heart, we were almost back to where we'd started, too.

25

She Saw Love Blooming

Lola

"AND THE FIRST CATEGORY...IS...BOOKS!"

The grin on Aiden's face was even bigger than mine. Finally, it was our time to shine.

After Ruth's blistering win at paper planes and Harry's narrow victory at the marshmallow toss—he'd stuffed more into his mouth than he'd landed in the cup—trivia was the time for us to make Ruth's dream come true. Her eyes never strayed far from the enormous hampers. The fact that the first questions were focused on books? Even better.

No one else in the crowd agreed. A heavy groan rippled around the room. The loudest protest came from Ruth.

"Books?" She stuck her nose in the air with an indignant huff. "Who *reads*?"

My eyebrows popped up. "Surely the undisputed Queen of Scrabble loves reading?"

Aiden grunted a laugh but was smart enough to dodge Ruth's frosty glare. He smiled at her, all innocence, and reached across the table for a pencil, ready to scribble down our team's answers.

Ruth waved away my question. "As if I'm going to waste my time reading some dusty book from ye olde times when a whole world of reality TV is at my fingertips."

"Yes!" Brooke bounced up and down, clapping her hands with excitement. "I knew I liked you! What's your addiction?"

"*Soccer Mum Socialites*," Ruth fired back. "Absolutely no question."

Aiden paused his scribbling. "Do you want us to win this round?" His eyebrow arched in Ruth's direction. "Yeah? I need to hear more of the questions and less of this." His hand waved at the space between the two gossips.

Ruth's dark eyes narrowed. She didn't appreciate being told what to do by Aiden. But one longing glance at the trophy and oversized gift hampers crowding the bar swayed her—to keep her voice down, at least.

She bent over and whispered to Brooke, "Did you watch the new episode last night?"

Aiden's pencil hovered over the answer sheet. His finger twitched, ready to croak at them.

Brooke arched forward, excited whispers tumbling out as if she were sharing the juiciest story in the world. "Did you almost die when they revealed the plastic surgeon was cheating with the nanny?"

"I never saw it coming! I thought for sure he was fooling around with his assistant." Ruth chittered with evil delight. "But the showdown when his wife pushed him into the pool was epic!"

Ryan joined the mix. "What about when his toupee fell off and bobbed along the water?" His shoulders shook with laughter. "I totally lost it. The nanny started screaming because she thought it was a rat. No rat is *that* ugly."

Every pair of eyes at the table snapped to the farmer—even Harry's, and he hadn't said a word all night.

Ryan gulped. "It's, uh... a fun show." A sheepish smile flashed.

"*You* watch *Soccer Mum Socialites*?" Ruth's jaw was still on the floor.

Ryan shrugged. "I don't mind reality shows. I've lived on the farm since the day my mama brought me into this world. I've learned a lot about different cities and people." He gulped and flitted nervous eyes around the table. "I, um, *well*—I auditioned for a show a few months back."

Squeals erupted in every direction. Aiden's disapproving scowl wouldn't stop them this time.

Ruth grabbed the sleeve of his shirt. "Which one? Which one?"

Brooke grinned. "I can *totally* see Ryan dancing up a storm on *It's All Ballroom*."

"Only if they have a new category for two left feet." Ryan spun his empty beer glass in nervous hands. "There's that show where they, um... help match farmers with, you know... a nice lady."

Disappointment etched on Ruth's face. "Are you...?" Her shoulders slumped.

He shook his head. "The producer and some crew flew down from Sydney. They liked my story. Pa thought I was completely bonkers, but he gave me his blessing. He thought it might be good for the farm... Good for me... But..." He shrugged. "After they left that night, I stood in the field, looking out over the valley, and something didn't feel right." His eyes dropped back to his empty glass. "Maybe my mama was looking down on me... telling me to wait because the right girl was waiting just around the corner."

His throat bobbed as he shifted his gaze to Ruth. She offered a shy smile in return before glancing over her shoulder at Aiden.

An unspoken question passed between them—maybe asking for his approval—and he clasped her shoulder. Yes. Growing bolder with the blessing of her best friend, Ruth's gold bangles jingled when she touched her hand on Ryan's knee. The farmer looked like he'd just about died and gone to heaven.

But the first blossoms of the budding romance didn't thrill everyone at the table.

Brooke slumped in her chair, silent devastation in her eyes when she snuck a sideways glance at Harry. His gaze stayed fixed on the beer sitting untouched in front of him, and he continued to sit hunched in his seat, silent, until trivia ended.

The Games Night master announced us as the winners before calling the next event.

"Musical chairs?" I groaned. "Count me out. I've got more left feet than Ryan."

Ruth flashed a hopeful smile at Aiden.

He grunted a firm no. "And you can withhold the powers of your wobbly chin for another night, Ruth. This old dog doesn't need to learn any new tricks." He jerked his head at the two sitting across the table. "Get the young ones up there."

Harry jumped out of the chair. He didn't need convincing from Ruth's puppy-dog eyes. And if Brooke was upset to see him scrambling across the bar, desperate to escape being so close to her, she didn't show it.

Determination shone in her eyes. She hiked up her chest, way too much cleavage spilling out. "This dress is about to pay for itself," she declared before charging off to win her prize.

Harry and Brooke were the perfect choices to get Ruth one step closer to her trophy. They cruised through the early rounds. Harry charmed an old lady from her seat with one of his dimpled smiles. Brooke dazzled another of the old-timers by bending over ever so slightly to check the heel of her shoe. Ruth's cheers only encouraged them to play dirtier. And, in the end, despite their questionable tactics, Harry and Brooke were the final two.

Only one chair sat in the middle of the bar.

The music started.

Harry's eyes narrowed on the seat. Brooke paid it no attention, another prize clearly on her mind. She circled the final hurdle to her victory with a wicked smile dancing on her lips and her fingers crossed behind her back.

The music stopped.

Harry dived for the chair. "Hell yeah! I'm the win—"

He froze, his mouth clamping shut when Brooke's bottom crashed into his lap. She wrapped her arms around his shoulders, and just when his face couldn't flame any redder, she smacked her lips on his cheek. For one long second, the pair shared a heated gaze, and when Harry's hand reached up to twist one of her curls around his finger, I was convinced he was about to kiss her so good she'd cry with joy for a month.

But the magic moment stalled.

Harry released the stray curl and wriggled out from under her.

"Shit, Harry..." Aiden mumbled, his hands going to his knees, pushing off the chair.

But if he was worried, he didn't need to be. Harry only got two steps away before his gaze landed on Aiden. One dip of his friend's chin, and Harry straightened his T-shirt, turned around, and strode back.

"Remember the first day we met?" he asked Brooke.

She tipped her chin up to look at him, her face still painted with shock. "Y-yeah," she stammered. "At the village store."

Harry nodded. "You came flying in, covered in dust, and your hair was all wild in this big, messy ponytail on top of your head. You barged in front of me at the checkout."

"And I said..." She swallowed her nerves with a big breath. *"Outta my way, pip-squeak. You can buy your stale old corn chips after I've sent a horde of cockroaches to heaven."*

"Yeah." Harry's laugh was almost dreamy. "When you stormed out of there, I turned to Ashley and said, *'That's the girl I'm gonna marry someday.'*"

"Really?"

"Yup. I've been stupid about admitting my feelings for you, but I'm done being stupid. So, I'm gonna kiss you back now," he warned, falling to one knee. "You better tell me if that's not something—"

Brooke's lips landed on his, and the bar erupted in cheers and stomping boots.

Aiden relaxed back in his seat, smiling.

I nudged my finger into his shoulder. "You had something to do with that, didn't you?"

"I'll take credit for giving him the courage to tell her how he feels," he said. "Doing it in front of the whole town is all on him."

"I think it was adorable."

Aiden slid a wary glance at me. "You want me to get hold of the microphone and tell the town how we first met? Would you forgive me then?"

"Don't you *dare*, Aiden McKinnon!"

The wooden chair creaked when he eased back. "I think about the morning at the clinic sometimes. You were as timid as a mouse. Scared of your own shadow." He tilted his head towards me, an expression almost like pride settling across his face. "And look at you now—the fearless Storm Queen who stole my umbrella and ruined my shirt."

"I gave your umbrella to Harry." I huffed an annoyed sound. "And I didn't ruin your shirt. I *washed* it!"

"And ironed it," he reminded me with a rueful smile. "Now I've got nothing else to remember those early days except up

here." He tapped his temple. "And every time I see you frowning at me. But…"

"But?"

"You're not frowning at me as much tonight."

"What am I doing instead?"

"Smiling."

26

He Saw His Nightmare
Come to Life

Aiden

THE DAY BEFORE MY twelfth birthday, I broke my arm in three places.

The whole thing was Ruth's fault.

We didn't know the creek was flooded until our bikes skidded to a stop on the muddy bank. Murky brown water blocked off our usual shortcut home from school. No way around. No way over.

I was happy to take the long way, but Ruth had the bright idea to cobble together a ramp out of old bits of wood so we could jump the creek.

Sure, I hauled over most of the wood, found a few good rocks, and built the ramp. But it was *Ruth's* idea.

She pedalled her pink BMX like a demon, dark hair whipping in the wind, and her lip curled with fierce determination. Her bike flew up the ramp, and she launched into the sky like a warrior princess riding on the back of a pink Pegasus.

"This was a bad idea!" she hollered as her bike soared over the creek.

She was ten and braver than any other kid in town—nothing like me. I was cautious, always plodding a few steps behind, taking the world in nice and slow, and overthinking everything. But that was one time I didn't need to worry.

A spray of mud signalled Ruth's safe landing on the other side. Her bike skidded to a stop, and she threw her head back, laughing. Another challenge conquered.

She cupped her hands around her mouth and shouted from the other side of the creek. "You coming, slowpoke?"

I eyed off the ramp and the distance across the creek. I wasn't convinced I'd make it. "I—I dunno."

"For reals?" She rolled her eyes. "You're *such* a wuss."

Twelve-year-old me was as thick as a stump, too. Hearing Ruth's taunt turned off all my good overthinking. I forgot she was a champion equestrian rider and the self-proclaimed Queen of Pony Club. I forgot how she was lighter than a feather, and I was already shooting up and spending half my afternoon in front of the fridge looking for more to eat.

If Ruth could do it, I could do it, right?

I definitely couldn't do it.

I pedalled like hell, got up the ramp okay, but had no clue what to do once my bike got airborne. I soared through the sky on nothing but silent prayers and the pride glowing in Ruth's eyes. Reality crashed me against the edge of the muddy creek bed, my head cracking against the edge, until I tumbled into the water with a splash.

Dazed and twisted in a mangled heap, I was alive—despite Ruth screaming like I'd croaked it—but my helmet was cracked clean in half, and the front wheel of my bike was bent all out of shape. My arm was even worse.

I limped home, one arm around Ruth, the other cradled against my chest, the pain searing so hot I couldn't speak. Shock and the promise of Mum were the only things that kept me shuffling along. It didn't matter I was twelve. Her cuddles still made everything better.

But Mum wasn't home.

My father's shadow blocked the final step to the back porch.

"Where the hell have you been?" he roared.

I swiped the mud off my cheek and held out my arm, but his words slammed down harder than I had in that creek.

"Man up. You're twelve, not two. Quit that sniffling."

I hugged my arm close to my chest and dropped my eyes to my muddy shoes. "Y-yes... S-sir..."

My stuttering only made him angrier. "Get your shoulders back. Don't be so damn weak." And when I tried to stand tall, but the pain shot through my arm so bad I whimpered, he shook his head, ashamed. "Four generations of police officers, and look what I ended up with—nothing but a bloody crybaby!"

In the end, my arm healed up okay. Mum took me to the hospital, and Ruth was jealous as shit because I got a week off school. I broke my arm another time playing football, too. No big deal. That was the thing about broken bones—they heal.

But whatever my father knocked out of me that day never came back. I shut down. No emotions. No weakness. Everything that hurt was buried so deep I wasn't even sure I knew how to feel properly anymore.

For a long time, it worked to live shut off from that part of myself.

But...

Did it *still* work?

My gaze shifted from the damp coaster I'd been tracing with my finger to the couples on the dance floor.

I was grateful when the Games Night master had announced a break for dinner and dancing. There was too much noise. I was running close to the wire, my nerves frayed down to only a thin thread, ready to snap. The music was quieter now, and without constant noise slamming me from all sides, I could finally patch myself up.

I might just make it.

Another frayed thread knotted back together when Ruth flashed me a crooked smile over Ryan's shoulder. The farmer was nothing like me. He was a good sort of man. He'd shimmied her bad foot onto his boot, and after anchoring her safely against his chest with a protective arm around her back, he took it slow and steady to waltz her around the dance floor with all the oldies.

"Aiden! Look!" Ruth's dark eyes sparkled as he spun her. "I'm dancing!"

Smiling, I nodded, trying to hide the tears stinging my eyes. We were still the same after all these years—me, plodding a few steps behind, always too cautious, so Ruth could charge ahead knowing I'd always be there to catch her.

Ryan carefully tipped Ruth into a bend. Her laugh lit up the room. I'd have to be thicker than I was at twelve not to see those two falling for each other. Not that I minded. Ruth had been suffering more than I knew. This was the hope she'd been searching for. Another chance. And the farmer had proven himself a good sort. I trusted him. He was nothing like Matthew.

"Ruth looks like she's having fun." Lola's hand touched my shoulder before she settled into the chair beside me.

"Yeah."

Her eyes flicked around the empty table. "Still abandoned here on your lonesome?" Her smile was as perfect as those little hands of hers. "I let the church ladies corner me by the bar to give you some space. You seemed lost in your thoughts."

I lifted a shoulder. "There's a lot to think about."

"Do you want to talk about anything? My offer's still open if you want to go outside. We can escape all the noise"—she nodded at the crowd shuffling on the dance floor and waggled her eyebrows—"and the waltzing."

I shook my head. Her eyes dropped to her hands. She was probably feeling as on edge as I was, but...*because* of me. My heart twisted like an old dishrag.

Why did I keep following my father's rules? When had locking away my feelings ever helped me?

Maybe, once upon a time, it'd made me a good police officer, but a group of men in suits had decided a long time ago my days in a uniform were over. And every stupid step I'd taken to keep acting the way my father had drilled into me had already risked losing the precious woman sitting next to me.

"Lola, I..." My words stuck in my throat, but I wouldn't let those old fears beat me. "I'm not good with words, but I'll try to speak up more. Explain myself more. Not just walk away and keep you guessing. I promise. And that's an *actual* promise. Not one of those loophole promises."

Lola bit her lip in a nervous smile. Sweet girl. The best thing that ever happened to me.

"Incoming!"

Brooke was a blonde blur, delivering drinks from a tray balanced on one hand like it was nothing but air. I bet she was a waitress before she whipped the clinic into shape. Her new ginger-haired shadow trailed only a few steps behind. The kid flopped into his chair, still grinning like a dopey idiot, and the second Brooke emptied the tray, he snatched her waist and dragged her onto his lap.

Brooke's delighted squeal was like a love-dipped nail driving into my skull.

"Oh, brother," Lola giggled. She bumped her shoulder into mine. "We've created a love monster."

I grunted. No kidding.

"Hold still." Brooke squirmed in Harry's arms and reached over to snatch a napkin off the table. She zeroed in on the outline of red lips staining his cheek. "I didn't realise. There's a big red ma—"

"Hey, back off!" Harry jerked his head away. "No one's messing with my kiss mark. Not even you, Princess. Why don't you fix me up?" He tapped his other cheek with his index finger. "Gimme one on this side, too?"

Brooke didn't need to be asked twice. She smacked a matching red kiss on Harry's face, and he looked around proudly, chest puffed out, grinning like a fool. The dumb look on his face only got worse when Brooke jiggled in a dance and hummed along to the music.

The kid was in heaven, but this was my worst nightmare. The waltz had faded into the beat of something louder, faster, and every pound of the heavy bass splintered through my ears like broken pieces of wood.

I struggled to get in a breath. I was okay. Yeah. Just music. I could ignore the beat speeding up just like I ignored Harry's god-awful bangers playing on the radio sometimes.

I was only just clawing back a shred of control when a burst of rainbow lights lit up the dance floor. My eyes darted around, scrambling to get my bearings, a twinge of panic jolting through my fingers. I wouldn't be able to talk myself out of this one. There was no escaping Hell's Disco.

My gaze snapped to the dance floor. Flickers of blue and red swirled over Ruth's face. Even though her smile still beamed at me across the room, I was dizzy, the bile racing up my throat like I was back on the highway ten years ago.

"Aiden?"

I could barely hear Lola's voice above the roar of blood in my ears.

My hand bolted down to the table for support, desperate to keep myself grounded, my fingertips bleaching white. Just a little bit longer. I could do it.

"Aiden!"

Was that Harry?

I couldn't tell anymore. The lights made my mind hazy, old and new memories blurring into one. I tried to count to ten, reminding myself to breathe—just like Lola had taught me—but panic surged through my veins. No matter how many times I told myself to calm down, no air reached my lungs.

"Dancers, it's time to take it up a notch!"

The piercing screech of the microphone being dropped sliced through my last fragile thread of control.

Images of that dark night ten years ago hurtled faster than the squad car. And when the only noise I could hear was the constant tick of the indicator as I pulled out onto the highway, I shuddered a breath, clawing frantically to drag myself from the memory before it was too late.

But when I closed my eyes, raindrops danced in the fog of broken headlights. And then I shouldered my way out of the crumpled wreck onto the broken glass littered all over the road...

Fuck.

I bolted upright out of my chair. The squeal of wood on wood only pushed me closer to the edge. The chair tumbled to the ground, but I didn't stop to pick it up.

I had to get out of there.

Nothing else mattered. Not Harry stumbling to his feet, confused, his face scrunched up. Not Lola's frantic call after me.

I just had to get the hell out of there.

Ruth couldn't see me break.

Not ever.

27

She Saw How Much He Struggled

Lola

I CRACKED OPEN THE door. Just a tiny peek.

Sometimes, it paid to be cautious. I was venturing into the uncharted territory of the men's bathroom, and as much as I wanted to find Aiden, I really didn't need the unexpected sighting of a random man's penis—or *worse*—when I was off the clock.

My eyes skipped over the stalls. No doors shut. Not a soul in sight.

I nudged the door open a tiny bit wider.

A light flickered above the washbasins, a broken sun blinking on and off above Aiden's hunched shoulders. His hands braced the basin, his head hung low, and even though water gushed out of the tap, he didn't turn it off. His eyes were closed, and his mouth moved in a slow, steady beat. My heart twisted. He was counting.

"Aiden?"

He didn't answer.

He wasn't ignoring me. He was lost in the other world he disappeared to sometimes—the one where he hovered on the edge of something sudden and scary. That was a world where I was powerless. Nothing I did helped him.

I crept a few steps closer. "Aiden?"

Silence.

Still oblivious to me, he let out a frustrated sigh that echoed off the tiles. He cupped his hands under the tap, water sloshing around the porcelain as he splashed some onto his face before the whole routine started again. His hands went back to the sink, he bent forward, his shoulders slumped, and his eyes screwed shut.

I counted with him this time. He probably couldn't hear the click of my heels over the water gushing from the tap. I gnawed on my lip. I didn't want to scare him. Should I call out again? I didn't. But should I have?

Even though I didn't know the secret buttons that sent Aiden spiralling to his unknown hell, and even though I crossed the tiles on timid feet, I never felt like I walked on eggshells like when I'd lived with Chris. Anything and everything had flipped Chris's switch. What happened to Aiden was different. Whatever darkness swallowed him up, he fought it every step of the way.

Beside him, still unnoticed, I touched his back. "Aiden?"

His head jerked up. "Lola—what? Why are you...?" Wild eyes darted everywhere like he wasn't sure where to look. "This is the *men's* room."

I waved him off with a smile and leant my hip against the basin. "This is what I do... Hanging out in bathrooms... Saving the day." I twisted off the tap with a flourish and a silly *ta-da*. "Would you look at that? I'm kicking more superhero goals."

Relief fluttered in my chest when Aiden smiled. It was only the hint of a smile, but I'd take it. It meant he'd taken one step further away from the edge of his dark abyss.

My eyes wandered around the bathroom. No answers there. Hints of past visitors stained the floor around the urinals. And what on earth was that smell?

I scrunched my nose. "The men's bathroom is kinda gross."

"Kinda?" Aiden's face cracked in a genuine smile. "Try all kindas."

My heart fluttered to see some of the hard edges of his face soften. There he was. Grumpy but talking.

What now?

I'd had my own lonely moment like this in a public bathroom. When my world had been crumbling around me, a kind stranger offered her help. What had she said to me? *I know you'll find your strength one day.* I had. It had taken me months and so many doubts and false starts, but I'd found the courage all by myself. How much easier would it have been with someone by my side?

"You hit a bit of a wall back there," I said.

"Lola, I'm sorry." Haunted grey eyes lifted to meet mine. "I already broke our promise."

"What happened out there wasn't you running away from a tough conversation. Something bigger was going on." I stroked the silver hairs around his temples. "Up here."

Aiden's head dropped. My heart was an empty echo in my chest. Was he going to shut down again? Storm off? Tell me to take the hint like he'd done outside the coffee shop all those weeks ago?

His voice low and uncertain, he kept talking. He kept *trying*. "I panicked. I don't let Ruth or Harry see this side of me—especially after everything Harry went through growing up. The few times something's happened that I haven't been able to control, he's chalked it up to me being a grumpy bastard. I guess I am." Aiden lifted a shoulder. "You're the only one who's seen...*anything*. And... Lola... I can't begin to tell you how sorry I am that you had to see me like that. I'm usually more careful. I've figured out how to manage it over the years."

Years?

I blinked back the tears threatening to spill down my cheeks. Aiden had been dealing with these panic attacks for *years*? And all by himself? He was so close to Ruth... Why couldn't he let her see? He must have felt so...*alone*.

"I have a routine." Aiden rushed on, as if he needed my approval to confirm that he was doing the right thing. "I keep the flashbacks under control. I can stop them before they start." His sigh was defeated. "Most of the time."

"Have you talked to someone about this?"

"Sure. A whole group of doctors tried fixing me. They couldn't wait to write down a diagnosis. Six men in suits sitting on a panel read it out to me before they ended my career. Everything I ever worked for." His laugh was bitter. "They took my whole identity with the swipe of a damn pen."

"Are you comfortable sharing your diagnosis with me?"

His head bowed. The silence stretched on and on. "PTSD."

My chest caved in. Post-traumatic stress disorder was a serious condition. Flashbacks. Nightmares. Uncontrollable anxiety. Police officers were prone to it. Had he suffered from his work? Something else? I couldn't imagine the horrifying things he must have lived through for his mind to splinter into a world so dark.

"Oh, Aiden—"

"Don't you dare pity me."

"I care about you. I *worry* about you. Have the flashbacks been getting worse lately? Like the day at the clinic? Was that your worst episode?"

"No." Aiden wouldn't meet my gaze. Even a hesitant touch to his shoulder didn't help ease the tension holding him together this time. "That...wasn't the worst..."

Dread prickled in tiny spikes all over my skin. He avoided my eyes as much as he avoided my question. He'd mentioned so many times that he wanted to protect me. Was that what he thought he was doing now? Was that what he'd tried to do before?

"Was the worst at my place?" I urged him cautiously.

"You...have a clock..."

"Is that why you left that night?"

"Lola, I wanted to stay. I'm usually so careful, but that night..." His fist clenched by his side. "I was so damn selfish. I ignored all the signs because all I wanted was to be with you, but... I stayed too long..." Frustrated, angry with himself, he thumped his fist into his thigh. "Everything went to shit. When the flashbacks get bad, I don't always know where I am or what I'm doing. I can't stop the memories. They're everywhere. *Everything.* I've lashed out before. Smashed stuff. Come back to the present with bruises on my hands." His eyes were almost wild again, and his breath was jagged, coming too fast. "I couldn't risk anything happening to you."

"Hey, it's okay..." I ran gentle fingers down his neck. The tension in his jaw eased. "If this is too much, we can stop. We can talk about something else. Anything you want. Ruth's quest for victory. Harry earning the love of the Sunshine Princess." I slapped my hands against my knees. "Hey, now, what about that cricket match last week?"

I had absolutely no idea about cricket, and Aiden knew it. A smile ghosted on his lips.

"Is your offer still open?" He swallowed heavily and glanced an apprehensive look over my shoulder to the door.

No one was there. Only the dulled beats of music drifting from the bar filled the silence of the bathroom. I finally understood. He was scared, still chained dangerously close to another flashback.

"I don't think I'm ready to go back yet." He confirmed my suspicion with a sad smile. "Maybe we can go outside for a few minutes. Shake the last of it."

I gave him my answer by lacing my fingers through his, and I tugged him away from the basin.

Aiden's eyes rounded, but he followed on unsteady feet. Every few steps, his gaze locked on our linked hands, his brows knitted together, confused, like he couldn't believe it. I floated along beside him. A shy blush crept up my cheeks. Maybe I couldn't believe it, either.

After we pushed through the side doors, the noise of the bar drifted further away. I wobbled along in the silly heels Brooke had chosen for me, trying not to sink into the grass as we followed the worn stone pavers to the garden.

I sat on one of the wooden benches and patted the spot next to me. Aiden stared at my hand. Then he stared at me. He didn't budge. I tapped my palm on the bench again. With a wary glance from the corner of his eye, Aiden eased down beside me.

"This isn't how I wanted tonight to go," he said.

"It hasn't all been bad. Ruth's kicking butt at this Games Night thing. I'm certain she's going home with that pamper hamper she's had her eyes on."

"She hates all that stuff, you know. Skin care and bath bombs—that's for *girls*." He smiled and bumped my shoulder. "She wants that one because it's the biggest."

I laughed. "Okay, well, what about how you helped Harry?"

Aiden grunted. "I should've kept my trap shut. All those dopey grins and the kissing and the squealing." He pretended to be annoyed, but I could see the smile in his eyes. "I had no idea that pair would be so..."

"Nauseatingly happy?"

"Yeah." His smile suddenly faded, and his eyes flickered uneasily between my face and his hands. "Those are all good things, but... I wish..." He trailed off, finishing his thoughts only with a shake of his head.

"What?" I prompted gently with another bump to his shoulder.

A splash of warmth darkened his cheeks. "I wish... I'd asked... if you'd dance with me."

My stomach dipped like I was already dancing. "I would've said yes." I grimaced. "But I wasn't kidding when I said I have more left feet than Ryan."

"Barb's years of forcing all those dance recitals didn't help, huh?"

I grimaced. "The dance school eventually asked her very gently *not* to bring me back."

"What about a slow waltz? I could teach you," he offered. "If you want to give it a try?"

"Now?"

Aiden's chin dipped. His silent yes.

He braced his hands on his knees, stood up, and pulled his phone out of the back pocket of his pants. A few swipes and taps at his screen, and music floated around us, soft and slow, like dandelion seeds disappearing on the night air. He offered his hand to me, and the guarded hope in his eyes bloomed into a satisfied smile when I rested my palm in his.

"Okay, this hand here"—he guided my hand to rest on his shoulder—"and mine goes here." His big palm anchored on my back. Apprehension clouded his eyes, and he whispered, "Is this...okay? Not too close?"

I wanted to whisper that it wasn't close enough. We hadn't taken a single step, but butterflies already danced and twirled in my stomach. I couldn't make any words come out of my mouth. I rested my cheek against Aiden's shirt, the linen warm from his broad chest, and his smell the familiar lullaby of fresh soap I remembered from all those weeks ago.

Aiden counted again, but this time, it wasn't to battle through a panic attack. He moved with quiet patience, leading me through the unfamiliar pattern, stepping to one and two, three and four, five and six. It was pure magic. He smiled—one of the rare genuine smiles that lit up his face, all the way to his eyes. Gorgeous. My heart stuttered.

All my careful focus on the confusing steps disappeared. My heel clomped down hard on his foot.

Aiden choked back a grunt of pain.

"Whoops." My shoulders hiked up around my ears. "Sorry."

"It's okay, love. I've got you." He pulled back to look down at me with a smile. "Want to try a little spin?"

My head bobbed in an eager nod.

He chuckled. "Sweet girl. One...and...two...and..."

Our hands rose, and I twirled, my dress fanning in an excited whirl. Dizzy in the best way, I laughed and melted back into Aiden, my head resting against the safety of his chest. The thump of my heart raced so much faster than the steady pulse of the music and the awkward shuffles of our feet.

Could he hear how breathless I was, even though we were barely moving?

"Thank you," he whispered. "For being there for me..."

He didn't need to thank me for that. "Thank you for the dance..."

And for the beautiful new memory that chased the fading nightmare even further away.

28

He Saw Her Compassion

Aiden

"I could've sworn..." Cocking my head, I lowered my book, listening.

Wind. Birds. Yeah, there it was again. A quiet knock tapped at the door.

I snapped my book shut and hopped off the couch. A glance at my watch, and my brows bunched together. A little after midday. Too early for Ruth. Her instructions had been *very* clear.

Ruth

> Be ready to bring lunch at two... unless something pops up.

And the mystery visitor wouldn't be Harry. He never bothered knocking. He just swung the door open and barged inside—usually with his boots still on, tramping dirt all over the hardwood floors.

My book slid across the dining table as I passed. The door eased open. I blinked.

I'm dreaming.

Lola stood on the veranda, her back to me, her eyes roaming the valley below. Blonde wisps escaped the high ponytail sweeping her hair back, and she was dressed simply in a loose white T-shirt, jeans, and sneakers. *Pink* sneakers.

I cleared my throat. That would wake me up. I had to be sleepwalking. "Lola?" I managed to croak.

She turned, her cheeks flushed almost as pink as her sneakers. "Hi!" A soft laugh. Was she nervous? "That view... It's so beautiful up here."

I stood there, my hand frozen on the door, my mouth hanging open. Words deserted me. Lola was at my house. It was like winning the lottery. No. What was better than that?

She was *at* my *house*.

Lola's smile wavered. "Do I look like a wreck?" Self-conscious, she reached a hand to smooth her hair. "It's windy this high up. And hillier. I'm not as fit as I could be." Another of her laughs tingled over my skin. "Maybe I should have agreed to go to one of those classes with Brooke."

Wait. Hold up, one second. "You walked here?"

She nodded. "It only took about forty minutes."

Forty minutes! Panic surged to life in my chest. "Lola, that's not safe! There's no path. You have to walk along the road." I speared a hand through my hair. "What if a car—"

"I'm fine." Her fingertips grazed my forearm to reassure me she was okay. "You have the only house this way. So, unless you or Harry are burning a trail up the mountain, I'm perfectly fine. Nothing to worry about! Anyway, forget all that. Sorry I'm late."

I frowned. "Late?"

"For lunch." She held up a pink container. "Dessert, as requested."

My frown didn't budge. I stared at her, more confused than ever.

"It's a brown butter cheesecake! Ruth said…" Lola trailed off, her shoulders sagging when she sighed. "You didn't know I was coming…did you?"

I shook my head.

"Ruth set me up?"

"I think she set us both up. I've got a chicken and leek pot pie in the oven, which I have a suspicion might be one of your favourites. The last time I baked a pie, Ruth accused me of being the reincarnation of Nana Wilks. It's old people's food, apparently." I shot Lola a wry smile. "She told me to bring it down to her place at two… unless something popped up."

And something had *definitely* popped up. The *best* thing.

Lola's sigh was defeated. "Aiden, I'm sorry. I wish everyone would stop interfering."

"I won't lie and say I'm sad you're here." I was damn near thrilled she was standing at my front door. "I like spending time with you. But if you'd prefer not to spend time with me, I understand. Let me drive you home, though. I'll be a wreck worrying about you marching along the road to get back to town."

Lola leant forward, just enough to get her head in the doorway. She took a big sniff. "If that's a chicken pie in the oven… And I've already baked this nice cheesecake…" The bite of her lip was all nerves. "It seems a shame not to enjoy them."

Was this happening? "You'll…stay?" Now I *knew* I had to be dreaming.

"If…you'd…like?"

I didn't even pause to check my mouth. "I want that more than anything in the whole world." A split second later, the stupidity of how desperate that sounded hit me, and I let out an awkward laugh. "Or, um… yeah. Sure. Stay." I lifted a shoulder.

Lola smirked. "No big deal, huh?"

I shook it all off with a smile.

A few twirls, arms everywhere, and her bag hung on the rack by the door, her pink sneakers were off, and the cheese-cake was safely deposited in the fridge.

"Oh!" Her tiny feet scurried across the wooden floor. "Look at all your books!"

"Uh, yeah... I enjoy reading."

"It's like a library! Oh!" Her hand shot out for *The Count of Monte Cristo*, but when her fingers brushed the spine, she quickly pulled her hand back. "S-sorry. I shouldn't—"

"Of course you should. Here." I slid the book off the shelf and handed it to her. "Would you like to borrow it?"

Her eyes swept over the cover. "Can I?"

"Yeah, of course. If you want, you can take the antique set—"

"Oh no! Not your special editions. This one will do. I just want to read it." Smiling, she hugged the book to her chest. "We've talked about it so many times. I'd love to be able to add my thoughts to our conversations."

She could add her thoughts about cement to our conversations, and I'd still listen. I just liked hearing her voice. And those laughs...

"Lunch will be ready soon," I said. "Can I get you something to drink? I don't have anything homemade to offer you, but I have some wine... Red... White..."

"White? If you have a Pinot..." Longing eyes drifted to the deck overlooking the valley. "Can we sit outside?"

"To answer your first question, I have a local Pinot Grigio you can try. As for the second, I'll leave it up to you to pick a nice spot for us... I'll only be a minute."

That minute ended up being five. I bent over the sink, sucking in air, trying to calm my nerves enough to get the bottle of wine open. It was only a damn screw top, but the sweat on my palms made getting the lid off almost impossible.

It wasn't my cock talking—although that appendage wasn't helping the situation. My heart thumped in my chest, pounding faster seeing Lola's things in my space, watching her fingers skim the wooden table I'd made, and hearing her contented hum when she flopped on the outdoor lounge. I loved her being there.

Don't screw this up, idiot. This can't end like last time.

After grabbing the bottle of wine, two glasses, and a rushed platter of cheese and crackers in my hands, I wrestled enough control back to head outside.

"Ruth sent me three pictures of potential locations for the Games Night trophy," Lola said, reaching for the wine glass when I offered it to her.

"Yeah? Which spot did you choose?"

"The shelf above her potted herbs. You?"

"The entry table. That way she can crow about it whenever someone stops by for a visit."

Lola grinned. "A solid suggestion." Her eyes darted to the side. "And, um... not to become the next church lady or anything, but..."

I sank onto the lounge beside her. Not *right* beside. A gap. A *respectable* gap. But close enough to smell her familiar coconut shampoo and whatever new perfume she wore.

"But?" I prompted.

"I *may* have spotted a hat on her dining table in one of the photos."

"A hat, huh?"

"Mmhmm. A hat that looks suspiciously like the one Ryan Hollyoak wears sometimes."

"You don't say."

"I don't. I'm only *thinking* I saw it there." She zipped her lips. "I won't be telling a single soul other than you." Her eyes drifted back over the valley. "I'm happy for them."

"Me too."

A comfortable silence settled between the two of us. There was never any pressure to fill the quiet with too many words. With a faint smile on her lips, Lola sipped her wine, twirling the glass in her fingers as she gazed over the rolling grass and tufted treetops.

Being with her was so effortless. Too easy. Dangerously familiar.

I ruined it all.

"It was my fault," I said.

Lola's head turned, a crease between her pale brows.

"Ruth's accident was my fault."

Staring at the mole dotted on my thumb seemed easier than looking at Lola after blurting out my darkest secret. She set her wine glass down with a clumsy clink, but she didn't bolt for the door. She edged closer on the lounge until her jeans pressed against mine.

My gut clenched in a tight knot. Why *was* Lola still sitting here? I slid a wary glance to her. Why did she push up her glasses and smile at me so sweetly instead of storming off in disgust? She *should* storm off. That was the reaction I was waiting for. That was the one I deserved.

Lola's hand squeezed my knee. "Lost in your thoughts again?"

I hid the surprise of her touch by shrugging.

"Do you want to talk more about what you said?" she asked. "If you want to try... I want to listen."

"I've, um... Yeah." I let out a slow breath, but my chest still felt too tight. "I've never really talked about this stuff with anyone before."

"Ruth's accident was such a long time ago. You've been carrying this on your shoulders all these years without talking to anyone?"

"Some things are better left unsaid."

I wanted to laugh at myself. Some things? More like...*every-thing*.

In the months since I'd screwed up with Lola, I'd only existed by floating from one of her smiles to the next. Before her, I'd barely existed at all. Ruth and Harry were all that had kept me going most days, and for a long time, that was enough. They were both important to me.

But honestly... I was *tired*. And, selfishly, I wanted more.

I wanted to cuddle Lola on my couch. I wanted to bring her eggs and milk because she always forgot to stock up. I wanted to hold her hand and kiss her on the cheek and tell her I'd missed her when she came home from work.

I loved that girl right down to her adorable pink toenails, and if I had any hope of ever being with her, I needed to be honest. That was what we'd promised each other, wasn't it?

But where did you start when you needed to tell someone *everything*? The beginning? Maybe not the very beginning—like how I was born in the back of a Mitsubishi Sigma on the way to my aunt's barbecue—but to the beginning that mattered.

"You, um..." I swallowed heavily. "You said you spent some time with Ruth while I was away?"

Lola's face brightened. "We hung out a few times."

"Did she talk much about her life on the mainland?"

"Ruth spent all her time talking about *your* life on the mainland. I've been subjected to her never-ending sales pitch. Let's see..." Lola started ticking my achievements off on her fingers. "School captain. Football captain. Model citizen. Oh my, and how handsome you looked in your tux for the high school formal."

I groaned. "She *didn't*."

"Oh, yeah, big guy." Lola grinned. "Ruth got out *all* her photo albums. She even showed me newspaper clippings of your heroic deeds."

I sank lower on the lounge. "Tell me you're joking."

Lola shook her head, but her smile faded, her expression becoming serious. "Ruth told me you were a police officer. All the photos and articles... You seemed born for it..."

"I was. There were four generations of McKinnon police before me. My father was so damn proud when I was promoted to sergeant." That was about the last time he was proud of me, too. "Ruth was a cop."

"She flipped through those pages so quickly, but I saw a couple of photos." Lola forced a tight smile. "I didn't ask any questions. She seemed—I don't know—not herself."

Those words were a punch in the gut. "Life was good until it wasn't. Does she still have any pictures of Matthew?"

"I'm...not sure... I don't think so. Who's that?"

"Ruth's ex-husband. He left...after..." My fist clenched by my side.

"After the accident?"

"*Because* of the accident. After the first couple of visits, he stopped coming to the hospital. That weak bastard said he couldn't deal with it. Ruth was so damn brave. She got through all the surgeries and all the rehab on her own."

"You were there, though."

I jerked my chin down in a nod. "Every day. I would've been there anyway, but it was the least I could do...after...after what I did."

A shudder raced through me. My gaze retreated to the valley and landed on the magpies nesting in the twisted arms of the eucalyptus trees, a jury of a hundred accusing eyes. My pulse surged.

No way. I was out of here. I was done.

But I barely got my backside off the lounge before Lola stopped me. Her fingers wrapped around my hand, and she held tight.

"Stay," she whispered. "You're brave, too."

Brave? Me?

The only thing firing courage in my veins was Lola. Her hand clutched mine, and her head fell against my shoulder. She was still there. Without her, I was shit scared to relive this moment.

"You were with her when it happened?" Lola asked.

I nodded. "Ruth and I were on duty together when dispatch called through some teenagers who'd stolen a car." My voice wavered and scratched like an old record wobbling around a worn-out turntable. "They were joyriding on the country highway and making a damn nuisance of themselves. A couple of drivers had reported near misses."

I scrubbed a flannel cuff over my eyes. It didn't help. The hot sting of tears still burned.

Fuck.

I struggled in a jagged breath. Nope. Didn't help. I bent over, the heels of my palms pressed roughly into my eyes.

Lola's hand touched softly on my back. "Aiden?"

I screwed my eyes shut. All my careful control was unravelling, and the more Lola soothed her fingers in a circle on my back, the quicker the threads untied.

"Visibility was shit. It was night. It was pouring. All fucking excuses. I should've known better. When I pulled onto the highway, it all happened so fast. Headlights headed for us in the wrong lane. A truck. I made a split-second decision. The only thing I could see was"—I swallowed—"was—"

"Oh, Aiden. This is too much for you. We can stop now."

No. I couldn't stop now. The truth wanted to flood out, and nothing was going to stop it. Not me trying to block it out. Not Lola jolting up from the lounge, her arms hugging around my shoulders and burying my face against the warm, protective curve of her belly. Nothing.

"I swerved right. A car pulled out from behind the truck. Those stupid damn teenagers. The truck had switched to the other lane, thinking they'd go past. I didn't see them until it was too late." I wrapped my arms around Lola, dragging her warmth as close to me as I could, burying my face deeper into her stomach as the first strangled sob escaped me. "If I hadn't gone right..."

My weight collapsed into her, the soft cotton of her white T-shirt growing damp beneath my cheek. How long did I cry? I never cried. My ribs ached, burning from the pain of those memories and the sobs that escaped me in tortured gasps after being trapped deep inside me for so many years.

"Aiden," Lola whispered as she stroked her fingers through my hair. "What happened was an accident. It wasn't your fault."

She was wrong.

I lifted my chin. "It *was* my fault. If I'd turned left..."

Lola cupped my face in her hands. "A *different* tragedy would have happened."

"But Ruth would've been spared. So would those kids not wearing their bloody seatbelts. I would've taken the hit, and everyone else would've walked away without a scratch."

"You don't know that."

"I do, Lola. I *do*."

"If they did an investigation—"

"I don't care if that exonerated me of any fault. Look at Ruth, Lola. Look at her! You can't say I'm not to blame when my best friend was...was... God, Lola. Those *kids*."

"Aiden, you need to be kinder to yourself. *Fairer* to yourself." She brushed the hair off my forehead, and her lips curved in a tender smile that any other day would've made my heart flip upside down. "I know you don't trust doctors, but you need to talk to someone about what happened." Her lips were even more tender when they pressed down on the top of my head.

I swiped at my face with the sleeve of my flannel. Not because the warnings of my father still echoed in my mind, but because Lola didn't think I was weak. Somehow, that made me feel stronger. She didn't judge me for falling apart sometimes, and she knew how it felt to be stuck in old memories on repeat.

"I used to see a shrink years ago," I said. "I stopped going. I didn't think I needed it anymore." Truthfully, I hated reliving what I'd done. "I've been thinking about going back lately. Maybe it'll help with the flashbacks...the panic attacks... But, Lola, talking won't change what happened that night."

"No, it won't, but it will help you deal with the nights still to come. Please, don't keep wading through the mud of these thoughts on your own."

"What about you?"

"I'm not a psychiatrist, but I'm here to talk any time you want. Thank you for trusting me enough to share that, Aiden. I know it wasn't easy."

"No, but..."

How could I explain that the iron grip around my chest had started to give? That somehow, just saying the words out loud, it felt safe to breathe again?

I think she knew. Somehow, Lola always did. Her gentle smile reappeared. "Here's what we're going to do next. You listening?"

"Y-yeah?"

"I'm going to sit on your lap and hug the absolute hell out of you because I think you need that more than anything. And when you've had your fill of cuddles, we're going to eat the amazing chicken pot pie you have in the oven, sip our wine, and talk. Books. The past. Anything you want—except *Soccer Mum Socialites*."

I chuckled. "And then?"

"We try the cheesecake, and well before the sun sets, you can drive me home."

"I love the sound of this day."

Especially the hugging part, but I kept that to myself.

29

She Saw a Future with Him

Lola

AIDEN SLID HIS REUSABLE coffee cup across the counter.

The girl taking his order blinked. A line furrowed between her eyebrows. "Uh..." She blinked again. "So..."

Something in her brain short-circuited when she looked at that cup. Was it because it was bright pink? Or was it the sparkly unicorns pooping rainbows that made her thoughts fizzle? Personally, I thought the cup was adorable.

Aiden shrugged away her confused look the same way he pretended all Harry's wacky gifts were no big deal. But if you knew when to look, a smile peeked from his beard when he presented the cup to the barista. It was the same smile he tried to hide when he showed me another pair of his silly socks or talked about the wonky birdhouse Harry had built him years ago.

Those smiles were proof of the final skeleton hiding in Aiden's closet—he was nothing but a sentimental softy.

The girl behind the counter fritzed back to life. "What'll you have?"

Aiden shook off a yawn. "A latte, please," he ground out. "Actually—wait." His fingers speared through his hair. "Make it a double shot."

My eyebrows popped up. This was new. How tired was he? "A *double* shot?"

Aiden barely nodded. Dark circles framed his eyes, and even though he often frowned, there was an extra heaviness to the lines around his mouth. "You're right. That won't cut it." He turned back to the barista. "Make it a triple shot, please."

He slumped his hip against the counter, one hand fumbling in the back pocket of his jeans for his wallet, his other hand fighting off another yawn.

Scratch tired—he was *exhausted*.

A sneaky grin spread across my face. Finally, this was my chance. The five times Aiden had paid for my coffee were five times too many. I was treating him whether he liked it or not. I darted forward. He didn't know what hit him. He was only just flipping open his wallet when my hand launched across the counter to tap my card and pay.

"Lola," Aiden's tired voice pleaded. "I invited you for coffee. I should pay."

I didn't bother trying to hide my frustration. My arms folded across my chest, and I stared him dead in the eyes. "You promised I could treat you next time," I huffed. "And that was at least three coffee dates ago."

Aiden's eyes rounded, suddenly wide-awake. "D-dates?"

"Oh." My eyes skipped nervously over the cookie jars lined up on the counter. "When you started inviting me out for coffee, I thought... Isn't this...? Were these not...?"

"Yes!" Aiden blurted. "I want that." He gulped. "If you do. Do you want them to be dates?"

Shyness forced my eyes to my sandals. All I could do was nod. When I dared to look up, a softness crinkled the corners of Aiden's eyes. He was smiling, too.

With our coffees in hand, we wandered side by side to the table in the back. I dropped into the chair by the window. Aiden collapsed into the one beside me. Even slumped over, he still looked comically oversized at the tiny café table. His big hand covered his face in another yawn.

I slid his coffee closer to him. "Didn't get much sleep while you were in Hobart?"

"Not a wink," Aiden grumbled.

"Were you worried about your appointment with the psychiatrist?"

"No." Another tired grumble. "My problem was Harry." He threw a helpless look over the rim of his cup. "That's the last time I let him tag along. He kept me up all night."

"Does he snore?"

"I wish. There wasn't much sleeping going on. He was like a twelve-year-old at his first slumber party. He gushed about Brooke for hours. Do I need to spend half the night figuring out if she likes macaroni? Yes. I do."

I laughed. "I think it's sweet how Harry is completely gaga over Brooke."

Aiden grunted. "You wouldn't think it was so sweet if his phone was shoved in your face at one in the morning. He blathered on and on about rings. Rubies or garnets. Princess cut or oval cut. I make furniture. What the hell do I know about jewellery?"

I sipped my coffee, careful to keep my face neutral even though I wanted to squeal. *Rings!* "Is Harry...?" I froze. Surely not. "It's way too soon!"

"It is." Aiden's smile turned coy. "You know nothing."

I pretended to zip my lips shut, but I wriggled in my seat, too much excitement bubbling in my veins.

Aiden's eyebrow arched. "Can you keep a secret, Lola?"

"Yes." A grin escaped. "Okay, no." I laughed. "I will *try*. Promise." I zipped my lips again.

Aiden flashed a smile, but it faded quickly. His finger traced the rim of his cup, and he sat silent, lost in his thoughts. It was a long time before he spoke again.

"My, um, appointment," he said. "I think it went well."

"So, the psychiatrist we found turned out to be okay?"

"Yeah, I think he's a good fit for me. He sees a lot of ex-cops and return veterans. The appointment was long. The shrink asked a lot of questions. Some of the questions... Yeah." His eyes lowered to his cup and stayed there. "Going back over old ground was harder than I thought."

"It would've been difficult to open up about what you've been through."

"It was. You've been seeing someone, too, though. It gets easier, right?"

"It does. The first few appointments I had were hard, but now it's like catching up with a friend who's a great listener. No judgement, just help. Take it slow and remember to be kind to yourself all the days in between." I sipped my coffee. "Will you keep going?"

He nodded. "Once a month in the city and on the phone the other weeks. I'm trying to be realistic. I know I'll never be a hundred percent. I doubt I was before the accident, either, but I don't want to keep pretending I'm okay. I want to get better."

"I'm so incredibly proud of you."

Aiden tried to shrug off the compliment, ducking his head so I wouldn't see the rosy hint on his cheeks. Too late. I saw it—and his red ears, too. Ruth had told me to look out for those.

"So, uh..." Aiden cleared his throat. "How have you been? How's the book going?"

My shoulders scrunched up to my ears. "I finished it last night."

"Already? It's a solid effort to get through *The Count of Monte Cristo* that quickly."

"Oh, Aiden, I couldn't put it down! I was hooked when I read the first page. I barely moved off my couch all weekend." Aiden's soft smile only encouraged me to gush even more. "How had I never read it before? How did I exist in the world before I knew Dantès and Faria? It was the most perfect of all perfect books. Thank you so much for letting me borrow it."

"Thank you so much for reading it. I'm glad you liked it."

I grinned over the top of my coffee. "What if I'd hated it?"

"Then we'd shake hands, part company, and never speak to each other again. I can't be friends with anyone who doesn't love the Count."

"Really?"

"Of course not." He laughed. "We can have different opinions. It doesn't bother me. Ruth hated *The Count of Monte Cristo*. She didn't even make it out of the Château d'If before she threw the book across the room. *Literally*." He lifted his hair to show me a faint triangular scar on his forehead. "You wouldn't believe the air she got on that thing."

My heart swelled. He rarely acted like this. Playful? Joking? This wasn't Aiden. Or maybe...this *was* Aiden, but a version of him that few people ever saw. Had Ruth seen him like this? Did she miss seeing this side of him as much as I wanted to see more of it? I grinned. Well, she probably didn't miss the reading part.

Aiden's hand covered mine, and he leant closer. *"All human wisdom is contained in two words,"* he recited softly. *"Wait and hope."*

My stomach twisted in a hundred knots. Even though I knew those were the last words in the book we both treasured, the guarded look in his eyes hinted that they meant so much more. He was waiting, hoping, but for what? For me?

"I'll wait." His steady gaze promised he would. "But do I have a right to hope?" He swallowed. "Will you ever be able to forgive me?"

"I forgive you."

He frowned. "But?"

"It's hard to forget what happened between us. I understand why you acted the way you did, but you know my story. I don't always trust myself to make good decisions. I see you're trying. I *know* you're trying. But my history... and our history..." I bit my lip. "I'm sorry. I know that's probably not the answer you want to hear."

"Forget what I want to hear. What do *you* want, Lola?"

My eyes popped open. "I want..." I faltered.

No one had ever asked me that before. What *did* I want? The fairytale? Maybe something even better? Should I let the words gush out and allow Aiden to choose if he wanted to be part of my fantasies?

Yes.

Just once.

Yes.

"I want a life with someone," I said. "I tell myself I'm brave... I'm strong... I know I can do it on my own, but I don't want to. I want someone who walks beside me, and holds my hand, but watches out for me so I don't stumble in the puddles. I want to be with someone who doesn't control me or dictate what I can wear, where I can go, or who I can be friends with. I never want to put my key in the lock and worry about what's waiting for me when I open the door. I want to laugh and share kisses and make love...every day...and...maybe"—I grinned—"get a cat."

He chuckled. "A cat, huh?"

"Yes. And I get to name him anything I want."

The smile on Aiden's lips faded almost as quickly as it had appeared. Was that too much? I nibbled down on my lower lip, nervous the longer he stayed lost in his thoughts.

Aiden's voice was strained when he finally spoke again. "I hate that bastard stole so much from you that you wish for simple things you should expect and not have to hope for."

"I'm happy to hope for simple things. For a long time, even that didn't seem possible. Every day it feels easier to want a little more, and every day I look less to the past and more to the future. I want you to be part of my future—I *do*. I'm just not sure if it's..." I trailed off with a shrug.

"Lola, there's no rush. Not for a relationship...or anything else. I like spending time with you, and I think you like spending time with me, too. You want more, you say so. You want to do your own thing, read your books, or watch that awful TV show with the girls, you say so."

"Really?"

"Your life is yours. I want to be a part of it, but I'm willing to wait and earn my place—whatever that place turns out to be."

"What if it takes me a long time to fully trust you?"

"Then it takes you a long time. I waited thirty-seven years of my life to meet you, and I've got a real nice place up on the mountain." He answered my confused look with a smile. "That means I'm patient, and I'm not going anywhere."

"What if I want to take things in the bedroom...*slow?*"

"Then we take things slow. Lola, we're working on your list here. I know I need to prove myself. And I know words don't mean much, but I'm going to say them anyway. I'll never try to control you. Keep your bank account. See your friends. Wear whatever you want and live your life any damn way you choose. You decide who's lucky enough to help you through the puddles and make special memories for when you're old and grey. I hope that lucky jerk is me, but if it's not, I hope we can still be friends."

My list. My wants. The memories I wanted to create. My heart twisted. If I were honest with myself, I already knew what I wanted. I was still scared, but I knew.

Right now, the only memories I wanted to make were with *him*.

Be brave.

I took a deep breath. "What if I want to go on a real date? Not coffee. Not lunch. A proper romantic dinner date."

Disbelief flashed across Aiden's face. Then a big smile. He shook off all the emotions by clearing his throat to finally say, "Then I guess we're going on a romantic dinner date."

"Anywhere I want?"

Aiden eyed me warily. "As long as it's nowhere near the church, we're going anywhere you want."

"Oh, darn," I teased. "And after I promised Yolanda."

Aiden almost turned green, but he didn't say no. "What about, uh..." He cleared his throat. "The bar? Or the little winery just outside town?"

I squirmed in my seat. A romantic dinner date. "Tonight? If you're not too tired?"

"I can't say no to you, sweet girl. Tonight." He tapped the rim of his coffee cup. "I might need a couple more of these, but Hollyoak's stupid horses couldn't keep me away."

I threw my arms around his shoulders and planted a kiss on his shocked face. A grin was on mine. That same grin popped out of nowhere for the rest of the day. Brooke, my patients—everyone noticed. But it seemed like no one was surprised to hear me squeal that I was going on a date with Aiden.

A romantic dinner date!

I hadn't been on a proper date since... I couldn't remember when. A lifetime of bad memories had passed, but I was determined to finally put them all behind me. I was looking forward to my future and choosing my own path.

I practically skipped home in the dark from the clinic.

Next door's curtains didn't flutter to the side like they usually did when I swung the gate open, but I still waved a quick hello as I raced down the stone path.

I pressed my shoulder against the front door, and with two powerful shoves, the stupid thing finally groaned open. My hand fumbled for the light switch as I slipped my bag off my shoulder, dumping it by the door as I toed off my shoes. One off, my body went still.

Something wasn't right.

I fumbled again for the light switch. I flipped it on. Nothing.

Down. Up. Down. Still nothing.

Balls.

The ancient bulb must have blown. It wasn't the first time, and it wouldn't be the last. The tiny cottage had seen better days, and I was forever finding things that needed fixing. All good. The back porch light was on, and enough rusty yellow light trickled down the hallway for me not to trip over my own feet.

I arched through the doorway to my bedroom and fumbled for the switch. Up. Down. Up. Nothing. I stepped back into the hallway, my eyes squinting at feet that almost disappeared in the dark. Was the power out? But...then...how was the porch light on?

My head slowly turned.

The kitchen loomed only a few steps away. A cold sweat prickled across my skin, my nerves coiling tighter with every step I padded closer, my mind screaming for me to turn back to the front door.

My eyes frantically bounced from shadow to shadow. The kitchen counters were bare. No pans glistened under the light flickering from the back porch. Where was the mess I'd made at breakfast? I'd stayed up too late reading *The Count of Monte Cristo*. I'd overslept and didn't have time to do the dishes.

Wait.

Did I?

I pushed up my glasses and pressed my palm into my eyes. Was I losing my marbles? Or was I just that tired? Maybe I should have had one of Aiden's triple-shot coffees...

I shuffled on wobbly legs the last few steps to the doorway. My hand reached for the light switch. Blood roared in my ears. *No.*

Fear raced like ice through my veins and froze me to the scuffed wooden floors. My knees were weak, my whole body shaking, but I couldn't make my feet move.

A silhouette darkened a seat at the dining table, sitting prim and tall, hands clasped. Nothing made him disappear. No matter how many times I blinked, he still sat there.

Terror clawed every inch of my neck to silence my scream before I could open my mouth.

"Hello, Lola." Icy blue eyes lifted to mine, the flicker from the porch just bright enough to light the edge of his cruel smile. "Did you miss me?"

30

She Saw the Devil

Lola

"LOLA." CHRIS'S VOICE WAS a sweetened razor. "I asked you a question."

He rose from the table like a snake, slow, deliberate, every movement calculated to intimidate. The mottled shadows of the kitchen didn't hide his slicked-back blond hair or the perfectly pressed lines of his crisp, white shirt and dark trousers. He'd always worn an expensive skin to conceal the monster underneath.

My glasses slipped down my nose, but I didn't push them up. And when the icy tips of Chris's fingers reached out to trail a line of goosebumps down my arm, I didn't flinch. I didn't dare.

His head tilted. Waiting. I knew this dance. He wanted a smile to go with the answer to his question.

I forced my lips to curve. "I—I missed you."

He pressed a soulless kiss to the corner of my mouth. "That's my girl."

His girl? Not anymore.

I wasn't the same shell of a person who'd escaped him six months ago. I was battered around the edges, but I was whole. I was my own person now. Even though fierce determination ignited inside me, I was careful to hide it. I had the scars to prove that challenging Chris never ended well.

His fingers coiled around my arm. He dragged me closer and squeezed me so tight against his chest that the sting of his expensive cologne burned my nose.

"Do you know how upset you made me when I came home from work and you weren't there?" The dulled ends of his fingernails bit into my skin. "Do you know how embarrassing it was explaining to everyone that you'd disappeared after another one of your...outbursts?"

"You said that when you came home that night, you—you were going to—"

"Oh, Lola. You've always been too sensitive. Why can't you ever remember anything the way it happened?"

I lifted my chin. Defiance boiled beneath my skin. I wouldn't let him rewrite that moment in our history.

Chris always called me crazy. For a long time, I'd believed him. But my memory still burned with the sharp flash of his eyes as he'd stood over me, belt raised, while I'd shielded myself with nothing but my own bruised arms. He'd said I'd made him late for work for the last time. The ice in his voice had been more than a threat. He'd meant it.

I remembered that moment better than I remembered what I'd had for breakfast. That was the moment I'd vowed he'd never put his hands on me again.

Another slimy kiss pressed to my cheek. "Be a good girl for once." His fingers twisted tighter around my arm. "Tell me you're sorry."

Never.

Chris's lip twitched. My defiance was unexpected, but his jaw clenched, determination flashing in his cold eyes. The cruel grip of his hand squeezing around my arm reminded me how dangerously close I was to unleashing his anger. I breathed through the pain, but his eyes narrowed, and his hand twisted and twisted.

He broke me.

"I—I'm sorry," I whispered.

I earned his brittle smile. "Good girl."

His fingers disappeared from my arm, and he stepped back, dead eyes roaming around the kitchen.

"Lola, this place is a dump." He pinched my favourite pink tea towel between two fingers and lifted it from the counter as if it were toxic waste. "It's like a condemned Barbie Dreamhouse. Pink. Flowery. Bullshit. And the mess you left in this kitchen..." Disgust curled his lip. "Some things never change."

My fists balled by my side. Maybe the cottage was run-down. Maybe it wasn't decorated with the soulless precision of his mansion on the waterfront. There was no exposed concrete, stark white walls, or ugly abstract art. This was my house. I'd fought for a place of my own and every pink tea cosy and fluffy pillow in it.

Chris's back turned as he continued listing his grievances with my decorating.

My eyes were wild in every direction. I needed a plan. It would only take one false step—one wrong word—to snap the thread of control holding back his rage.

I'd only have one chance.

I needed more time.

I touched a cautious hand to his arm. "Chris?" His eyes snapped to mine, anger swirling, barely contained, and I fought the urge to cower back. "You must be tired after your flight... I could make you some coffee...or...something to eat?" I took a step towards the fridge, but his hand shot out and yanked me back. "I have some cake—"

"We'll get something on the road," he hissed. "It's time to go."

"G-go?"

"Yes. Go. Home. You've frolicked about on your ridiculous escape to the country long enough. We're going home. Tonight."

"T-tonight?"

"Did you get even stupider since you moved to this backwater? Yes. T-t-t-tonight. I have a suite booked in the city." He bent his head closer to whisper, "And when we get there, you can spend the rest of the night proving to me just how sorry you are."

I wasn't going. He'd have to drag me kicking and screaming all the way to the city. I didn't want to be chained to some cold, posh suite with a monster looming over me, stealing love from me he'd never earned.

I wanted to twirl in my pretty dress and slip on the high heels that I could barely walk in so Aiden didn't have to bend so far to nuzzle his nose in my hair. I wanted to be at the winery. I wanted to be on my romantic date.

My heart twisted.

Was Aiden already waiting for me? He was always early for our coffee dates. Was he nervous? Did Ruth talk him into wearing another shirt he hated just to impress me? And when I didn't come, would he think I was trying to hurt him the way he'd hurt me all those months ago? The world swayed and blurred. I couldn't bear the thought of that.

That couldn't be our ending.

Chris's eyes bulged when I tugged my arm back. "No," I said, ignoring the flare of his nostrils. A warning. But I needed to risk his wrath. I needed more time. "I can't. I need things—clothes—to pack."

"Nothing in your wardrobe is worth bringing. Like this thing." He flicked the hem of my shirt. "Hideous."

The cruel comments no longer stung, but my options for bargaining for more time were running out. My mind raced. Chris was too clever. Too cunning. He'd see through me if I lied. The truth was risky, but sticking as close to it as possible was all I had.

"I had p-plans tonight... M-my friend will be waiting...for...for me."

"Then let her wait!" Chris spat. "I've waited six fucking months, Lola! Do you have any idea how much money I've wasted chasing you halfway across the country? Do you have any idea how much fucking grief your father gave me? Do you? No one else would put up with the insane shit you've put me through! You should be on your fucking knees thanking your lucky stars that I still want your pathetic little arse."

"Chris—"

He shoved me towards the back door. "We're going."

"Please. It's a small town. Everyone knows everyone. A-and...m-my friend... You know the type... She's *such* a worrywart." I was ashamed that I couldn't stop the fear weaving through my voice. I wanted to be strong—the girl I was yesterday. "She'll call the police if I don't show up. Please..."

I twisted away from Chris, heading to the doorway. A flutter of hope flickered in my stomach. Another step away. Getting closer. If I could get my phone, I'd have options. Brooke. Ruth. They'd come. They'd help me.

"I'll just message her—"

"Do you think I'm stupid?" Chris's eyes narrowed. "No calls. No messages." He yanked me back against his chest. "We're going. Now."

Tears trickled down my cheeks. I was failing. I was running out of options. "Can I get my bag? Or...my...p-purse? What if I need to show ID at the airport...or...or...something?" I pointed down the hall. "I dropped it by the front door when I came home."

Chris arched his neck to look past me. Even in the dark, he'd be able to see the pink lump. He scowled, thinking it over for a moment, and then his chin dropped in a nod. He loomed closer at my heels than my own shadow as I padded down the hallway.

My eyes zeroed in on the old brass doorknob.

A thousand plans raced through my mind, and a thousand times, I failed. That stupid door was heavy and always got stuck. There was no way I'd manage to open it before Chris got to me. No way.

But it wasn't locked.

I knew it wasn't.

And it was my only chance.

I surged forward, sprinting down the hallway, reaching out, my hand curling around the knob, twisting, turning, and with a yank so hard it jolted me back a step, the door was open. Streetlights blazed through the gap. My eyes went wide.

I did it!

A palm landed flat on the door, and the glimpse of freedom slammed shut.

My blood turned to ice. I glanced over my shoulder. "C-Chris—"

His hand shot out so fast and so hard that when the slap connected with my cheek, my face snapped to the side, my body spun, and my shoulder cracked against the front door. My knees buckled.

He kept coming.

A scream tore from my throat when the burst of fists struck my fragile body. The world went fuzzy. My glasses were missing. My shirt was ripped, and I tasted the sweet metallic burn of blood on the back of my tongue, but I wasn't going down without a fight. I clawed at Chris's face and kicked my legs. My heel smacked into his nose. The sickening crunch flipped my stomach upside down.

Chris reared back. "Fuck!"

I didn't waste a single precious second. I scrambled to my feet and bolted down the hallway, but...where to? My eyes were panicked. I'd never make it to the back door. What other options did I have? My bare feet skittered along the wood floor into the bedroom, and my hand flew out to rip the drawer from the nightstand. Frenzied, my whole body shaking, I dropped to my knees and sifted through the mess that spilt across the floor.

No!

Panic speared my temples. My eyes skipped over the hazy outline of my junk again. Tissues. A book. The scrunchie Ruth had made me. I blinked back tears of frustration. My heart rocketed when the silver glint I desperately needed was nowhere to be found.

No!

A cruel laugh bristled the back of my neck. "Looking for your knife, Lola?"

My body went still.

Chris's footsteps were slow on the wooden floor. "Did you forget? I tidied up for you." He slithered closer until his breath was hot on my ear. "I found all your secrets. I touched all your pretty things. Did you think I wouldn't check your drawers? How stupid do you think I am?"

Desperate, I fumbled through the junk. Even a pen would do. My fingertips brushed over smooth metal. Relief sparked in every battered bone in my body. Chris hadn't found all my secrets. I'd bet he'd seen the pink glittery tube and scoffed at it like he did at everything else I liked.

I silently flicked off the lid of the pepper spray and watched it roll under the bed.

"How stupid?" I whispered. "Pretty stupid."

Confusion flashed across his face. I raised the pink canister, gritted my teeth, and pressed the nozzle. White fog spewed out. The foul smell burned my lungs, but I held my finger down, my aim steady on his bloody, swollen face.

"Fuck!" His eyes squeezed shut, and his arms thrashed wildly, smacking nothing but air. "You little bitch!"

I launched off the floor, onto the bed, clawed my way across the comforter, and tumbled off the other side. I scrambled back to my feet. My shoulder clipped the doorway as I flew out of the room.

And I ran.

"Lola!"

I ran for my life, down the hallway, into the kitchen, my eyes glued on the back door. My heart raced in my chest. Muscles burned in my legs. The pounding of Chris's steps behind me drowned out mine. I didn't slow down.

"Lola!"

The back door was right there.

I was so close.

A scream pierced the air. Was it mine? Pain exploded between my shoulders. My lungs seized. Something hard had slammed into me, and I tumbled, sliding across the kitchen floor like it was ice. My head hit the back wall. Dazed, dizzy, I never had a chance to recover. Chris was already on top of me, pinning me under his weight, his hands wrapped around my throat.

I never gave up. Any hand or foot that I wrestled free clawed and kicked. I fought.

But Chris was strong.

So strong.

All I could see was the feral glare of red-rimmed eyes as he stole the last breaths from my lungs.

That was all.

Until a flash of silver sliced through the darkness behind his head like a shooting star. I murmured a silent wish.

Please don't let this be my ending.

The swish of a frying pan flew out of nowhere to smack against Chris's skull.

The claws disappeared from my neck. His face whipped around, frantic eyes searching the dark for his attacker, and I scurried out from underneath him. I gulped in huge, desperate gasps of air as he forgot about me, lumbering to his feet, unsteady, almost tipping over. The bite of rust was in the air. Blood oozed through the fingers he clutched to the back of his head.

Another silver streak flashed.

The frying pan slammed with a sickening crack against the side of his face, and he wilted down the kitchen cabinets. Even though he sprawled out in front of me, motionless, my pulse still raced. I was ready. Ready to run. Ready for him to lurch back to life. He didn't. There was no more fight in him. Only his chest rose and fell in shallow heaves.

Yolanda's bunny slippers shuffled forward.

"Did I get him?" She smoothed back her wiry grey curls. Popping her hand onto her hip, she peered down at Chris. Her slipper kicked the heel of his expensive shoe. Not a peep. "Reckon I got him good."

I only nodded. Everything ached, and when I pressed my palm against the floor and pushed up, my arm shook, and my legs wobbled like I'd never be able to stand again. The frying pan clattered to the counter. Yolanda was coming to help me—bunny slippers and all. A loud thump stopped her in her tracks. Her eyes darted over my shoulder to the front door. My eyes flew to Chris. He was still passed out.

Another thump. A thundering crash. Wood splintered. Something was broken.

"Lola!"

My heart surged back to life.

Aiden.

Yolanda barked a laugh. "Your cavalry's a bit late." A smirk cracked her thin lips. "Although better late than never with that one."

"Lola!" The panic in Aiden's voice tore at my heart.

"I..." I wanted to shout back, "I'm here, I'm okay," but my voice was hoarse and broken.

Heavy steps charged down the hall.

I stumbled to the doorway on legs still too shaky to hold my weight. The relief swelling inside me was the only thing dragging me forward. Into the hallway. To him.

The front door hung wide open, barely still on its hinges, and the streetlight outside glowed enough for me to see the man stall at every doorway until his frantic eyes locked on me. His last few steps faltered. Worry etched every line of his face.

I stumbled to him just as he collapsed to his knees.

Aiden's throat bobbed with a heavy swallow. "I—I couldn't remember if I was supposed to pick you up. I heard you—" His eyes screwed shut, and he shook his head. He wouldn't be able to finish that train of thought. "I heard you from down the street. I didn't think I'd make it...but...you're...you're okay." He smoothed back my hair, and wild eyes scanned my face. "No. Not okay." His fingertips fluttered along my cheek, my jaw, my neck—all the places where the snake's claws had been on me. "Oh, love. Where are your glasses?"

Tears streaked down my cheeks, but I was smiling. That sweet, perfect, grumpy man.

I threw my arms around him.

And then I kissed him.

I kissed him with every bit of fire and fight still burning in my belly so he'd feel just how much he meant to me. It was the kind of kiss that showed him I forgave him and let him know that his face was the one I wanted to see every day—for coffee, for romantic dates, for everything.

"Oi! Lovebirds!" The bunny ears of Yolanda's slippers flapped as she sped past. For a frail old lady, she was fast on her feet. "Plenty of time for smooching outside."

She dug her phone out of the deep pocket of her dressing gown, mashed at the screen, and pressed it to her ear.

"Calling the cops?" Aiden asked.

"The cops?" She scoffed over her shoulder. "It's Tuesday. I'm calling the pharmacist."

Aiden shook his head with a laugh. "I'll explain later," he promised, helping me to my feet.

He dropped a kiss on the top of my head and then anchored his arm around my waist. I was safe. He was with me, patient, never hurrying me to move faster to the door.

Outside, Yolanda barked into her phone. "Carlie, that you? You tell the sergeant to put his pants on and haul his arse to my place... Nah... Not *later*." Yolanda rolled her eyes at us. "Right now... Tell him to send the paramedic as well. The doc's had a problem with some bastard from the city."

A problem.

I turned my head, my gaze searching through the broken door, down the dark hallway, and into the kitchen. The shadow of expensive shoes was the only hint of the man who'd tortured me for eight long years. But the nightmare was over. I was finally waking up.

Aiden's arms wrapped around me, and he hugged me close. "Don't look back," he whispered.

Silently, I nodded.

I didn't let my eyes linger on my past for another second. I wound my arms around Aiden and pressed my face into the warmth of his chest. The rumble of his soft, contented sigh swelled inside my heart. Together, we were a patchwork of just enough broken pieces to make one whole.

Aiden was my future.

31

He Saw the Woman He Loved

Aiden

WHEN ALL THE LIGHTS around my house were out, and the whole world was asleep except me, I replayed my favourite memories.

Lola. Me. Her cottage. The Storm. Dancing. My confession. Her forgiveness. The perfect moments before the nightmares started again for both of us.

I drifted somewhere between the heaven of remembering Lola's kiss on my lips and avoiding the hell of my past when a scream ripped through the silence.

Lola's hoarse, aching cry always tore my chest wide open. It never got easier to hear her pain.

But I didn't throw my legs over the side of the bed and race to the other room. I reminded myself not to panic. I fixed my gaze on the black lines of nothing out the window and...waited.

Feet pattered across the hardwood floor.

I never had to wait long.

My bedroom door creaked open. Light splintered through a crack just wide enough for Lola's head to poke inside. Neither of us spoke. We didn't need to. After three nights of her staying with me, we'd figured out a routine. I peeled back the covers. She scurried across the room, dove into the bed, and wriggled across the white cotton sheets until she was safely tucked in beside me.

Only one of her eyes peeked at me. The puff of the pillow hid the other. And even though icicles with pink toenails sent a shock wave of goosebumps up my legs, I loved how close Lola was when she tangled around me and the tip of her nose tickled mine.

I rested my forehead against hers. "Another bad dream?"

She blinked at me with a wordless nod.

"Oh, love..." I whispered. "You've been so brave."

"I don't feel brave," she whispered back. "I feel like I've taken a hundred steps back to exactly where I started when I moved here six months ago. I feel safe here with you, but soon... I'll be on my own again... and...and... I'm scared, Aiden."

"He can't hurt you," I whispered before sealing the promise with a kiss on her forehead. "Not anymore."

"I don't want to look over my shoulder my whole life."

"I know you've been worrying, but Chris was refused bail. He's locked away until the hearing. We've got time before we need a new plan of attack." My thumb stroked her cheekbone before I kissed her there. "Sometimes knowing that won't help, so you just tell me...or Ruth...or Brooke. We'll be there. You'll never be on your own."

"Can I come stay with you sometimes?"

"You can stay with me whenever you want."

Lola sighed with a little purr of relief, snuggling into me like a kitten, her head burrowed in my neck and her fingers tracing my collarbone. "And tonight?" Her voice was cautious. "Promise me you won't disappear again?"

I swallowed, but the knot stayed stuck in my throat. Lola's fingers stilled on my neck. My silence unsettled her. I'd give that girl the whole damn universe if it were possible, but I couldn't promise her that.

"Aiden?" I hated the cautious way she said my name. "I don't like when you sleep on the lounge... or...or worse..."

The words slammed into my chest. *Or worse.* "Lola, if this is about last night—"

"You know it is." She propped herself onto her elbow, frustration pinching her voice. "I've been trying to talk to you all day, but you keep avoiding me by banging around doing who-knows-what in your garage."

"I told you," I protested weakly. "I'm working on something."

"Yes, your big secret project." Her giggle faded when she touched her hand to my cheek. "Aiden, I was worried. When I found you last night...you were sleeping slumped over the bath..."

"I'm just... My brain's in overdrive. It's not your fault. It's not. But the night of your attack...when I heard you...my brain...and not getting there in time... So much old shit spewed to the surface..."

"More flashbacks?"

"Yeah."

"Why didn't you wake me up? I could've helped." Her voice ached with hurt. "I've helped before, haven't I?"

"Always, love. Always. But you shouldn't have to prop me up all the time. You're dealing with so much—*too much.*"

"Our pasts aren't going to magically disappear one day. We have amazing moments together, but we need to learn how to make space for our challenges, too. I never want you to feel like you have to deal with everything on your own."

Instead of listening to her, I dug my heels in like a stubborn ass. "I won't let my problems be another burden on your shoulders."

Lola huffed in frustration. "Do you want me to pretend that I'm okay? Hide my nightmares from you?"

"Of course not. I want to be there for you. Help you."

"Why do you think you should expect any less from me?" She silenced me from muttering about how worthless I was by pressing her fingers gently to my lips. *"When we have suffered for a long time,"* she recited, *"we have great difficulty believing in good fortune."*

A chuckle rumbled from my chest. This girl. "You sweet-talking me with quotes from *The Count of Monte Cristo*, Lola?"

"For a book that's allegedly your favourite, you haven't taken much of it to heart." Her face was still hidden in the dark, but I heard the smile in her voice. "Believe, Aiden. Please? Don't you think we've had enough suffering in our lives? Things *can* get better. I know that for both of us."

"I want that, but—"

Her fingers pressed back on my lips. "No buts. I'm not asking you to be perfect or to pretend that you have no past or no problems. All I'm asking is for you to be mine. That's all. Just...mine."

Hers? I was floating. Dreaming. Was this happening? Not that she even needed to ask. "I was always yours."

"Good." She kissed the corner of my mouth. "So, next time you're struggling, you wake me up. We can count together. Or have a cup of tea. Or cuddle here and talk. Whatever you need. Just...please...*stay*."

A weight heavier than a thousand oak trees was stacked on my chest, but I swallowed back the fear. I trusted her. I wanted this. All of it.

"I'll stay," I promised.

She flopped onto the pillow and shimmied closer to wrap herself around my body. Her feet weren't ice on my legs anymore. She was a warm tangle of sunshine and hope. I loved that. I loved her. I wasn't sure how I ended up such a lucky bastard, but I was never letting her slip through my fingers again.

Lola talked a little about looking forward to spending time with Ruth for lunch the next day and finding a new place to live, but her voice soon trailed off in drowsy murmurs. Then, she snuffled quiet breaths on my neck.

I couldn't say what happened after that. I fell asleep with the love of my life in my arms, and my past no longer haunting every dream.

·♥·♥·♥·♥·♥·

My eyes opened, squinting into the blur of daylight.

Sunrise burned over the mountains, and the white-hot spears of light through the fading purple sky told me it was later than when I usually got up at the butt-crack of dawn.

But I wasn't bothered. I was flying.

I'd kept my promise to Lola.

I rolled over, and my palm landed flat on a cold pillow. A smile tugged at my lips. I'd expected that. Lola's breakfasts were one of my favourite parts of this strange routine we'd created since she'd been staying with me.

She was Breakfast Boss. I was Helper Lackey. Sometimes, I was Mr. Eye Candy. Either way, Lola ran the show, and if she kept flashing me that dazzling smile while she flipped pancakes, I'd never change a damn thing.

So, I took my time making the bed, stuffed around in the bathroom, threw an old T-shirt over my plaid pyjama bottoms, and eventually wandered down the hallway to see if she wanted help with anything. She wouldn't, but I'd offer anyway.

I poked my head into the kitchen. No Lola, but...
Hell.

A Lola-sized cooking bomb had gone off. Almost every bowl and measuring cup I owned was piled on the counter. Flour was—my eyes darted around the kitchen—yep, *everywhere.* A fluffy white mountain in a mixing bowl. Smatters on the benchtop. A handprint on the fridge door. *Everywhere.*

I chuckled. Even the perfect woman needed at least one tiny flaw. Actually, was that a flaw? Nah. It gave me another reason to hang out with her.

I grabbed the blue dish rag off the sink and started to mop up the mess. My eyes drifted out the kitchen window. Fog over the valley... And a blur of red wobbling through the grass to the chicken coop.

Oh... Shit...

I flew out on the porch, then jumped down the back stairs and bolted after Lola. I instantly regretted forgetting my shoes when the sharp chill of the dewy grass spiked my bare feet.

"Lola!"

She paused, turning, a huge smile lighting up her face. "You ran out of eggs!" My red flannel shirt swam around her like a tent, and there was only a hint of knobbly knees and skinny legs peeking out from the top of my enormous gumboots. "I can't make pancakes without eggs."

I pecked a kiss above the smear of flour on her cheek. "Where are your glasses, love?"

"I don't need them to find a few eggs." Her nose scrunched up as she squinted at the coop. "I can see those clucky ladies just fine."

"Oh, yeah?" I smirked. "But can you see the snake?"

"The"—she gulped—"s-snake?"

"Yeah. Great big tiger snake." I pointed to the brown lump curled by the coop door. "See him? He's a regular. Comes up here looking for the mice who steal the feed. He's got himself an all-you-can-eat buffet with a real nice view."

"How about we skip pancakes this morning?" She laughed. "What about some toast?"

"I love toast."

A gentle tap on her bottom got her moving. The snake wouldn't bother her if she didn't bother him, but I wanted Lola back inside—*safe*—all the same.

With her hand steadied on the top of the outdoor lounge, she bent over to wrestle off the gumboots. Not that it did much good. She toppled over with an airy laugh when she yanked off the first one, but I caught her before she could fall out of the second. That earned me another one of her magic smiles.

My heart thudded in my chest. I wanted more moments like this one and our cuddles at night. I wanted to buy Lola her own gumboots—pink ones—so she could collect eggs every morning. I wanted to clean up the mess she made cooking breakfast. More than anything, I wanted to see her smiles. Real smiles. For me. And not just the bits of me I wasn't too scared to show her. Her real smile for the real me.

And maybe because those thoughts muddled up my brain, my dumb mouth blurted out, "I love you."

Lola stood frozen on the porch, drowning in a sea of red flannel. Her eyes widened. No shy smile, though. Her mouth dropped open in shock.

Great.

Just. *Bloody*. Great.

I tugged at the hem of the T-shirt. Why did I always make everything so awkward? Why couldn't I have surprised her over a nice dinner or something? This was the wrong place and *definitely* the wrong time. Why was I—

Lola launched herself at me, arms around my neck, kissing me like she was trying to knock me over—and it worked. My calves hit the edge of the outdoor lounge, and I tumbled back with her in tow. She landed in my lap, laughing, then cupped my face in both hands to keep me still as she peppered frantic kisses across my cheeks and nose.

"Really?" she breathed.

"Really."

"Since when?"

"Since forever."

"Tell me again."

My palms covered the pretty pink flush of her cheeks. I held her gaze to tell her how she was my whole world—*properly* this time. "I love you, Lola."

Her cheeks burned even pinker. "Oh."

She took the lead. I didn't mind. I liked her bossy. She straddled my lap, teased me with her hungry, demanding kisses, and when that wasn't enough, she tortured me by starting to rock her hips against me so achingly slow. I couldn't have stopped the pained groan even if I tried. Her fingers fumbled on the button at the neck of the old flannel she wore.

Oh, sweet hell. Is she...?

"Lola, you..." My voice was rusty. The words wouldn't come out. "We don't have to do this."

"I want to." She fidgeted with the next button. "Do...you?"

My breaths turned ragged. Thinking wasn't possible anymore. My gaze locked on that one undone button because I was coming undone myself. I didn't deserve this. I didn't deserve her. But—*hell*—I needed that woman like I needed oxygen.

I managed to choke out a simple, "Yes."

Lola bit back a smile and started to flick off another button. And another. All of them. I didn't blame her for not shucking off the flannel and tossing it to the ground where I wanted it. Icy air drifted across the porch, needling goosebumps across my bare arms. But the glimpse of her pale skin, prickled from the cold, and the soft curve of her belly peeking through the gap of my old flannel shirt? Goddamn, that drove me wild. My cock was already harder than a damn rock.

I let my index finger trace the line of opened buttons, then drift lower, over the sliver of her pale skin exposed to my greedy eyes.

Every inch of Lola was so...soft.

My hands were rough, scarred, and calloused from years of hard use. But she never flinched away from my touch. She gasped those soft little sounds as I kissed her and dragged my fingertips over her skin. She loved the light touches best—over her breasts, down her waist, along her hip, and where the bumpy edge of her knickers hugged her skin.

Lola tugged at the waistband of my pyjamas and tore her lips away from mine, only to demand, "Off."

I loved her confident like this, but... "Lola, is it...too...soon?" She'd only just escaped that monster. The deep purple bruises were fading on her skin, but I could still see them, trace them, remember her fear...

"We've waited months," she murmured, kissing my neck.

We weren't talking about the same thing, but I wasn't going to spoil one of the best moments of my life by reminding her of the man who'd tried to end hers.

She shimmied out of her white knickers, kicking them off her ankles onto the porch. Then she shoved down my pyjama bottoms, impatient, a little rough, but so damn perfect I ached to be inside her all the way to my soul.

"Tell me again," she whispered.

It didn't matter that my cock was throbbing and kept hostage in her tightly wrapped fingers. I'd happily tell her a hundred times. "I love you."

"Are you okay if we do this without a—"

"Just let me be inside you."

I'd imagined this a thousand times—her on top of me—but nothing compared to the real thing. Hot. Slick. Impossibly close after months of believing I'd never touch her again. But her sweet, breathy sigh in my ear when my cock was buried inside her just the way she wanted? That sound alone nearly finished me.

Lola pressed kisses up my throat, her legs locked tight around me, hips rolling in a slow, torturous rhythm. She took her time, drawing out every last drop of pleasure from my body to make herself feel good.

The first night I made love to Lola, she was quiet, almost timid. We moved slow. Took our time. Explored each other for hours. But now?

Now, she didn't hold back. She told me what she needed with a strong, proud voice. And I couldn't get enough. Kiss her neck? I grazed the skin with my teeth and soothed each spot with a kiss. Tease her breasts? With my tongue, my mouth, my fingers, all of them.

"God, that's so…" Her fingers clawed at my chest, holding on as she rode me even harder, wetness grinding against my belly. "You're such a big beast of a man. So…so… strong. But *I'm* the boss today."

Yeah, she was. "You're the boss of me every damn day."

She moaned and dug her fingers so deep into my shoulders I started reciting the seven times table to make sure it wasn't over in one second flat.

Lola demanded everything I could give her until her eyes clamped shut as she came hard enough to knock the breath from both of us. The raw sound I let out when I followed seconds later had her curling into me, her legs locked tight, owning the moment. And maybe she did.

She owned all of me.

I smoothed away the messy strands of wind-swept gold, desperate to see her face. Still panting, she laughed when I kissed the tip of her nose. My sweet girl with the glasses too big for her face. She found me gutted, empty, and still chose me. She gently led me through the darkness to find pieces of myself I thought I'd lost forever.

"Guess what?" Lola pecked a kiss on my cheek. "I love you, too."

And this time, she ruined me.

But in the best way possible.

32

She Saw Her Happy Ending

Lola

My eyes drifted from the road, flicking a glance in the rearview mirror. Aiden's black beast of a truck trailed a safe distance behind me, but I still caught a glimpse of him tapping the steering wheel, agitated, on edge.

I jabbed the button to activate my phone in the console. The speakers bleeped with each ring. I glanced in the mirror. Aiden frowned before the phone connected.

"You doing okay back there?" I asked, eyes still on him.

His expression stayed stony. "Focus on the road, love." His voice was strained. "I'm fine."

Frowning, I flashed him a wave and hung up.

Aiden worried too much about me driving. Even though I hadn't owned a car for six years, I wasn't that rusty. I was cautious. Sensible. But Aiden's past stalked at his heels. It was early days for him in therapy, and even though he tried so hard, the flashbacks still happened. But we were working through it—together.

The speakers chimed with an incoming call.

Aiden's warm chuckle made my heart skip a beat. "Keep to the speed limit, Leadfoot Lola."

I glanced at the dash.

Leadfoot Lola?

Hardly. I only crept a few over the speed limit, my pulse jumping with the excitement of getting to my new house. But I eased off the accelerator and darted a look in the rearview mirror. No tapping fingers. One hand sliding off the wheel.

Aiden was okay.

Not like the drive back from Hobart last week.

Aiden had driven us to the city. We'd spent two days having crazy-good sex in a three-star motel, reading books, and laughing our heads off when we tried to cook a romantic brunch in a shoddy microwave. On attempt two, Aiden had exploded an egg. What a mess.

Somewhere in all that, we'd found time to buy a new car.

My new car.

Some people would never understand how important it was for me to walk into the dealership. I'd been caged for years, my every move, every breath, picked apart. The car was my freedom. And ironically, that freedom came from the one thing still hidden at the bottom of the faded pink pillowcase—my old engagement ring.

The last reminder of Chris disappeared into the hands of a jeweller in the city, and I drove home in a brand-new car instead of the used Toyota that Aiden had helped me pick out from the online listings.

But the drive home had been a nightmare.

A perfect storm of hell brewed for Aiden that afternoon. I hadn't been behind the wheel in years and lurched to a few sudden stops, getting used to the brakes. He was tired, and his nerves frayed too close to breaking after an appointment with the psychiatrist. He trailed in his car behind me, and everything was okay...until it wasn't.

The weather turned halfway home. Charcoal clouds swept in off the ocean, and rain pelted in white sheets across the highway. Aiden unravelled in seconds and swerved off the road to battle through one of the worst anxiety attacks I'd ever seen. His skin drained white, and the pained cries that wrenched out of him when he slumped over in the front seat almost broke my heart.

Even when he could finally choke out words, his head stayed bowed against the wheel.

"I can't get better," he said. "I *can't*."

"We could try count—"

"It doesn't fucking work!"

"Aiden—"

"It doesn't always fucking work, Lola! Please. I'm a fucking failure. Leave me to rot here where I belong. Just go."

"What's our rule?" I huffed at him. "What's the one thing you can't do?"

Guilty, tear-stained eyes turned from the steering wheel. "I'm not pushing you away."

I snorted. "Yeah, right. Try again, big guy."

"You're better off without me."

"Nope."

"Please go."

"Nah."

And when my gentle encouragement had still failed, I'd called in the big guns.

The lovebirds met us on the highway. Harry drove Aiden home. Brooke sped along at the back of the convoy in her shiny convertible. And me, well, I zoomed at the front, music floating in my own little piece of freedom.

Everything had worked out.

I'd shown Aiden that life wasn't about struggling on his own. He had friends he could rely on. I did, too. But I had a sneaking suspicion I'd have to repeat that message a few more times until it was burned into his stubborn brain.

I zipped my car into the driveway and shut off the ignition.

"There she is," I murmured, a proud smile spreading across my face.

The old farmhouse was a beauty. Bigger than the cottage and farther out of town, the house was an easy walk to Ruth's for all the Mexican fiesta nights I could handle. A tray of pumpkin seedlings and pea shoots waited beside the front door. She'd promised to help me plant a vegetable garden of my own.

I pushed open the car door, hopped out, and clicked the fob to lock it. *My* car. I skimmed my fingertips over the shiny paint, savouring those new car feels, until Aiden's arms circled my waist. Happiness fluttered in my chest when he kissed the back of my neck.

I twisted around, looping my arms around his shoulders. "Hey, you." I tipped up on my toes and brushed my lips over his cheek.

Aiden raised an eyebrow. "What kind of hello is that?" His beard grazed my skin as his kiss lingered, deep and loving, but ending too soon. "Love you."

"Love you more."

"You sure we have to go to this barbecue?" he murmured, squeezing my hip. "I've got this real nice bed—"

A shriek from across the yard cut off his naughty train of thought.

"Hey, hey, hey!"

I ducked a guilty glance around Aiden's shoulder. Brooke stood in the front doorway with her hand on her hip. Her other hand had a death grip on a clipboard.

"Yolanda warned me you two would waste time with that"—she flapped a furious hand in our direction—"kissing nonsense. Cut that out. We're on a schedule."

Aiden tilted his head, his voice low by my ear. "Who gave her a clipboard?"

I was quick to cover my smirk behind my hand. "She gave *herself* a clipboard."

Aiden muttered a curse under his breath, and I choked back my laugh when Brooke flashed a ferocious glare in my direction. Wow. She was *not* playing around anymore. This morning she'd been bossy, but now she was in full-on organising meltdown mode.

Her foot tapped impatiently. "Well? You two gonna stand there all day? I thought we had a house to move into. No?"

She barked orders from the list of jobs pinned to her clipboard. My eyebrows popped up. Harry crept out of the darkness of the hallway behind her, and his index finger pressed over his lips, warning us to keep quiet.

Aiden started whistling and looking up at the sky. A grin burst out of me.

Brooke's eyes narrowed. "Are you two even listening? We're already behind schedule. The barbecue starts in exactly one hour, and we still have—"

The high-pitched squeal she shrieked when Harry's hands clamped around her waist jolted through Aiden like a lightning bolt. My hand shot to his arm, and he sagged into me, his muscles relaxing under my touch. He shook out his clenched fist.

Harry planted kisses over Brooke's neck until he spun her around. "You kicking butt and taking names, Princess?"

She pouted. "I'm trying, but they're ruining my schedule."

"Aw, yeah? And you're working so hard to keep us all on track, huh? What do you need, Princess? Want a shoulder rub while you talk me through your list again?"

Her red lips curved in a smile. "What about more kisses?"

Harry grinned. "Yeah, I've got a never-ending supply of those for you."

His lips were on her in a flash. She melted against him like butter on toast, but his eyes stayed open, darting over to us. He raised his eyebrows. Waited. Raised them again.

Wait... What?

Exasperated, he frantically waved us through.

Whoops.

Distracted by Harry's sloppy public display of affection, Brooke didn't notice us slip past her and the never-ending list of jobs stuck to her clipboard. We escaped inside the farmhouse and headed for the kitchen.

Out of the frying pan and into the fire.

Ruth stirred a pot on the ancient cooktop. Was she making chili? I sniffed the air. Whatever bubbled on the stove smelled *yummy*. Her head turned ever so slightly. She knew we hovered in the doorway, but she refused to acknowledge us.

Aiden coughed into his fist.

Ruth's head whipped around. Her dark eyes narrowed, and she snorted an indignant huff over her shoulder before turning her back.

Aiden sighed. "Ruth."

"Don't you *Ruth* me." She furiously stirred the pot. "I'm still not speaking to either of you."

"Ruth, we talked about this."

"*We* talked about *this*? Oh no, we did *not*." She whirled around, the spoon in her hand flicking angry splatters of chili around the kitchen with every word. "This is a travesty. A *crime*! Aiden, how could you let this happen? Lola"—she flashed her sweetest smile at me—"it's not too late to change your mind. Aiden has a huge place on the mountain and—"

"Ruth," Aiden warned.

She ignored him. "Lola, he *desperately* wanted you to move in with him instead of buying this place. He talked about nothing else for hours. He misses you, and he's *so* lonely—"

"Ruth!" Aiden scrubbed a hand down his face. "Stop."

"Never! You two are perfect together. *Perfect.* I don't know why you're wasting time pretending like you're not utterly mad for each other by living in separate houses."

"We've only been dating for a few weeks—"

Ruth snorted. "You've been in love with Lola for months." She glanced back at me with a smile full of sunshine. "For *months.*"

"Stop." Aiden's command was gentle but firm. "Lola and I... This is all new. For both of us. We need time to get ourselves right before adding any extra pressure." He squared up, hands on his hips, and fixed her with a glare. "Not that it's any of your business."

"Until the day you put a ring on that woman's finger"—Ruth pointed her spoon at me—"you're absolutely my business. And, well... yeah, okay, probably after that, too. Less, though. Promise."

Aiden grunted.

Ruth's lips curved in a calculated smile. "Have you shown Lola her surprise yet?"

My eyebrows popped up. "What surprise?"

Ruth chittered an evil laugh. "I'll show *you* none of my business," she muttered, giving the pot another stir like a witch brewing something wicked in her delicious chili cauldron. "I'll have you pair married in no time."

Aiden frowned at the back of her head. "Uh, yeah, a surprise." He lifted his shoulder. "It's just a little, um... Come on. I'll show you."

He led me through the kitchen, past Brooke's colour-coded moving boxes lining the hallway, to the spare room door. His hand rested on the knob. He drew in a breath so deep, you'd think he was about to jump off a cliff.

"If you don't like it, I can change it," he said, nudging the door open.

I stepped inside.

My jaw dropped. *"Wow."* This couldn't be real. It *couldn't* be. "Just... *wow.*"

The spare room had been turned into a library. Not just any library—my dream library. Built-in shelves stretched to the ceiling, complete with a ladder for any hard-to-reach books at the top. Pink curtains framed the window. A white sofa was nestled underneath, loaded with soft, squishy pillows, and a pink shag rug covered the battered wooden floor.

I wanted to spin and twirl like a girl in a teen movie montage. I wanted to drop onto that rug and make snow angels with my arms. The library was...*perfect.*

Aiden watched me cautiously from the corner of his eye. Why was he worried this time? Couldn't he see how much I loved this room?

"It started with the bookcase in the middle," he said. "The special project I was working on when you stayed with me." He rubbed the back of his neck. "Once I knew this was the house you'd chosen and I got the measurements, I, uh... I guess I got a bit carried away."

I shuffled to the wooden bookcase in the middle. It was different from the others. I pointed to it. "This is the one you started first?"

Aiden nodded and stuffed his hands into the pockets of his jeans.

My fingertips danced along the smooth top of the bookcase. The other shelves were white and were a high-end, fancy design—probably the type Aiden installed for his business. The middle one was long and low, made of striking red wood, its knotted top distinct and imperfect, yet somehow still beautiful.

Aiden had *made* that. No—he'd *crafted* that. All of it. For me.

Tears pricked my eyes. I lifted my glasses to scrub them away with my wrist. "Aiden, you're so talented."

He lifted a shoulder like the compliment was no big deal, but the tips of his ears burned red, so I knew it was.

"And you made all this?" I squeaked. "For me?"

"Not the sofa or the soft furnishings. Brooke helped me order those so they would get here in time. And Ryan helped me hide it all on the farm until moving day."

My feet flew across the floor. Aiden's hands shot out from his pockets just in time to catch me as I slammed into his chest. I wrapped my arms around him, holding on tight, rising onto my toes, and kissing him until his breaths were ragged.

"I adore this," I told him. "I adore you."

His beard couldn't hide the big white grin stretching across his face.

I walked around the room, touching all the new and pretty things. When I glanced at Aiden over my shoulder, he stood awkwardly by the door, hands back in his pockets, eyes on his shoes.

"Aiden, what Ruth said—"

"Ignore her. She has a terrible habit of always expecting to get her own way."

"Are you upset that I want to keep living on my own?"

"Of course not."

"And you know I didn't make that decision because of you...or us? After Chris..."

After Chris, I was scared. I wanted the freedom to be myself and not worry about living under someone else's rules every day. Ruth was right—maybe it was a little silly. Aiden and I were probably going to spend a lot of our nights together, but it was important to me that one of the options was my own house.

Not forever. But for now, at least.

Aiden didn't need me to explain any of that. He didn't always say a lot, but there was a knowing in his eyes. "Where we see each other or spend time together isn't the important part. Your house. My house." He shrugged. "Maybe not that motel with only a microwave." He grinned. "All I need is you. Everything else, we can figure out along the way."

"I like the sound of that."

We didn't speak anymore, just smiled and laced our fingers together as we headed down the hall, through the kitchen, and onto the back porch. Aiden's hand slipped out of mine, and he grinned at me over his shoulder before hopping down the stairs to the yard.

I paused on the landing.

A fresh shimmer of tears blurred my eyes, but I didn't blink them away. The feeling was perfect. A moment to be cherished. Everywhere I looked, I saw how much my life had changed.

I'd first set foot in Richmond seven months ago with one suitcase, wearing clothes that were almost rags, not a friend or even hope to my name.

But today...

Brooke perched on Harry's lap on the bottom step. He nodded as she read out the long list of jobs on her clipboard. They were so young, so in love, glowing with the kind of happiness that made everything around them so much brighter.

My other protector, the farmer, unstacked a pile of outdoor chairs until Ruth's cane clicked beside me. Ryan jumped up the stairs two at a time to grab the plates and cups stuffed under her arm, and then, after offering her his hand, he carefully guided her down to the pavers. She laughed, and when her head dropped to his shoulder, his face lit up like the sun. An undeniable connection was building between them, too.

My parents stood with Yolanda, conspiring a trip to Cradle Mountain, and other friends crowded around the yard, sipping drinks and laughing, waving hello when they saw me.

And then there was him.

Aiden.

The man who gave me hope in those early days when I was still waking from a nightmare. The same man who shattered my heart then slowly, piece by piece, week by week, rebuilt what he'd broken, stronger than ever.

Watching Aiden reminded me of the morning we first met. He wore the same red-checked flannel shirt, and his dark brows furrowed to blot out the sun, but there was a lightness to the way he moved now. His past wasn't crushing down on his shoulders anymore.

And when his gaze lifted, and he saw me still standing at the top of the stairs, he didn't scowl.

He smiled and mouthed, "I love you."

So much had changed. I had, too. Maybe to some people, I'd always be Lola from the City. But I wasn't the newcomer anymore. And I'd never be an outsider again.

I could love. And I was loved in return.

My version of happily ever after.

Epilogue

Aiden

Three Years Later

"Time to go, sleepyhead."

The summer sky hid behind my closed eyes, but the warmth of Lola's voice swelled in my chest. I loved waking up to my wife's voice. Loved it. She sounded sweeter than honey drizzled on crumpets. Better than the pancakes she'd cooked me for breakfast. I never got tired of hearing her voice.

That didn't mean I was opening my eyes, though.

I kept 'em shut real tight. Kept pretending I was enjoying a peaceful doze on the porch. My back ached from sitting crooked on the outdoor lounge, but my legs were stretched out, and a book lay open on my chest. *The Murder of Roger Ackroyd.* Bruce and Barb had given it to me when they'd stopped by on their latest tour around Tasmania.

"Aiden." There was a frustrated huff in Lola's voice. Loved that, too. Loved her bossy. "I know you're awake."

I cracked one eye open.

Lola's body blocked out the sun streaming over the mountains. It didn't matter that she glared down at me, hands on her hips. She still looked like pure heaven in her new dress. I reached out to flick the hem, but she playfully smacked my hand.

I looked up at her with my saddest puppy-dog eyes. "Do we have to go?" I grumbled.

"Yes."

"And I have to wear...this?"

I pointed to the outfit. Colonel Cotton Paws was curled up and purring on my lap. Hopefully, his ginger fuzz had ruined the ugly pants Lola had made me wear.

Why did the women in my life insist on dressing me? And why did they always choose scratchy, wool outfits like accountants wore? I liked jeans. They looked good. Went with everything. Apparently, sometimes you had to wear *something nice*.

Fine. For Lola, I'd suffer, but that didn't mean I had to like it. I was stripping those pants off and shoving them into some dark corner in the back of the wardrobe the second we got home.

When she gave me a sassy cough to get moving, I raised a brow and asked, "Are you sure this *visit* to the farm isn't a surprise party you're all springing on me?"

"A party? No, of course not." Lola's teeth gnawed on her bottom lip. "You hate parties."

Yeah, she was dragging me to a surprise party.

My lip curled. "Is there going to be singing?"

"Singing?" Lola's nose wrinkled, and she bit down harder on her lip, but a smile still broke through. "Why would there be singing?"

Great. Just *great*.

A surprise party with damn singing, too.

It was my birthday. Why couldn't I choose what we did? What was wrong with spending a day at home on the couch watching TV with my beautiful wife?

I tried my luck one more time. "Is the grumpy birthday troll at least getting a cake out of this?"

Lola hid her eyes behind her hand.

"Did you bake my cake, love?"

Her smile only got bigger.

My hand captured her waist, and I dragged her closer, ignoring her protests and the grumbled meows of the Colonel. He took the hint to skedaddle back to his sunny perch in the living room. Lucky. Lola's bottom landed in my lap a second later.

Now, *that* was more like it.

"Can I have a birthday kiss?" I murmured in her hair.

She playfully swatted my shoulder. "You've already had plenty of birthday kisses."

"Earlier doesn't count. That was my midnight birthday kiss."

"After that."

"Nah, morning birthday kisses don't count, either." I flashed her a lazy grin. "I need my lunchtime kisses now." I flicked the frill of her dress. "Preferably without all this on."

Lola's hand cupped my cheek, her lips only a whisper away from mine, and just when I thought I'd won and we were heading back to Naked Town instead of the Hollyoak Farm, she pecked me on the lips.

"That's barely a kiss," I grumbled. "What type of awful birthday is this?"

She laughed and hopped off my lap. "The best you're getting, you old grumble bum. Now, get moving, it's party ti—" She slapped a hand over her mouth. "I didn't say that."

I chuckled. She'd always been rubbish at keeping secrets.

I followed her to the car without too much complaining. My hand dug into my pocket for the keys, and I tossed them to Lola. Her eyebrows popped up over her glasses.

"You can drive." I shrugged. "The birthday boy needs a day off."

Lola grinned at me like it was her birthday. It was a special treat for her to drive my car. It wasn't that I didn't trust her—I still didn't completely trust myself.

Three years of seeing the shrink, and I was light-years from where I'd started, but some things still weighed heavy on my shoulders, and no amount of talking seemed to help. Driving was the worst. I was a terrible passenger. I stressed Lola out with all my worrying.

Today, my feet were entirely on solid ground. I felt good. Relaxed. Tired and a bit blissed-out after too much sex. She could drive without me bugging her about slowing down today.

That didn't mean I didn't tug on her seatbelt to make sure she was strapped in safe, or that she didn't squeeze my thigh once or twice during the drive to the farm. My sweet girl, always showing me in small ways that she was there for me. I hoped she knew how much that meant to me.

"Glad to see you smiling again, love," I said with a smile of my own.

Lola's eyes stayed on the winding mountain road. "I'm sorry. I know I've been"—she waved a hand around—"out of sorts and moody."

"Don't apologise. You've had a lot on your mind. Chris applying for parole..." I shook my head like that would somehow scatter the frustration sinking deep in my bones. "I know that was hard for you."

The car slowed. "He's barely served his sentence!" She pushed her glasses onto her head and started to scrub furiously at frustrated tears already spilling down her cheeks.

My heart lodged in my throat, so I said something dumb. "Lola, love, your makeup—"

"Shit." She dabbed carefully at her face. *"Shit.* I know." She huffed out a strained breath. "I'm sorry—I just—I should get over it. That part of my life is ancient history. But it feels like there was no justice at all. He dragged me through hell in court and only pleaded guilty at the last second because the prosecutor gave him that bullshit plea deal. Seven years was nothing to start with!" The strain in her voice made my heart ache. "And then to be eligible for parole so soon..."

"They denied his parole," I reassured her. "We've got another two years before he can apply again, and when that time comes, we'll fight that bullshit application, too. He's just getting desperate because he keeps landing himself in trouble with the other inmates. You made sure he'll never practice law again. His money's gone. But he needs to serve his full sentence. I'm with you. Every step of the way."

She nodded and tossed a shaky smile in my direction before she focused back on the road. "I know. I love that you're on my team. I just hate that Chris can still upset me like this. After all these years...and after everything he did..." She sighed. "I don't want him to keep having that power over me. I don't want to waste any more of my life on him."

"I understand. We'll keep fighting until the day you find your peace." I gave her knee another squeeze. "Together, right?"

She smiled and offered me a firm nod like we were sealing the deal. "Together."

Lola turned down the driveway and parked the car. After she arched over to check her face in the rearview and was satisfied she didn't look like a panda, we walked together hand in hand, our steps crunching on the long gravel pathway to the front porch of the Hollyoak farmhouse.

Balloons, streamers, and bunting floated everywhere the breeze could catch.

Not a surprise birthday party, huh? Sure.

Poppy waited on the top step. She was barely two, but that tiny girl was the spitting image of her mama. Dark curls sprang up everywhere, and she was all dolled up in her sparkly tutu dress, her chubby belly jutting out. She twisted back and forth in her party shoes and frilly white socks, her dark eyes already on me. Little devil.

She grinned a toothy smile and raised her hands.

I bent down to her. "Want something, little one?"

She punched her fists about her head. She didn't say much—more like her daddy—but I knew she was asking me to pick her up. She loved having a front-row seat for all the action, and no one could get her higher or closer than her "Unnie Ay-Yon."

Poppy stuffed her chubby fingers into my beard, babbling away about who-knows-what as I lumbered inside, then down the hallway. She was like a doll in my arms, propped on my hip, and I paused with her to look at the splashes of colourful photos that Ruth had flooded all over the walls of the Hollyoak farmhouse.

Three years of new memories.

The first photo I looked at was one of the six of us when we'd won Games Night. It was a turning point in my life in so many ways. That was the night I'd finally admitted I loved the girl of my dreams and truly let other people into my life.

And it had been the six of us ever since.

My eyes glanced over the other photos. Ruth and Ryan's shotgun wedding, once news of jellybean Poppy had shocked us all. The six of us smiling on the beaches of Fiji for that magic week away when Harry and Brooke had eloped. Ruth beaming a proud smile the day she'd started her pony club. Harry and Brooke when they'd bought their first house. Ryan and one of his dumb, hairy cows. Lola holding the keys to the clinic when she'd taken over. And of course, Poppy. There were truckloads of photos of our Little Miss Poppy.

A smile tugged at my lips when I looked at the newest photo at the end.

Lola and I on our wedding day.

There was nothing fancy about our wedding—just a small shindig at our place on the mountain with a few friends. The wedding was another one of those days when I was told I couldn't wear jeans, but Harry was the one who convinced me to chuck on the suit.

One of my best friends. My best man. In a lot of ways, the better man. I still teased him about being a kid, but honestly, he was the one who'd helped me grow up in a way no one else could at one of my lowest points.

He was a big part of why that beautiful woman had come wobbling along the grass towards me in her puffy pink tea dress, holding those damn daisies and making me scrub a waterfall of tears off my face because I just felt so...*blessed*.

No word of a lie—Harry ribbed me so hard because I'd cried more than Yolanda.

That crafty old broad had constantly nagged me and stuck her nose where I didn't want it. She was convinced right from the start that the love of a good woman was what I needed. She'd said it was the only thing that got her husband through some dark days after he'd come back from the war. For a long time, I'd thought she was full of shit. Turned out, she was right—I just hadn't met the right woman yet.

Lola was the gift worth waiting for.

And God help me if the waterworks weren't stinging my eyes all over again when I looked at that photo of us.

Ruth waddled beside me, her belly growing rounder with another Hollyoak on the way. Her head fell onto my shoulder. "That's my favourite, you know."

"Really? You like it even more than the one of your grinning husband and his dumb cow?"

She laughed. "Miss Bernice is actually a big deal in the farming world."

Poppy shoved a flurry of chubby fists at my mouth. I smooched little kisses on each toddler punch. She giggled. "I'll take your word for it," I said to Ruth.

"How do you feel now you're officially forty?"

"Old."

"You already acted like a grumpy old ass."

"Old-*er*."

Ruth smirked, but it faded, and she was quiet as she glanced over the wall of photos. "Do you remember the night all those years ago when Matthew filed for divorce? The night I tore the house apart? When I chose to move down here to Tasmania?"

My chest squeezed tight, all the breath stolen from my lungs, but I nodded.

"I never thanked you for coming with me," she said.

"You don't need to."

"I *want* to. You were always there for me when no one else was. I know I put on a brave face, but for a long time, I was angry at the world and everything that had been taken from me. My family. My dreams. But *now*..." She turned a wistful gaze to me, her eyes shining with tears, but her lips curved up in a smile. "Aiden, did you ever imagine it would turn out like this?"

No. Not for a damn second.

But when the singing started, and my wife walked towards me holding a birthday cake, her face lit up with a smile even brighter than the sparklers stuck into the top, friends and family crowded behind her, I knew why everything had worked out the way it did.

It was all because of her.

The End

About Aubrey

Aubrey Whitten writes contemporary romances with an Australian twist. She has a soft spot for flawed characters searching for second chances—whether in life or love—and crafts heartfelt stories with warmth, humour, and a dash of romantic steam.

Aubrey lives in the sunniest part of Australia and juggles writing around a busy day job and the joyful chaos of her small but mighty family.

Connect with Aubrey

www.aubreywhitten.com
www.facebook.com/AubreyWhitten

Made in the USA
Middletown, DE
22 August 2025

12779140R00182